Outstanding Praise For Robert J. Conley's
FUGITIVE'S TRAIL

"Robert Conley is possibly one of the most underrated and overlooked writers of our time, as well as most skilled. Versatile: Poetry, Humor, historical, Western, Mystery, even Horror. Now, Kid Parmlee. Neither a traditional general Western character, a super-hero or anti-hero caricature, he is simply Kid Parmlee, a human being. In his pathetic way, Kid Parmlee is not a very good person, but also only as bad as survival requires. Simple, yet clever, good and bad, sad and funny, failure and success . . . 'The Kid' holds up a mirror to the human condition."

—Don Coldsmith, author of
the Spanish Bit Series and *Bearer of the Pipe*

"Kid Parmlee ain't much shucks with the King's English, but he's loud and clear when he talks with his six-shooter. Robert Conley spins a fast-action tall tale salted with Western humor."
—Elmer Kelton

"Cherokee writer Robert Conley is one of the most inventive writers America has ever had. In Kid Parmlee he has created a second-hand Billy the Kid who will charm your damned ears off and send you down a trail of fun, frivolity, and adventure. Go buy it right now, read it and enjoy it."
—Max Evans, author of *The Rounders*,
The Hi-Lo Country, and *Bluefeather Fellini*

**St. Martin's Paperbacks titles
by Robert J. Conley**

The Devil's Trail

A Cold Hard Trail

Fugitive's Trail

THE DEVIL'S TRAIL

Robert J. Conley

St. Martin's Paperbacks

This is a work of fiction. All of the characters, organizations, and events portrayed in this novel are either products of the author's imagination or are used fictitiously.

THE DEVIL'S TRAIL

Copyright © 2002 by Robert J. Conley.

All rights reserved.

For information address St. Martin's Press, 175 Fifth Avenue, New York, NY 10010.

ISBN: 978-1-250-09415-5

Our books may be purchased in bulk for promotional, educational, or business use. Please contact your local bookseller or the Macmillan Corporate and Premium Sales Department at 1-800-221-7945, ext. 5442, or by e-mail at MacmillanSpecialMarkets@macmillan.com.

Printed in the United States of America

St. Martin's Paperbacks edition / February 2002

St. Martin's Paperbacks are published by St. Martin's Press, 175 Fifth Avenue, New York, NY 10010.

10 9 8 7 6 5 4 3 2 1

Chapter 1

My ole maw used to always tell me, "Melvin, allus be keerful a getting something what's just exact what you wants it to be." I never really knowed for a long time just what the hell she was a-talking about, but I reckon I found out all right. Now maybe you never heared a me atall, but then maybe you did, and if you did then likely you recall that ole Red, she was just about almost my own gal. A course, she made her living a whoring, and that's all right with me on accounta ever'one's gotta make a living somehow, but aside from that little ole thing, well, she was kinda my gal. Anyhow, whenever my old paw final and for sure a-headed back for Texas and Maw, like what I told him to go and do, and my new pardner ole Churkee headed on to get him a look at the Churkee Nation what he hadn't never saw on accounta being borned out in Californy and all, and we was all of us a-walking around free with cleared-up names and all, well my original ole pard, ole Zeb Pike, he wanted to go on back up in the hills and sniff out some gold.

"I don't know, Zeb," I tole him. "I ain't feeling like it just now."

"Well, how come not?" he said. "What the hell's wrong with sniffing out gold? Tell me that. Ain't I allus steered you right on that?"

I had to allow as how he had all right, but then I said, "I just ain't a-feeling like it, is all. After what-all we been through, well, I just kinda wanta lay around town here for a spell and take it easy-like. Hell, I got money in my jeans. Whenever I ain't got no more, that there's the time I'll be ready to go back to work."

"Sniffing gold ain't no work," Zeb said. "It's a downright pleasure. It's the biggest pleasure in life. It's better than getting drunk. Hell, it even beats a good romp with a whore."

"I don't know about that," I said.

"Hell, you're just a snot-nosed kid."

I couldn't argue none with that.

"You go on back up yonder in the mountains, Zeb," I said. "I'll wait for you right here. Or if I get ready and you ain't come back yet, I'll go on up there a-hunting you."

"You couldn't tell up from down in them mountains without I was along with you to lead you by your nose," he said.

I grinned at him. "I reckon you're right about that, ole pard," I said.

"Then come on and let's us go," he said.

"Tell you what," I said, "let's have us some whiskey and think about it some more."

You see, I knowed that if I could get enough whiskey in ole Zeb, why, he'd plumb forget what the hell we'd been a talking about, and then, I figgered I could kinda sneak off and hide from him for a spell, and then he'd maybe go on off up in the mountains without me and leave me alone for a while. I just wanted to hang around town with ole Red until I got all my—well, you know, till I got plenty of funning around to last me for a while. Anyhow, we went on over to the saloon and got us a bottle. We was standing at the bar a sipping our whiskey—well, I was anyhow. Zeb was kindly gulping. We was standing there when ole Jim Chastain, the sheriff, come in and stood there right beside me.

"Howdy, Kid," he said.

"Buy you a drink, Jim?" I said.

"Sure," he said.

We got us another glass, and then me and Zeb and ole Chastain, we all went over to a empty table and set our ass down there with our glasses and a bottle. I was being kinda tentative-like on accounta I weren't atall sure for certain that ole Jim didn't still have it in his mind to kill me for what I had did to him a little while back, but I guess he never, 'cause he picked up his glass, and he drunk with me all right. I figgered then that he had done got all his revenging on me did once and for final that time he throwed me out the upstairs winder a the hotel and me stark, staring-ass nekkid in front a the whole town in broad daylight. I'd had to rid outa town nekkid on horseback with ever'one in the whole world a laughing their ass off at me. I reckon that satisfied him all right.

Anyhow, I had stayed outa town for a spell a-cooling off and letting my skin turn back white from its humiliation red, and then I had gone on back in on accounta I sure did want to see ole Red, and I guess you know how come. So me and ole Zeb had been back in town for a while, but we hadn't yet run onto ole Chastain till just this very minute I'm a-telling you about. Anyhow, we was all drinking together pretty good, and so it seemed like as if ever'thing was all right. Red come back down the stairs just then, and she seed us, and she come on over to set by me. I sure was proud, I can tell you.

Ole Zeb, he got liquored up right quick, and me, I just kept a-sipping real easy on accounta I was wanting to go upstairs with ole Red, and I sure didn't want to be too drunk to do nothing once I got my ass up there with her. Zeb kept a talking about gold, and I just kept a-sipping and doing my best not to get drawed into no conversation with him about it. Final I couldn't hardly stand the tenseness a the situation no more, and I looked old Chastain square in the face.

"Jim," I said, "would you say that things is square up even betwixt me and you for the things we done each other in the past, or is you still a-wanting to kill me dead?"

"Kid," he said, "I got you last, and I got you good. As far as I'm concerned, it's all over."

"Yeah," I said, "well, actual, you got me first and you got me last."

"But you got me twice in between," he said.

I couldn't hardly argue none with that. You see, what had happened was, in case you ain't heared, ole Jim, he arrested me and Paw and Zeb for something what we never done. He tuck our guns and marched us right down the mainest street a Fosterville with our arms a stuck straight up in the air for ever'one to see. It was humiliating as all hell at the time, but only I just didn't rightly know at the time how much humiliating a feller can be made to suffer.

Ole Red, she had slipped me my six-gun later on, and I had busted our ass outa jail, but only I had gone and left ole Jim locked up in his own jail cell nekkid as a new borned babe. He wanted to kill me for that real bad, and I don't blame him none for it. Then I had went and caught him again. He had rid out with a posse after our ass, and he had got separated from the rest and I had did it to him again. Left him out in the countryside nekkid as a jay. Well, then he sure enough did want to kill me deader'n a cold turd.

Then when the situation was final resolved, and me and Paw and Zeb had our names all cleared up, ole Jim had did what he done to get even with me, what I already told you about. So thinking it all over, if ole Jim was satisfied with how he got to be even with me without killing me, I reckoned that I was too. I stuck out my hand, and he shuck it. All them hard feelings was in the past, and we was friends again. Of a sudden just then ole Zeb stood up, and he were a bit wobbly.

"Come on, Kid," he said. "Let's go to the mountains."

I was some tired a arguing with him.

"I ain't going, Zeb," I said.

"Well fuck you then, Kid," he said. "I'll go by myself."

He turned and staggered across the room to the door and on outside. I figgered that he'd pass out somewhere along the way to finding his horse and ole Bernice Burro, and I'd see him again come morning, but I was kindly hurt that my ole pard, and my best pard at that, would tell me what he told me and that in front a both ole Jim and Red. I reckon I kindly blushed up some at the feel of it. Red, she musta seed it on my face.

"He didn't mean it, Kid," she said. "He'll be back whenever he sobers up."

"I don't keer if he does or don't," I said, and I reckon I had me a hellacious pout on my face. I sure didn't mean what I had just said. Why, ole Zeb, he meant more to me than my own paw, or even my own ole maw. He had did a whole lot more for me than either one a them had ever thought a doing. Paw, he didn't give a half a shit about me, not till I become some notorious as Kid Parmlee, the one they called "a regular Billy the Kid," what name I never keered for much. And I was a thinking, in spite a what ole Red had said a-trying to make me feel better, that ole Zeb would do just exact what he said he would do. He'd pack up and head for the mountains all by his lonesome.

So you see what I was talking about whenever I first started on this here? I had wanted ole Zeb to leave me be, and it sure as hell looked all of a sudden like I had got just what I wanted. Only once I got it, I weren't atall sure for certain that I really wanted it in the first place. I reckon my ole maw had been right about that one, but only I had to go and learn it for my own self the hard way.

Well, ole Jim, he excused hisself after two drinks and went on about his business, whatever that is. I never could rightly figger out what a sheriff's business was whenever they wasn't no trouble a going on for him to get after. So me and ole Red, we was left setting there just the two of us, and Red, she kindly laid her soft hand on top a mine and looked me in the eye with her big green eyes.

"Kid," she said, "you wanta go upstairs with me?"

"Business or pleasure?" I said.

"I'm done working for the day," she said. "I started early."

"In that case," I said, "let's us go on up."

I picked up the bottle, and she picked up two glasses, and we headed on up to her room. Whenever we got inside, I latched the door and blocked it up real good with a chair. I didn't want no one causing us no rude disturbance nor interruption. I thunk about that there time ole Jim had caught me unawares. We put the bottle and glasses down on a table what stood there beside the bed, and then I tuck her in my arms and smooched her real good. It was nice all right, but it wasn't nothing compared to the gloriousness what was to follow.

Come morning, we was laying in bed side by side, stark-staring nekkid and sound asleep, and we had us a surprise awakening a gunshots out in the street. I jumped up right quick and moved over to the winder what had a kindly lacy curtain on it, and keeping my nekkid self to one side, I moved that there curtain just a bit so I could peek out. I seed a man with a sack in one hand and a gun in t'other come a running outa the bank. He had done shot twice, and I seed him shoot a third time. He shot into the bank, and then he mounted up on his horse, and it was only then that I seed that there was actual three of them. The one I was a-watching was the third one to come outa the bank, I guess.

I grabbed for my own Colt, and I cocked it a running back to the winder. I throwed that winder open and tuck aim, but only I never did shoot. Them three was done riding hard, and all I'd a did was I'd a wasted a shot. Then I seed Chastain a running toward the bank. Red was a setting up in bed. Final she said, "What is it, Kid?"

"Sure looked to me like three fellers just robbed the bank," I said.

I put my gun away and went back to the bed and set down beside her. I give her a good smooch.

"I sure had me a wondrous time last night," I said, "but I reckon I'd best get dressed and go on down."

"What for?" she said.

"Well, if I seed what I think I seed," I said, "ole Jim'll be gathering up a posse to go after them owlhoots. I reckon that now that me and Jim is friends again, I had oughta go along with them."

Sure enough, ole Chastain was out in front a his office a-shouting orders for all able-bodied men with guns to get their horses and join up with him right there. I didn't bother telling him that I was a coming along. He was busy enough. I done had my Colt strapped on, so I just hurried on over to the stable to get Ole Horse saddled. I did notice that Zeb's critters and all his tack and stuff was gone. I couldn't slow down to feel sorry about that, though. I got Ole Horse saddled, and then I rid on down to the sheriff's office.

Jim was a-setting his saddle ready to go, and setting right beside him there was ole Lewis Throne, the actual president a the damn bank. They was three or four others ready there, too. I kindly pushed my way through to get on the other side a ole Jim from where Throne was at.

"You 'bout ready to hit the trail?" I asked him.

"With you here, I'm ready," Jim said. "Anyone else comes along, they can try to catch up with us."

"Well, let's go get the bastards, then," Throne said.

We rid outa town fast, and we only slowed down in order to make sure that we was still on the trail a them three. We was, but they was a-moving fast. I could tell by the tracks their horses was a-leaving.

"We got to slow our ass down," I said. "We don't want to go killing our horses."

"The robbers aren't slowing down," Throne said.

"We ain't worried about them killing their horses," I said. "They keep on a-going like they're going, that's just what they're a-going to do. That'll just make it easier for us to catch on up to them."

"The Kid's right, Lewis," Jim said. "Let's follow them easy for a while."

"They've got a lot of the bank's money with them," said Throne, in a kinda huff.

"Some a that's my money," one a them other men said. I didn't know him by name.

"We'll get them," Chastain said. "Slow and easy."

We moved out taking my advice and Jim's orders, but ole Throne and a couple a the other riders was real obvious impatient with the pace we was a setting. Me, I was feeling pretty good. I was a-riding beside ole Jim again, and him not even a-wanting to kill me no more. I liked ole Jim, and so I was real glad a that, and I was glad a the opportunity to give him a hand at something and to show him once more that I really was a good citizen and a friend a his and all like that. Jim, he never said nothing, but I kindly felt like as if he was glad to have me along, too.

Well, we moved slow and easy for a spell, all the while a-keeping our eyes on them tracks, and then we decided that we could let our horses stretch their legs out again, so we whipped them up and moved out fast for a time. We still hadn't saw no sign a the culprits, just only their horses' tracks on the road. They was headed south. Final we had to slow it down again. We rid along slow again for maybe a mile, and then I seed them tracks turn off the road and head cross-country a-moving east.

"Looky there, Jim," I said, a-pointing.

"I see it," he said.

Me and him led the way, and the rest follered. The tracks was harder to foller out there off the road like that, and that slowed us down even more. We went on like that for a couple a miles, and then one a the fellers in back said, "I never thought it'd take us this long."

"I'm for going back," another'n said. "We've gone too far from town."

Chastain stopped his horse and turned to face the rest a the posse.

"Who wants to go home?" he snapped.

They was sullen for a bit, and then the two what had done spoke up admitted that it was them.

"Go on, then," Jim said. "We don't need you."

Them two set there for a minute or so. Then they turned their mounts back west and rid off. In another few seconds, another one follered them. Jim looked at what was left.

"What about you, Horace?" he said.

"Like I told Lewis a while back," said the one called Horace, "some of that money is mine. I'm sticking with you."

"Lewis?" said Jim.

"I'm staying after the sons of bitches until we have the bank money back," Throne said.

Ole Jim looked over at me then.

"Kid?"

"I'm a sticking by you, Jim," I said.

"All right then," he said. "Let's ride."

Well, we rid that day away, and we was a-getting some hungry, I can tell you. You see, we had ever'one of us figgered that we'd catch up with them three way sooner than what time a day it was. I noticed ole Throne turn up his canteen and dribble the last few drops into his mouth. I could also see that ole Jim was beginning to look some worried.

"If we don't come across them soon," he said, "we'll have to stop for the night."

"Are you sure we're even following the right tracks?" Throne said. He was some agitated.

"I'm sure," I said.

"There's another problem," said ole Jim.

"My God, what is it?" said ole Throne.

"In another ten miles or so," said Jim, "we'll be out of my jurisdiction. I'll have to turn back."

"And just let them get away with my—with the bank's money?" Throne said.

"There won't be anything I can do except wire the law out this direction," Chastain said. "If I was to arrest someone outside of my jurisdiction, the judge would let them off."

"Well, what the hell are we waiting for?" said Throne. "We have to catch them before they get beyond your reach."

We rid like hell for as long as we dared to, for the sake a the horses, and by that time the sun was right low in the sky too, and it were getting kindly dark. Real reluctant-like, Jim called a halt, and we made us a camp for the night, only it weren't none too comfy, on accounta we hadn't planned for no long ride much less for no camping out. Hell, we didn't even have no coffee, and even if we hada, we didn't hardly have enough water amongst us to boil it in. Ever'one was kindly grumbling. I got ole Chastain off to one side.

"Listen, Jim," I said. "Don't get too settled in here. I'm fixing to ride around a little and see if I can't find us a better spot. One with some water at least. I'll be back."

Well, I didn't get no argument out a Jim, and so I rid on out, and by and by I did actual come across a nice little stream, and by God, if there weren't a pretty little antelope a-getting itself a drink there. Well, I kilt it right then, and I cut its throat and strung it up by its hind legs in a tree there. I built a little fire, and then I gutted that critter and cut it up some and spitted some meat over the fire. I even found a little ole plant what Zeb had showed me once what I didn't remember what to call it, but you could pull it up and crush up its roots and boil it and get yourself something that tasted most nearly like coffee. The only thing was, I couldn't figger out what we had with us to boil water in.

Anyhow, I left that fresh meat a-cooking and rid back right quick to where I had left the others a-waiting.

"Mount up and foller me," I said. "I got water, and I got meat a-cooking."

Chapter 2

The next morning we had a breakfast a antelope meat and water just like what we had et for supper the night before, and ole Jim, he reckoned that we could ride a few more miles yet before we was plumb outa his what-he-called jurisdiction. We rid on a-follering them tracks, and we still hadn't even ketched a glimpse a them outlaws.

"We have to go faster," Throne said.

"We'll kill our horses," I said.

"Those outlaws are moving fast enough to stay well ahead of us," Throne said, "and I haven't seen a dead horse on the trail yet."

We rid on a ways with him a grumbling, and then we come to another little clump a trees beside a little watering hole. We rid on in there to take advantage a the place, and it was there where we found the answer to the pace them owlhoots was a-setting. The tracks was clear enough. Those bastards had stashed three extry horses in there, and whenever they come to that place, they had switched their saddles onto the fresh horses and then rid on out. The three wore-out horses was there a-grazing and drinking water and such.

"That does it, Lewis," ole Chastain said. "We'll never catch them now. Not before they're out of my reach. We'll have to turn back. I'll send wires out all over the area. Maybe someone'll pick them up for us."

"God damn it," ole Throne said, and he tuck off his hat and throwed it real hard to the ground.

"Jim?" I said.

"What is it, Kid?"

"What if I was to keep on after them? What would a judge say if I was to ketch up to them and bring them back to you? I ain't got no jurisdiction, do I?"

Throne give ole Jim a real anxious look.

"Well," Jim said, "you'd be acting like a bounty hunter. I don't see any problem with that. But there's three of them, Kid."

"I've tuck on worst odds," I said.

Then I reckon what ole Jim had said about bounty hunters had kindly stuck in ole Throne's head, on accounta he said right away, "If you bring back the money, the bank will pay a reward."

"How much, you reckon?" I asked him.

"Well, say five percent."

"I don't know what that means," I said.

"Say they got off with, oh, ten thousand dollars," Throne said. "Five percent of that would be five hundred."

"Five hunnerd for bringing back ten thousand?" I said. "It don't hardly seem worth it. Hell, I might just as well go on back to Fosterville and then go on up in the mountains and find ole Zeb and sniff around for gold with him. I'd make me more than that real easy."

"All right, ten percent," Throne said.

"You heared him, Jim," I said.

"I heard him."

"Ten percent," I said. "All right. You two can head on back, and I'll keep after them. I'd suggest you rest your horses up a bit right here though afore you head back."

"What about you?" Throne asked me.

"Hell," I said, "I'm a taking these here three extry horses along with me. They'll recover all right a riding along without no weight on their backs, and I'll be able to switch off ever' now and then. I'll ketch them bastards, all right."

Well, it weren't long afore I was a-riding along on the trail a the bank robbers on Ole Horse and a-leading me three extry horses. The trail was still clear enough, so I knowed they was ahead a me still. After a few miles, I stopped and tuck the saddle off a Ole Horse and throwed it on one a them others. I mounted right back up and kept a going. Come dark, I come on a little town just ahead a me. I rid on in.

First thing I done, I found the stable and put up Ole Horse and them other three for the night. I went on ahead and paid the man in advance on accounta I didn't have no idee what time a day or night I might decide to take on off again. Then I asked him if anyone had come in and stabled three hard-rode horses lately. He said they hadn't. I went a walking down the street and a looking at the horses what was tied there at the hitch rails. I didn't see nothing suspicious, so I headed for the saloon. It was just the one.

I went in and bellied up to the bar and ordered me a whiskey, and while I sipped at it, I looked over the crowd real good. I didn't see no one suspicious nor no one what looked like the ones what I had saw ride outa Fosterville after they robbed the bank. I finished my whiskey, and I asked the barkeep there if he had saw three strangers a-riding through town during that very day.

"Come to think of it," he said, "there were three such earlier today."

"They leave on out a town?"

He give a shrug. "I ain't seen them for several hours," he said.

"If they was to stay the night here," I said, "where might they find them a place to sleep?"

"Right down at the end of the street," he said. "Widow Sam's Boarding House. It's the only place in town."

I thanked the man kindly and walked out and on down to the widder's boarding house. She come to the door and squinted out at me after I knocked, and I asked her had them three come in for rooms for the night. She said they ain't, so it seemed that they had rid through, and they was still out on the trail out in front a me somewheres. I didn't see no profit in trying to foller their tracks in the dark, so I went ahead and asked the widder if she had a room for me. She said she did, so I paid her, and she showed me my room. I crawled in the bed and went right to sleep. It had been a long day a hard riding, I can tell you.

In the morning I bought myself a breakfast, and then I went into the little gen'ral store they had there in that one-horse town, and I bought me some supplies so that I'd be better prepared for a long trail ride. I made sure that I got me a coffee pot and some coffee, too. Then I got Ole Horse and them other three, and I headed out. I picked up the tracks a them bank robbers easy enough. I moved along pretty fast with four horses, and it was just a little bit after noon whenever I come to another little town. I was a-hoping that they mighta figgered they had rid far enough away from Fosterville that they could stop and rest a bit. I rid on in real easy-like.

Real soon I seed the saloon, and it was right smack next door to the sheriff's office of all things, so I stopped and tied my horses in front and started towards the saloon door, but just then I seed this character dressed like a real fancy dude cowboy a-ambling down the sidewalk, and he slowed up right there in front a the sheriff's office. They was some dodgers posted there, and that was what got his interest. I watched him squint at them a bit, and then I seed him reach for one, and just as he ripped it off the wall, I kindly reckanized one a the pictures on it.

"Hold on there a minute," I said.

The feller turned and looked me in the eyes, and he had a cold stare all right. His hair was real dark brown, just almost black, and his eyes was green. He had a smooth kinda baby face, roundish, and he was a wearing black mostly. His trousers and vest and boots and hat was all black, just only his shirt were a kindly light blue color. He had two Colts strapped on, too, and they was a hanging in black leather holsters off a black leather belt.

"You talking to me?" he said.

"I don't see no one else standing there," I said. He weren't a very big feller, but a course, he was bigger'n me. Most ever'one is. 'Cept a gal now and then.

"All right," he said. "What can I do for you?"

"I'd kinda like to get me a look at that there dodger you tuck off the wall," I said.

He looked at it hisself, and then he give me a cold-eyed stare, and he said, "I don't mind." He handed me the dodger, and I sure enough reckanized the bastards. Well, I reckanized one for sure, him being the last to come outa the bank at Fosterville. I never did read too good, but I could read enough for that dodger. The Dawson Gang, it said. So that's who I was after: the Dawson Gang. I had heared a little bit about them before. Then I seed that someone was offering five hunnerd apiece for the three a them bastards. That on top a my ten percent sounded pretty good. I give the man back the dodger.

"Thanks," I said, and I turned to head for the saloon door.

"Hold on," the man in black said. I stopped and looked back, and he come a-walking up aside a me. "Can I buy you a drink?"

I was some suspicious, and I reckon I showed it, but I said, "Sure," and me and him went on in together. We bellied up to the bar side by side, and he asked me, "Whiskey?"

"Yeah," I said.

The barkeep come over, and blackie, he said, "Two whiskies."

The barkeep come up with a bottle and two glasses, and before he could pour any whiskey out, the man in black stopped him. "We'll take the bottle," he said, and he paid for it and picked it up along with the glasses and headed over for a empty table. We set there across from each other. I watched him while he poured the drinks, and then he pushed one glass over to me and set the bottle right square in the middle a the table where either one of us could reach it whenever we tuck a mind to.

"How come you to be so generous with a total stranger?" I asked him.

"I'm curious," he said.

"What about?" I said.

"Your interest in the Dawson Gang."

"I might be the same kinda curious on you," I said.

"In that case," he said, "let's introduce ourselves and then have a polite conversation. I'm Richard Cherry."

"They call me Kid Parmlee," I said.

"I've heard of you," he said. "They call you a regular—"

"Don't say it," I said, interrupting him. "I know what they call me, and I don't keer for it none."

"I don't blame you," he said. He tuck a sip a his whiskey. "What's your interest in the Dawsons?"

"How about you tell me yours first?" I said. "It was you what set up this here palaver."

"All right," he said. "I'm a bounty hunter. The Dawsons are worth five hundred each. I mean to get it. I'd hate to have a run-in with someone else who has the same idea."

"Well, I'll tell you this much," I said. "I never even knowed they had no reeward on their heads, but I have been a-tailing them for a spell."

Well, that left him hanging, I can tell you. He downed the rest a his whiskey and poured hisself another. "Do you mind telling me why you've been tailing them?" he asked.

I never was one to give away too much information to no stranger, but he had bought the whiskey, and he had told me what he was up to. I thunk it over, and I couldn't see no harm.

"Them three robbed the bank over to Fosterville," I said. "I joined up with the posse a-chasing them on accounta the sheriff there, ole Jim Chastain, is a friend a mine. Well, we come to the end a the line on accounta ole Jim's jurisdiction, you know, but I told Jim I don't have no jurisdiction, so I kept on after them."

"That's it?" he asked.

"Well, mostly," I said.

"You said they robbed the bank."

"That's right."

"They get away with it? I mean, did they get out of town with money from the bank?"

"Yeah," I said. "They did. Ole Throne, he's the bank president, he rid along with us till we come the end a Jim's line. He was a-wanting that money back pretty bad."

"How bad?" Cherry asked me. Well, he had me in a corner. I had to tell him.

"Ten percent," I said.

"Do you know how much they got away with?"

"Ain't got no idee," I said.

He drunk some more whiskey, and I did too, and in a minute he said, kindly musing-like, "Kid Parmlee."

"That's me," I said.

"Yeah," he said. "I've heard of you, all right. They say you've killed a good many men. How many is it?"

I thunk about ole Paw a-counting, and then I thunk about that there Texas Ranger what had made me ashamed a keeping count. "I don't rightly know," I said. "That ain't a decent kinda thing for a man to keep a count on. It's a right smart number, though."

"I'll bet it is," he said. "Say, Kid, you still mean to go after the Dawsons?"

"That's the only reason I'm way out here in the middle a nowhere in this damn little one-horse town," I said. "I'm a-going after them, all right. I promised ole Jim I would, and I don't quit whenever I get onto something. I ain't never yet."

"I was afraid of that," he said. "Well, I mean to go after them, too."

"Listen here, Cherry," I said.

"Call me Dick," he said.

"Listen here, Dick," I said, "I promised to bring back the bank money to Fosterville, and I mean to do that. You'd best not get in my way a the doing of it, neither. Not if you know what's good for you. You know I've kilt me a mess a men, but you don't know the worst of it."

"What's that?"

"I've shot the ears offa a couple of them too."

"On purpose?"

"Damn right."

"That's good shooting," he said. "I never tried it, but I don't think I could do it. Likely I'd just put a hole in their heads."

"So what the hell do you say?"

"I'm not backing off."

"Well, I ain't neither," I said. "Are we a going to have to shoot it out betwixt the two of us and all over them three worthless bastards?"

"I hope not."

"Well, like I said then, stay outa my way."

"Have another drink, Kid," he said, and he went and poured it.

"You ain't a getting me drunk," I said.

"I mean to get me drunk," he said. He poured his own glass full again and drunk it down right quick. I figgered that I could go on ahead and sip on another one if he was a-glugging it down like that. I tuck me a sip. It was good whiskey, but only I was a-meaning to get on back out on the trail. They was still about a half a day a riding time left.

"Well, you just go right on and do that," I said. "Me, I got places to go. Thanks for the drinks."

I stood right up then and started in to leave the saloon, but he come right after me. I was clean out onto the sidewalk, though, afore he ketched up to me. He put a hand on my shoulder and spun me around, and I come up with my Colt a tucked right under his chin. He kindly friz up and helt his hands out to his sides.

"Whoa," he said.

I put my Colt away.

"What do you want?" I said.

"I got a proposition for you."

"I'm a-listening."

"Let's team up. There's three of them against one of you—or one of me. If we team up, it'll be three to two. Much better odds. You agree?"

"I agree that it's better odds," I said, not committing myself to nothing.

"All right," he said. "You've been after the Dawsons for ten percent of the bank money they stole, and you don't even know how much it is. Why, I've heard of bank robberies where a smart teller stuffed a bag full of one-dollar bills, and the robbers ran off with it not knowing about it till later. They had a big bag full of bills but not much money. I know that there's fifteen hundred dollars on their heads. If we catch them together, we split the reward money and the ten percent from the bank. How's that?"

"I don't know," I said. "I wasn't figgering on partnering up with no one. 'Specially not no stranger."

"I'm no stranger," he said. "We drank whiskey together. And think of it this way. You didn't even know about the reward. You still wouldn't know about it except for me. You wouldn't even know you were after the Dawson Gang if it hadn't been for me. Come on. What do you say? It's better than shooting it out."

Well, he had a good argument there. I had to admit that. He had did me a kinda inadvertent favor by going up to that there dodger and calling my attention to it. And two against three was a whole lot better than one against three. Then there was that extry fifteen hunnerd what I hadn't even counted on, in fact, hadn't knowed about. I thunk it through real quick-like. If I was to turn him down on his offer and go on by my own self after them Dawsons, why, it was pretty damn clear that he was a-going to do the same thing, and then whenever one or the both of us ketched them, there would almost for sure be a fight betwixt the two of us over which one was a-going to get the privilege a taking them in and claiming all the reewards.

"Well, hell," I said, sticking my right hand out for ole Cherry to take a-holt of, "I reckon I got myself a new pard."

Chapter 3

Well, now, I was a-wanting to head right on out on the trail after them damn Dawsons, but my new pard, he weren't in no such a hurry to get going. He had done had some drinks, and he was a wanting to have hisself some more, maybe go right on ahead and get hisself drunked up right smart. Now, I could understand that impulse sure enough, but I was awful anxious to get that bank money on back to Fosterville in order to show ole Sheriff Jim Chastain just how all fired serious I was at really being a good citizen and all. I told that to ole Dick Cherry, and then I added a kinda threat what I really thunk would work on him, being as how he had horned in on my game anyhow.

"Hell," I said, "if you ain't all that serious about it, I'll go on after them all by my own self. It's just that I thunk that was exact what you didn't want me a-doing."

Well, that got his attention all right. "Kid," he said, "I'll have to let you in on something. I was going to keep it to myself, but you forced my hand."

"What the hell you talking about?" I asked him.

"When you first spotted me looking at that poster on the Dawsons," he said, "I wasn't really looking for them. That poster just caught my eye. It was the first time I ever saw anything on them. What I was really doing was looking for the latest information on ole LeRoy Girt. He's right here in town, and he's worth a thousand bucks all by himself. I meant to get him myself and then ride out with you after the Dawsons."

"You son of a bitch," I said. "You was a-meaning to start off our brand-new pardnership right off by cheating me outa five hunnerd bucks. I oughta shoot off your damn left ear just for the hell of it. I've did it before, you know. Shot ears off."

"Cool off, Kid," he said. "I was after Girt before we met. I figured that our partnership was starting with the Dawsons, but now that you're threatening to go after them without me, I decided to let you in on this other deal. We get Girt first, we can take after the Dawsons with an extra five hundred each tucked in our jeans. What do you say?"

"You say he's in town?"

"I can point him out to you right now."

"And he's for sure wanted?"

"Come on," he said. He led me back over to the front a the sheriff's office where them dodgers was all a posted, and he poked a finger at one a them. It was for LeRoy Girt all right, and it had his picture right there with one thousand dollars writ right under it. He was wanted for murdering and robberying. It seemed all right to me then. Oh, yeah, it also said "dead or alive." I tuck it that meant it was all right to just walk up behind the bastard and shoot him dead without even giving him no warning nor nothing like that. 'Course, that weren't my style, but it could be did and still be all legal, all right.

"Where is he at?" I asked.

"First of all we have to come to an agreement," ole Cherry said.

"I'm a listening."

"We take Girt, and we split the reward fifty-fifty."

"Agreed."

"Then we spend the night right here and get us an early start in the morning on the trail of the Dawsons. When we get them, we split the fifteen hundred the same way—fifty-fifty."

"And we take the stoled money back to the bank in Fosterville?"

"Of course. And split the reward from the bank. Same as all the rest."

I thunk on that for a spell, a-scratching on my head and shuffling my feet around some. "They'll get that much more farther away from us," I said.

"They don't know we're after them, do they? We'll catch up to them easy enough. Besides, I think I know where they're headed."

"How come you to know that?"

"They're headed east, aren't they?"

"Yeah," I said, "I reckon. They was the last I knowed, and I for sure never seed them double back and cross my path."

"I know the country east of here," Cherry said. "There's only one place they could be headed for."

"Where is it then?"

"We got a deal? We do it my way? Head out in the morning? Together?"

"Hell," I said, "all right. We got us a deal all right. Now tell me where it is they're a headed to."

"They'll be headed for a little town called Snake Creek. It's the only place east of here within reach. I imagine they'll stop over there to rest up and play around for a spell. We'll catch them there."

"You better be right what you say in all your speculating," I said. "Okay. What do we do now? Where is this Girt at right now?"

"He's right in there in the saloon," Cherry said. "He's sitting at a table in the far corner all by himself. He's been there for a couple of hours, so he's likely drunk. You and me together can take him real easy."

"Let's go do it, then," I said.

I hitched at my britches and headed into the saloon, and ole Cherry, he was right along behind me. We went on inside and bellied up to the bar. Kindly casual-like, I glanced around way back to the darkest and fartherest corner a the room, and sure 'nough, there set a feller all by his lonesome a-sipping at a whiskey glass. Nobody was a-setting at no table nowhere near where he was at. They was a bottle a-setting on the table in front of him. I turned back to the bar and said in a real low voice, "That him back there?"

"That's him," Cherry said.

"How you wanta do this?"

"I figure if we come at him from both sides at the same time, we can take him without any trouble. I'll walk down to the end of the bar and then along the back wall. I'll be coming up to him from his left. You go on over to the far-side wall and come at him from that direction."

"I get his right side?"

"I'll take his right side if you want."

"No," I said. "That's all right. We'll take him like you said."

"Are you ready then?"

"We going to try to take him alive?" I asked.

"You can ask him to give up if you want to," said Cherry. "It'd be a whole lot easier to just shoot him though."

"I'll ask him to give it up," I said. "Any man oughta be give that chance. Don't do no shooting before that."

He give a shrug. "Have it your way," he said, and then he turned away from me and went to walking alongside a the bar. I let him go on like that a ways before I turned around and kindly looked towards the other side a the room. I picked up a glass and a bottle and headed on back thataway. Whenever I got clean back to the wall, I put the glass and bottle on a table like as if I was about to set my ass down there, but only I never. Instead a setting, I turned again and commenced to walking along the wall a-headed for that there Girt feller. I seed that ole Cherry was a-doing the same thing back at the back wall. We was a-coming at him from both sides just the way ole Cherry had planned it.

Well, Girt weren't total drunk. He seed us, and he knowed what was a-happening all right. He shoved his chair back and come right up to his feet, his gunhand a-making a motion. I hollered right up. "Give it up, Girt. Ain't no call for killing." He stopped still. So did I and ole Cherry, he did too.

"You lawmen?" Girt asked.

"We ain't lawmen," I said, "but we aim to take you in."

"Bounty hunters," he said, and it was like as if he spit out them words like they was real distasteful.

"Call it what you like," I said. "Unbuckle your gunbelt real easy-like and let it drop, and there won't be no shooting."

"Fuck you," Girt snarled, and he went for it. Well, as usual, I was faster. I whipped out my trusty Colt and snapped off a shot what tore into his right chest. I was a little off. It didn't kill him, but just then ole Cherry shot, and he hit him, too. His shot went into Girt's heart, and the ole outlaw fell back against the wall, and then kindly slow, he slud down to set on the floor with his chin a-resting on his chest. He left a smear a blood down the wall where he had slud. He was dead all right.

Well, we collected our blood money, but the local sheriff, he didn't like us none too much. He let us know right for sure that he would be real happy whenever we got our ass outa town. He didn't keer too much for bounty hunters. To tell you the truth, I never had keered too much for them my own self, and I felt kindly funny-like putting that money in my pocket. Hell, I hadn't even knowed that Girt feller.

"What are you looking so down about, Kid?" Cherry asked me as we was a walking out on the sidewalk.

"Nothing," I said. "Just only that I just now helped you to kill a man what I didn't even know and what wasn't doing nothing to me."

"He was a cold-blooded killer, Kid. Don't give it another thought."

"If what we done was so all-fired noble," I said, "then how come the sheriff to act like he done towards us? Tell me that. How come him to want us to get outa town?"

"Is it any worse that we killed Girt than if that sheriff had done it?" Cherry asked me. "And how about this? Girt was sitting in the saloon, and that sheriff wasn't doing a damn thing about it. We did the law's job, and I say, it's justice that we got paid for doing it."

Well, I never could argue like that, so I just kept my yap shut, and I walked along with ole Cherry till we come back to the front door a the saloon. We went back in there, only this time we got us a bottle and two glasses and set our ass down at a table. I felt kindly like ever'one in the place was a looking at us, and likely I was right. They had just a little while back seed us kill a man in there. They knowed we had money, too, on accounta the reeward. Pretty soon, sure enough, a little old gal come over and set down right beside ole Cherry and commenced to rubbing on him and making over him like as if he was General Grant or something. She never paid no attention to me atall. I figgered it was 'cause I was so skinny and scrawny and never did look like much nohow.

It didn't take long before them two stood up and headed for the stairs what led up to the whore rooms. That gal was a hanging tight onto ole Cherry's left arm and a-giggling all the way. I couldn't help myself, but I started in to thinking about my ole Red back in Fosterville, and I developed me a powerful urge on accounta the thinking. There I was a-setting by myself there with a bottle a whiskey. I sipped me a little more. The whiskey was good enough, but it weren't what I was really a-wanting. I guess you know what I mean.

I kept a-watching around a-wondering if that little gal up-stairs with ole Cherry was the only gal a-working in that place. But I never seed no other gal a tall, and so I just kept on a-drinking, and by and by I was pretty damn drunk. Well, I stood up kindly wobbly, and I went a-weaving my way over to the bar. I was kindly self-conscious staggering around like that in front a all them folks. It was a good thing too that I come to the bar as quick as I done, 'cause I needed to ketch myself on it to keep from tumbling on over.

"I think you've had enough," the barkeep said.

"Hell," I said, "I know I've had enough. Where can I rent me a room to sleep it off in?"

"Right here," he said.

Well, I paid him, and he give me a skeleton key to one a them whore rooms upstairs. I tuck it and turned to head for the stairs. I had made my way about halfway down the length a the bar when a big, ugly character come up from a chair and walked over to the bar smack in my way. He stood a-facing me, and I swear he was so bow-legged that his legs was two inches apart there where they come together. I could see that he was a-looking for trouble.

"You don't look so dangerous now," he said.

I stood a-swaying, and I kindly blinked my eyes at him, and I said, "You talking to me?"

"That's right," he said. "You're drunk and all alone, and you don't look so tough like that."

"Mister," I said, "I want a bed. I don't want to do no killing just now. Why don't you go on and set your ass back down and leave it go? I'm drunk all right, but I'd have to be plumb passed out before I couldn't kill you in a blink."

"You're pretty cocky, ain't you?" he said. "For such a little shit."

I was feeling plenty woozy by then, and I was afeared that I was might near ready to fall over on my face. I sure did want to get rid a this bully before that was to happen.

"Listen, shithead," I said, "either set down and shut up, or go for your gun."

Well, he went for it, but he didn't even have it outa the holster before my Colt was cocked and pointed right straight at his nose, which was a pretty big one. He stood there skeered to move, and he went to shaking.

"I oughta kill you," I said. "I've kilt aplenty for less reason. I've shot their ears off, too. Once I even shot a man's thumb off. You want me to shoot off your thumb for you?"

"No," he said. "No. I—I'm sorry, mister. I take it all back."

"Go on and slip your hogleg outa the holster," I said. "Real easy. Toss it behind the bar."

He done what I said. "Now drop your britches down around your ankles," I told him. He was that skeered, he done that, too. I walked on around him then and left him with ever'one in the place a-laughing at him. I managed somehow to keep on my feet and make it all the way to the stairs. Then I used that railing to hold my ass up and help me climb. Pretty soon, I found my room and went inside. I locked the door and fell down on the bed. Right away, I passed on out, and if I dreamed any dreams, why, I never had no recollection of them the next morning.

When I woked up the next morning, my head was kinda hurting, but I splashed some water in my face and straightened my clothes up some and walked on downstairs. Ole Dick Cherry, he was already down there, and he was a-wearing a whole new set a clothes and was all slickered up real nice.

"You don't look to me like you're fixing to hit no trail," I said.

"Well, I am," he said.

"Like that?"

"What's wrong?" he asked me.

"Nothing, I guess. Let's find us some food and eat and then get going."

He agreed, and we hunted us up a eating place what was open early and went inside. It was kindly busy, but we found us a table all right, and pretty soon we had ordered up eggs and ham and biscuits and such. We started out with coffee, and we finished up the same way. When we was all did, we paid up and headed for the door, and just as we was about to go out, that feller what I had the run-in with the night before come in. We like to run into each other. He stopped still.

"Excuse me," he said.

"That's all right," I said. He stepped aside to let me and ole Cherry go on by. I started to go on, but I stopped. "What's your name?" I asked him.

"Marlowe," he said. "They call me Moose."

"Well, Moose," I said, "after last night, it come to me that we had oughta be interduced proper. I'm knowed as Kid Parmlee."

Well, I reckon that there Moose Marlowe had heared about me all right, on accounta whenever I said my name, he went kindly white in the face.

"Be seeing you around," I said, and I walked on by him and out the door. Ole Cherry follered me. We went on down to the stable and fetched out our horses along with them three extry I had brung along, and pretty soon we was on the trail.

"Right smart of you bringing along those extra horses," Cherry said.

"It was the Dawsons what left them behind," I said.

"Real thoughtful of them."

I laughed at that. "Yeah, it was, weren't it?" I said.

We rid along a bit farther without saying nothing too much, but only I was a-watching the trail, and I seed them same hoof marks what I had been follering all along. I didn't say nothing, but I knowed then that ole Cherry had been right about where them Dawsons was a-headed. We was on their trail for sure. I was just a-hoping that he had been right about the rest of it, that they would lay up at that there Snake Crick like he had said.

Then kindly outa nowhere, ole Cherry said, "What was that between you and Moose Marlowe back there?"

I told him more or less what had went on the night before betwixt the two of us, and he laughed at the thought a Marlowe standing in the saloon with his britches down, but whenever he got hisself over that, he got kindly serious like again.

"Kid," he said, "you made yourself a dangerous enemy in Moose Marlowe."

I give a shrug. "I wouldn't say that," I said. "Hell, I was staggering drunk last night, and I outdrawed him real easy. I made him do what I said, and he just only stood there a-trembling. Then this morning whenever I told him my name, I seed him go all white. Didn't you see that?"

"I saw it all right," he said.

"He's so skeered a me, I won't have no trouble from him even if I was to see him again."

"He's afraid to face you," my new pard said, "but he won't be afraid to shoot you in the back or to pay someone else to do his dirty work for him. I know him. I've known him a long time. He's like that. He's a coward and a bully, and he holds a grudge. Last night when he went for his gun, you should've killed him. You're too soft, Kid."

Chapter 4

Long about nightfall I knowed that me and ole Cherry was going to be obliged to set us up a camp for the night, and it might near had me agitated on accounta I figgered that if them Dawsons was still a-running hard, which a course they mighta been, they would be well ahead of us by then. By morning they'd be long gone and we might never ketch up with them atall. The only thing I was a-counting on and a-hoping for was that Cherry would turn out to be right about what he said that they would stop over for a spell to rest up some in that there Snake Crick, and we would come right up on their ass whenever we was to get on in there. That's what I was a-hoping, but I was still some uneasy on accounta they was a problem there, too. The longer them bank-robbing bastards was to be a-laying and playing around in Snake Crick before we was to ketch up to them, the more a that there bank money they would most surely get spent and the less our reeward would come to. That bothered me somewhat, but even more it was a-bothering me to think that I wouldn't be able to keep my promise to ole Chastain and even ole Throne that I was a-going to bring all a that money back.

But anyhow, we come across a good camping spot before long what had a small grove a trees and a little spring a running right there. It had some good grass, too. The real surprise though was that it had done been used and that real recent-like. We figgered on accounta the road weren't much traveled and 'cause a the tracks what we was a-trailing that it was them Dawsons what had camped there. That eased up my mind some. If they had camped the night there then they wasn't quite as much ahead of us as I had thunk they might be. They was apparent relaxing some, thinking they had done outdistanced their pursuit.

Well, me and ole Dick Cherry, we tuck and built us up a little fire and cooked some food and boiled some coffee, and then we et. We seed to it first, a course, that our horses was all staked out with a plenty a grass to graze on and near enough to the water. We was kindly tired out from the long day's riding, but it was still some early for sleeping, so we set up a-drinking coffee and a-chattering some.

"Whenever we come on them Dawsons up yonder at Snake Crick," I said, "how you reckon we had oughta play it? You got some idee along them lines?"

"They don't know you, do they?"

"They never seed me in their life far as I know. I seed them once though. I was upstairs a looking out a winder whenever they robbed the bank in Fosterville. I seed them a coming outa the bank and riding outa town."

"Well, they don't know me, either," Cherry said. "It ought to be easy for us. I figure we'll just play it by ear. Maybe we catch them one at a time apart from each other. I say we just see what happens and take it from there."

"Sounds all right to me," I said. "Anything you say, why, I'll go along with it. Say, you been in this bounty hunting business for long?"

"Couple of years," he said. "I didn't plan it. It just sort of happened. I worked as a cowboy for a while when I was a kid. Then I got kind of handy with a six-gun and hired on as a gunhand in the middle of a range war. The way things turned out, I gunned a man who was wanted. When I collected the reward, it came to me that there were a lot more men on those dodgers with prices on their heads. It just seemed like the thing to do."

"I reckon so," I said. And it did seem reasonable enough, and I was a-thinking on it for my own self. The only thing was that it was still somewhat distasteful in me to think on shooting someone down what I didn't know just on accounta someone would pay me money for the doing of it. With the Dawsons it was different. I kept on a telling myself that I was a-doing that for ole Jim Chastain and for Fosterville what had sorta become my own home town. Well, it was the most home town I ever knowed.

Anyhow, we give it up just a little after that and turned our ass in for the night. It come a little cool before the night was over, and we come out from under them blankets early and made us some coffee, but we hit the trail without no breakfast in our bellies. Cherry said that we wasn't none too far from Snake Crick, and we could wait till we got there and get us a full-cooked meal for a change. I went along with that, but then it was damn near noon whenever we final seed that little ole town up ahead of us, and my belly was grumbling something fierce.

Of a sudden, I hauled up on my reins and pulled Ole Horse to a dead stop.

"What's wrong, Kid?" Cherry asked.

"It just come to me," I told him, "that we're stringing along them three horses what them Dawsons left behind on the trail. If we was to ride on into town with them, them outlaws is bound to reckanize them, and that might could make them some suspicious of you and me a-coming in with their horses like that."

"Hell," he said, "anyone could've come across the horses along the way and picked them up as strays."

"That's right true enough," I said, "but still, it ain't worth taking no chance with. Besides, we don't need them no more. I'm a-turning them loose."

"Suit yourself," he said.

So we rid on into Snake Crick just the two of us on our two riding horses. I was kindly sneaking my eyeballs around a-looking over the town and the folks what was out on the street, but I never seed no Dawsons out there, and looking over the horses at the hitch rails wouldn't do no good, on accounta I hadn't never saw the horses what they was a-riding after they had made their switch. Well, we hauled our ass up in front of a rooming house and went in and got us a room. After we stowed our gear, we tuck our horses to a stable at the far end a the street. It weren't too far, though. There weren't much to that there Snake Crick. From the stable we walked on down to a eating place and went inside.

It was crowded in there on accounta it was just about the only place in town to get grub, and it was noontime. We managed to find a table though, and we ordered us up some eggs and stuff. The feller in the dirty apron what tuck our order argued some with us. He said that it was long past breakfast time, and the cook was a-whomping up steaks and beans and such, but we argued right back, and we final got our way. Well, the way it come about was like this here.

"It's noon," the man said. "He's done quit cooking eggs. Have a steak like ever'one else."

Then ole Cherry, I coulda shot his ear off, he said, "Listen, friend, my partner here is none other than Kid Parmlee, and he's a regular Billy the Kid. If he wants eggs, I'd fix him some eggs."

Well, that done the trick but only what else it done was it let ever'one in the whole damn town know just who the hell I was and that in a real short time. It don't take long in a one-horse town for word to spread, you know. I wanted to cuss ole Cherry real good, but only they was all kinds a ears a-listening, so I just kept quiet, and since the secret was done let out, I closed my eyes down to slits to look my most meanest.

So we finished our breakfasts and paid and left that place, and I tell you what, folks give us plenty a room whenever they seed us a coming their way. I never realized till just then how well I was knowed. There we was a ways from the mountains and from Fosterville where most a my activities had tuck place, but them folks in Snake Crick had heared about me all right. To tell the truth a the matter, it kindly puffed me up some, and I begin to strut pretty fine.

"Let's check out the saloon," Cherry said. I said that sounded okay to me, and so we went on over there. It weren't far. It was crowded pretty good, too, and before you go to thinking that Snake Crick was bigger'n what I said it was on accounta I keep on a saying that we run into crowds, well, they wasn't all that many folks. It's just that they was only one eating place and just only one saloon, so ever'one in town had to go to the same places, you see.

Anyhow, we bellied up to the bar and ordered us up a bottle and two glasses. We had us a drink a standing there, and then we hunted around the room for a table. We found one back against the far wall, and we went over to it and plopped our ass down there. We poured us another drink, and while we was a-sipping at our whiskey, I was a searching the room a looking at all the faces in there. Then I seed them.

They was clean across the room from us, but I could tell it was them Dawsons all right. They was doing just like what me and Cherry was a doing. I thunk about it, and I figgered we coulda kilt the three of them right then without no problems, 'cept only that the place was so crowded, we might get some innocent folks kilt in the process. I sipped some more whiskey. Then I said to Cherry in a most near whisper, "Anyone in here look familiar to you?"

"I can't say they do," he said. 'Course he had never saw the Dawsons, just only their pictures on that there dodger he had stole offa the wall that time I first met up with him. Me, I had saw them in the flesh.

"Well," I said, "they's in here all right, but afore I point them out to you, I want you to agree with me that this here ain't the time nor place to do nothing about it. They's too many folks in here."

"I agree," he said. "Now where are they?"

I give him a quick description and told him whichaway to look, and he seed them all right without calling no attention to the looking, so then we both knowed for sure that they was in town, and we both knowed what they was a-looking like. We agreed then, still a talking in low voices a course, that we'd keep our eye on them, and that if either one of us was to ketch ary one a them out alone, why, we'd just go on ahead and deal with it and tell the other'n later. I was worried that they was a-spending that there bank money, and I decided to go on ahead and say something about it to ole Cherry.

"You know, ever' damn time they buys a drink, they're a spending a little more a that there bank money."

"They might have had a little money in their jeans before they robbed the bank," Cherry said, "but chances are, you're right."

"The more of it they spend, the less we get to take back to the bank," I said, "and the reeward for the money is a percent. You know what that there means, I reckon."

"The more they spend, the less we recover, and the less we recover, the smaller the reward."

"Yeah. Something like that."

"Well, Kid, you're the one that said not to start anything in here. We could take them easy right now and stop all that spending. But you're calling the shots."

"I don't like it none," I said, "but we got to wait for a better time and place."

He give a shrug and picked up his glass and tuck a little bitty sip a whiskey. I done the same thing.

"I got me an idea, Kid," Cherry said.

"What's that?"

Well, he whispered his idee into the side a my head, and it sounded like a pretty good one to me, 'cept only for one thing.

"You done let the whole town know just who the hell I am," I said, "and we done been seed together."

"Men have falling outs all the time," he said. "No one will think anything about it."

I thunk on it a bit more, and he seemed to make sense, so I agreed to it. He tuck hisself another sip a whiskey, then got up and left the place, both of us a-hoping that them Dawsons hadn't noticed nothing. We figgered that our chances was pretty good on accounta them not knowing us atall and the place being as crowded as what it was. I sipped on my drink a little more, and then I got up and walked back to the bar. I tuck my bottle and glass with me, and I stood there with my back to the bar a-looking out over the crowd. I put on my meanest and cockiest look.

In another minute or so, here come ole Cherry back into the bar, and he made a big show a spotting me there. He stopped still. He looked mean and mad. He crouched down like a pissed-off panther, and he held his hands out ready for a fast draw.

"Kid Parmlee," he called out in a loud voice, and the whole place got real quiet of a sudden.

I looked over at him real casual-like and most unconcerned. "You a-talking to me?" I said.

"That's your name I called, ain't it?"

"That's what some calls me," I said. "What's on your mind?"

"A killing," he said.

"One that's been did?"

"One that you did," he said, "and another one. One that's about to happen. Step out away from that bar."

I stepped out and faced him square. "You oughta give that there some more thought," I said. "For one thing, if you go to shooting in here, someone innocent is liable to get hurt. For another, I don't even know you, and that means I don't really want to kill you, but if you don't back off, I will."

"I ain't backing off."

"You're making a big mistake."

"Hell, I know all about you. They call you a regular Billy the Kid. I guess you're the same kind of back-shooting bastard as he is. You don't scare me."

"All right, mister," I said. "Make your play."

Ole Cherry went for his shooter real fast, but I was some faster. My Colt was cocked and pointed right smack at his heart, and he kindly friz up with his drawed but not hauled up level yet. It was pointed at the floor about halfway betwixt the two of us. We just stood there for a long pause like that, him a-looking real skeered-like.

"You gonna raise up that there shooter or put it away?" I asked him.

"You got me, Kid," he said. "I never believed you were really that fast. I'll put it away."

"I could go on ahead and kill you," I said. "I got me a whole room a witnesses what seed you go for your gun first. You aiming to slip up behind me one a these times and do me in thataway?"

"No," he said. "You beat me square. I give it up."

"Then go on and put your gun away."

He did, and he turned around a-hanging his head and walked on outa there. It sounded like as if ever'one in the place let out all the breath they had been a-holding all at one time, and then they all commenced to talking again, but only they was most a them a-looking right at me. I tried to ignore it by turning around belly to the bar and picking up my glass to sip at it. Almost immediate, one a them little whore gals was a-hanging onto my left arm. I turned my head to give her a look at, and she weren't bad if she hadn't a been painted on so thick. She was a-looking up at me with great big blue eyes.

"Kid Parmlee," she said. "I've heard of you. I'm Sparky."

"I bet you are," I said. "Buy you a drink?"

"I was hoping you'd ask."

She called for a glass, and the barkeep brung her one, but I never poured none a my whiskey in it. Instead, I picked up the bottle and my glass. "Not here," I said.

"I have a room upstairs," she said. "You want to go up?"

"Let's go."

We turned away from the bar and headed for the stairs, her still a-hanging onto my arm. I handed her the bottle. She done had the fresh glass, and that meant that all I was a-toting was my own glass what I had in my left hand. I was a-keeping my right free just in case, you know. Whenever we come to the stairs, I stopped and tuck me a look around the room, like as if I was a-making sure that no one was fixing to try to get the drop on me. Then I turned back and me and that gal went on up to her room.

It was nice furnished with all kinds a pink and frilly stuff in it. She tuck the glass outa my hand and put it and the other glass and the bottle on a table what was there by the bed. Then she give me a look that had questions in it. I said, "Let's have us a smoke and a drink."

I tuck the makings outa my pocket while she poured the two glasses full, and I was just about to pour some terbaccy onto the paper, but she come and tuck it all away from me, and then she rolled up the best looking cigareet I had ever seed rolled, and she licked it real good, too. Then she tucked it in betwixt my lips. I pulled a wooden sulfur match outa my pocket, and she tuck that and struck it and held the fire to my cigareet. I sucked it started, and she blowed out the flame on that match, and her lips did pucker real pretty. She tucked the makings back into my pocket. Then she tuck

the cigareet outa my mouth and had herself a puff on it
before she give it back to me. We was a-setting side by side
on the edge a the bed by that time.

Well, I finished up my drink, and she finished hers, and
we put the glasses down on the table there. Then we passed
that there smoke back and forth till it was might near burned
up. She tuck the butt and snubbed it out in a tray there on
the table.

"Sparky, huh?" I said. "That don't sound to me like a
right name."

"Kid don't sound like a right name to me, neither," she
said.

I grinned at her. "You got me there."

Then she leaned in towards me with her eyes most nearly
closed and that there real inviting pucker on her lips again,
and I couldn't help myself. Ole Red come to mind, and I felt
a real sharp pang a guilt come on me. It tuck a powerful
effort on my part, but I forced that guilt and them thoughts
about ole Red right outa my head, and I went for them luscious lips. My, my, but she was sure sweet. After we had
drooled all over each other real good, I broke loose a her
bear hug and went over to check if the door was locked real
good. It were. It had a bolt on the inside what was slud home.
I turned back around, and ole Sparky was a-standing up beside the bed and stripping off her clothes. I walked back over
there and tuck off my gunbelt. I hung it up there on the post
a the bed, and I tossed my hat off. Then I set down on the
edge a the bed again and pulled off my boots. When I looked
up again, ole Sparky was stark-staring nekkid. She come at
me.

I tell you what, I never had no better time in my life than
what I had that time with ole Sparky. She sure enough lived
up to her name. Whenever we was final all done, and it were
a while, I was all wrung out like a bandanna what had been

a mopping a sweaty brow all day long out on the hot prairie. I wasn't having no thoughts about ole Red nor no other gals nor nothing, not ole Cherry, nor the Dawsons, nor no bank money. There wasn't nothing in my mind but just how I was a-feeling and what wonderful things had just been did to me. That's all.

Well, it were quite a spell, but final I was up and dressed again, and I went back down the stairs into the saloon. Ole Sparky, she had done gone down ahead a me, and by the time I got down to the bar, she was a making up to some cowhand there. She seed me though, and give me a wink. I had come outa that room up there so dizzy with wondrous feeling, that I had went and left my whiskey bottle behind. Whenever I got to the bar, that thought come to me. I was trying to decide was it worth it to go back for it, or should I just buy myself another drink at the bar. I hadn't made my mind up yet whenever someone stepped up beside me right close. Well, that always makes me some nervous, and I turned right quick and give a look.

"Can I buy you a drink, Kid?"

I'll be goddamned if it weren't one a them Dawsons.

Chapter 5

Now that what had just happened was just exact what ole Dick Cherry had planned on a-happening, but then it had come about so fast that it tuck me plumb by surprise. I was a-fixing to answer ole Dawson, but he talked again afore I could form me any words to say.

"I got two brothers setting over yonder," he said. "We'd be proud if you was to join us. We got a bottle. Good whiskey."

"Well," I said, "you got the advantage on me, mister. You know my name."

"Oh," he said. "Sorry 'bout that. I'm Clem Dawson."

So we shuck hands, and I said, "I don't see no reason why I can't take advantage a your kind hospitality."

"Good," he said. "Come on over."

I follered ole Clem Dawson over to the table where his two brothers was a-setting, and he interduced them by the names a Bo and Arny. We all shuck hands, and me and ole Clem set down. Clem grabbed the bottle by the neck and poured us drinks all around. I tuck mine up and sipped at it.

"It's good stuff," I said. "I thank you."

We set there a-drinking and making small talk till way nigh onto supper time, and I was the leastest drunk a the bunch, on accounta I was just a sipping the whole time, and they was a-gulping. If they noticed, they never said nothing about it, but the reason I was a doing thataway was on accounta I sure didn't wanta lose control a my faculties nor a my reflexes or nothing. After all, even though they didn't likely have no idee, I was a-planning on prob'ly killing them three.

"Hey," Clem said, "let's go over to the eating place and have us some steaks."

All three a them Dawsons stood up then, but I was still a-setting.

"Come on, Kid," Clem said. "It's on me."

"All right," I said, and I stood up to go with them, but I was a-thinking that he was a fixing to spend more a that damn bank money, and I sure didn't like that. I wondered if maybe I might could take all three of them somewhere betwixt the saloon and the eating place. I wondered too where at ole Cherry might be. If he was to come outa the shadders somewhere along the way, why, me and him could sure take them, and we'd get it did before they was to spend any more a that cash. But we got on over to the eating place, and I never seed no sign a my pardner.

We set down and ordered up some good steak dinners, and we was a-drinking coffee whilst we waited for them to be brung out to us. I was a-thinking about what the cost a them four meals was a-going to come to, and I was also a-thinking about what in the world ole Clem might have on his mind a-bringing me along with them the way he done.

"Kid," he said, like as if he was just about to go and answer the question what was inside a my head, "I never seen a faster draw than what you pulled back there."

"I had some practice," I said.

"I reckon," he said. "Can I ask you a question?"

"Go right on ahead," I said. "If I don't like it, I won't answer it."

"How come you didn't go ahead and kill that son of a bitch?"

"Didn't need to," I said. "I'd ruther a sent him crawling outa there in front a ever'one. Hell, folks sees killings all the time. They don't see what I done to him ever'day."

Clem laughed a little at that, and so did his brothers.

"I reckon that's true," he said, and his brothers nodded their heads and said, "Yeah. That's right."

"It did make a hell of a good show," Clem said.

Well, our steaks come out about then, and we all commenced to eating and cut out the talking. They was good steaks too, but only I was still a-thinking about how that there bank money was a-dwindling down in the Dawsons' pockets. I didn't enjoy my meal near as much as I had oughta. We finished up and slurped down another cup a coffee each, and then ole Clem, he looked at his brothers one after the other, and he said, "Well, boys, what do you say?"

Bo and Arny looked each other in the eyeballs, and then Bo give a shrug, and then Arny said, "Yeah, Clem. I think so."

I give them all a sideways quizzical kinda look, and ole Clem, he grinned at me real big. "Let's go on back over to the saloon," he said. "This ain't no good place to talk."

I follered them back to the saloon, and Clem picked out a table there what was well away from any might-be-listening ears. He sent Bo to fetch a bottle and some glasses, and he kindly rared back in his chair a looking at me.

"What the hell is this here all about?" I asked.

"Just hold on a little bit," Clem said. "I'm fixing to tell you."

Bo come back then with the bottle and glasses, and Clem poured drinks all around. My head was a-trying to add up them figgers, but it weren't doing much good at it. Clem lifted up his glass and said, "To new friends." His brothers lifted their glasses high, and just to be friendly, I lifted my own up but only not as high and not as enthusiastic as what they was. I was a mite too curious to show out enthusiastic.

We all tuck us a drink after that, though. Then ole Clem, he looked around to make sure they weren't no one a-listening, and then he leaned across the table some at me.

"Kid," he said, "how'd you like to throw in with us?"

"You mean—like pardner up?" I said.

"Yeah."

"I don't know," I said. And then I lied to him just a little. "I like to go it alone."

"Four men's better than three," Clem said. "It's sure better than one."

"That all depends on just what it is you got in mind to do," I said. "I'm doing all right just my own self."

"You got plenty a money?" he asked me.

"I got some," I said.

"The thing about money is it always runs out. There ain't never enough of it."

"I do all right."

I could tell that I was some frustrating ole Clem at my playing hard-to-get, but I sure didn't want him and his two brothers a-thinking that I was too anxious. He decided to take another direction in his next run at me.

"You got any lawmen on your trail?" he asked me.

"I've dodged a few," I said, a-thinking at the time how clever I was a-answering him thataway and not telling no lie.

"If a posse comes up on you," he said, "the more company you got, the better off you are."

I couldn't argue none with that. I just tuck me another sip a that whiskey.

"Well," Clem said, "what do you say?"

"Just exact what is it that you have got in mind," I asked him, "other than fighting off a posse?"

Clem looked at his brothers, and they all grinned at each other. He looked back at me.

"Banks," he said.

"Banks?"

"Bank robbing."

"That there's a risky business," I said.

"Not so much with four men," said Clem. "And one of them as good with a gun as you are. Well?"

"I don't know," I said. "I got money in my pockets, and you don't seem to be hurting none. Why take a chance?"

Clem sighed kindly heavy and glanced at his brothers again. Then he looked back at me. "Listen, Kid," he said, "this town might not look like much, but there's some big ranches around here, and hanging around the little time we been here, I happened to pick up on the news that there's been a couple a big deposits made in the local bank. We could get rich enough to retire. Move to New York or Boston. Mexico City or Paris, even. Well, come on. What do you say?"

"I don't know nothing about them places you named," I said, "but I don't reckon I'd be knowed none too well in Houston, Texas, or El Paso. Maybe out in Californy."

Then I realized that I was almost a-thinking serious on what ole Clem was a-proposing to me, and I had to remind myself just what it was I was supposed to be up to.

"You in, then?" Clem asked me.

"I'm a-thinking on it," I said. "Let me sleep on it. Let's get together for breakfast in the morning and talk some more. Tell you the truth, I'm kindly tuckered out. I can't hardly think straight tonight. If I get me a good night's sleep, I'll be all right in the morning for such thinking."

"All right," Clem said. "We'll meet for breakfast over at the eating place. We'll talk it out there."

I excused myself then and left the saloon, but I thunk that I overheard ole Clem tell his brothers as I was a-walking away, "We got him, boys."

Whenever I got over to the rooming house where me and ole Dick Cherry had got us a room, I was glad to find Cherry in the room, and I was even more glad that he had tuck a bottle in there. I made him pour me a drink afore I went to telling him what had tuck place. Then I laid out the whole story for him about how ole Clem Dawson had come to me and had final made me that offer to join up with them and go to bank robbing.

"They mean to take the bank right here in Snake Crick," I said.

"When?"

"They ain't said yet. We're s'posed to talk some more in the morning. I ain't even said I'd join up with them."

"Damn, Kid," he said. "It's perfect. With you right in the middle of them and me coming at them from the front, we could take them real easy."

"I don't know," I said. "I don't like it."

"What's wrong with it?"

"What if something was to go wrong and the local law was to think that I was really with them Dawsons? I been a wanted man afore, and I don't like it none."

"Tell you what," Dick said. "You meet the Dawsons in the morning and agree to join them. I'll go see the sheriff and tell him what's going on. I'll let him know that you've infiltrated the gang in order to help catch them. Then when you find out the exact plans, the time of the planned robbery, you let me know, and I'll let the sheriff know. We'll all be ready."

Well, I agreed, but I weren't none too happy about it. I was putting a awful lot a trust in ole Cherry what I hadn't really knowed all that long nor any too well. If it had a been ole Zeb or ole Churkee, why, I wouldn't a never even hesitated none. But I just weren't sure a Dick Cherry. Anyhow, I agreed and there weren't no turning back from that. Well, I drunk me some more whiskey, and I never just sipped at it, neither, and then I final went on to bed, and I slept pretty good without no tossing nor turning. I was up early the next morning.

I got myself dressed and walked on over to the eating place. It was so early that there weren't hardly no folks in there yet. They sure weren't no Dawsons. I was kindly hoping that they wouldn't show up, but I ordered me up some coffee and told that there greasy-aproned feller that I was a-waiting on someone, and I would order up my breakfast whenever they showed up. I had me three cups a coffee afore they come in.

"You get a good night's sleep, Kid?" Clem asked me.

"Pretty good," I said.

"You give any more thought to our proposition?"

"I give it some."

"Well?"

"I figger you're the boss a this here outfit, Clem," I said. "I been a-bossing my own self for too long. I don't take too well to no ordering around."

"Hey, Kid," Clem said, "the way you handle that gun, I never figured on ordering you around. Join up with us, and you'll be an equal partner. I'll tell you the plans I made, and if you don't like them, we can talk them over. Make changes if we have to. You and me will agree on everything before we ever go into a job."

"I can't think of no more objections," I said. "Count me in."

We shuck all around on that, and just then ole greasy apron come over, and so we ordered us up a fine big breakfast a eggs and ham and biscuits and gravy and taters and such, and whenever it was final brung over to us, we all four commenced to eating like as if we hadn't et in at least a week. Then we went and tuck us a ride outa town.

Clem knowed where he was a-going, and he led the way to a little crick what I guessed was Snake Crick, and we all dismounted there by the water. Bo pulled a bottle outa his saddle bags and handed it to his big brother. Clem uncorked it and tuck a slug, then handed it to me. I had me a swaller and give the bottle over to Bo, and he drunk some and passed it along to Arny. The whole time we set there a-talking, we done thataway with that bottle.

"Here's how I figure it, Kid," Clem said. "We'll hit the bank first thing in the morning when it opens. There's not too many customers in there that time a day. Maybe there won't be any. We'll have our horses all saddled and ready out in the street. Arny'll stand ready with the horses. Bo will stay outside by the door a keeping watch. You and me will go inside. We'll have us a couple a big sacks, and we'll pull our guns and make the teller or the banker or whoever it is in there to fill them up with big bills. Then we'll leave, jump on our horses and skedaddle outa town. Sound all right to you?"

"It don't sound bad," I said. "What if someone comes up from outside and figgers out what's a-going on?"

"Then we might have to shoot our way outa town. It's a chance you take."

"Yeah. Which way outa town we going? You have a place in mind to go to?"

"I'm thinking about heading south," Clem said. "We've been operating in these parts and moving east. Last bank we hit was over in Fosterville. You know the place?"

"I've been there," I said. "I think I heared about that bank job."

Bo grinned.

"You heard about us, did you?" he said, and it was like as if he was real proud a that fact.

"Yeah," I said. Then I looked back at Clem. "South, huh? How far south?"

"I been thinking about what you said, Kid. Houston, maybe, or El Paso."

"Think about this here," I said. "What if we was to double back? Head right back for Fosterville? Wouldn't no one be a-looking for you to do a fool thing like that. Then we could just keep a-going, right through Fosterville, and head on out to Californy. I'd kindly like to see that ocean out yonder."

"You can see ocean down at Houston, Kid," Clem said.

"Is that right?"

"Sure. The Gulf a Mexico."

"Is it for sure ocean? Right offa Texas?"

"For sure. I promise you."

"If I go all the way down to Houston with you," I said, "and I don't see no ocean, I'll shoot your both damn ears off. You hear me? I've shot off ears before."

"I believe you, Kid, and I promise you, if we get to Houston, you'll see ocean."

"Is there sand there where it laps up?"

"Great big waves rolling up onto a sandy beach," Clem said. "With all the money we'll have, we could get us a real nice place right there on the beach and listen to those waves a-rolling up all day long and all night long, too."

"All right, by God," I said. "We'll go south. To Houston. Now, one more thing. When are we going to pull this job off and head for the ocean?"

"First thing in the morning," he said. "Soon as the bank opens."

"All right," I said, "but let's get out earlier than that so we can get us some breakfast. I don't want to be riding out on a long trip like that without I've had me a good meal. There ain't nothing worse than a long trail on a empty stomach."

"Agreed," Clem said. "And right now, we'll go on back into town, and we'll do some shopping for everything we'll need for that long ride. Trail food and such."

We all had us one more pull on that bottle, and then we mounted up and headed back into Snake Crick. Clem and his brothers went into the general store, and I told them that I had to go on to my room and pack up my stuff. I wanted to be all ready early the next morning. It was damn near noon by the time we come back from our ride, and I suggested to Clem that maybe I shouldn't oughta be saw no more with him and his brothers till in the morning whenever we hit that bank. He agreed on that, and I was glad for it. I fetched a couple a steak dinners under towels and tuck them to the room. Dick was there a-waiting.

He was sure glad to see that steak, and me and him tore into our meals. We hardly said a word till we was done, and then we washed it all down with a little whiskey, early in the day as it was. Final we set back and relaxed, and he asked me what all had tuck place. I asked him first if he had went to see the sheriff.

"I did," he said. "I told him that the Dawsons had recruited you to help them rob his bank. I showed him the wanted poster on them, and I told him that you had been trailing them since they robbed the bank at Fosterville. He knows your sheriff Chastain, and he got a little friendlier when I told him the whole story. He still doesn't like bounty hunters, though. Anyhow, he decided that if you were a member of Chastain's posse who just didn't want to quit, then you aren't a real bounty hunter, so it's all right. Now, what did you learn?"

"We're hitting the bank in the morning," I said. "First thing when they open the door. You and that sheriff had best be ready, and you'd best be outa sight."

"Don't worry," Cherry said. "We'll be ready and well hidden."

Chapter 6

Well, sir, it were early the next morning when I went and met up with them Dawsons for a good, big breakfast. Like I had told them, you don't wanta go robbing no bank and then heading for a place like Houston, Texas, way off to hell and gone like that with no empty belly. 'Course, I didn't really have no intention atall a heading for Houston nor no other place just that soon. My real intention was to make like I was a-going to help them rob the bank and then for actual help my new pard ole Dick Cherry and the sheriff a Snake Crick—what I never did know his name nor keer to—stop them Dawsons from the robbing. They could give it up and go to jail or we could kill them dead. It didn't really make no never mind to me, but the point is that with a maybe fight a-coming up, 'special maybe some killing, well, I wanted to be well fed for that, too.

We was a-setting in the eating place a-sipping on a last cup a coffee each when ole Clem Dawson, he looked me square in the eyes from acrost the table. "You ready for this, Kid?" he asked me.

"Hell, yes," I said. "I'm a-raring to go. What about the three a you?"

"We've done it before," Clem said. "We're all ready."

"Well, don't you go to worrying none about me," I said. "Hell, I've tuck on a whole damn army before."

And that was might near the truth a the matter. 'Course, it were a army a outlaws, not a regular army in suits and all that, but they was a whole mess a the bastards. And, well, I did have me a little help that time, but not too damn much of it. You can believe me or not. I don't give a shit, really.

Clem pulled out a pocket watch, and I wondered who it was he had tuck it away from. He looked at it, and then he said, "It's time, boys. Let's go."

We all of us got up and follered Clem outa the place. 'Course, he stopped on the way out to pay the bill. We didn't want no trouble over such a matter as that to interfere with the big plans. We walked outside and on down the street and acrost it to the front door a the bank, and just as we was about to get to it, we seed a feller in a suit unlocking the door. We give each other a look and walked on over there. Early in the morning afore we had gone to the eating place, we had tied our four horses to a hitch rail just acrost the street from the bank, and they was still there just a-waiting for us. Clem give a nod to Arny, and Arny peeled off from the rest of us and walked over to wait with the horses. The plan was that whenever he seed us a-coming outa the bank, he would loose the reins of all four horses so they'd be ready for us for a fast get-outa-town. The other three of us kept on a-walking.

When we come to the front door a the bank, Bo turned around and leaned against the wall real casual-like, and he tuck the makings outa his pocket and rolled hisself a cigareet. He was to make like he was just a-loafing around and smoking but actual, he was a kinda lookout. Me and Clem went on inside. I stopped just to one side a the door, and Clem, he went on over to the counter. The feller what had unlocked the door was standing behind the counter, and he looked up at Clem and grinned.

"How may I help you, sir?" he said.

Clem whipped out his six-gun, and I done the same thing. Then Clem brung a sack out from under his coat and throwed it on top a the counter.

"Just fill it up," he said, "and don't try funning me with small bills."

The grin went offa that ole boy's face right quick, and he went to shaking. "Yes, sir," he said. "Yes, sir. Please don't shoot."

Well, with his hands a-trembling and all, he went to opening drawers and hauling out bills and stuffing them in that sack. By and by, ole Clem said, "That's enough of that. What's in the vault?"

"Why, I—"

"Just open it up," Clem snapped, "and be quick about it."

Ever' now and then, I would glance outside through the winder to see if anyone was a-coming toward the bank door. That there was a part a my job. I never seed no one a-coming though. We was lucking out on that part a the deal. Anyhow, I had just give one a my looks out the winder, and when I turned back I seed that there bank feller a-stuffing money into the sack from outa the vault. Clem give a nervous look back in my direction ever' now and then. Final he figgered that we had done spent enough time inside the bank.

"All right," he said. "Hand it over."

"There's still more money—"

"That's enough," Clem said. "Hand me the goddamn sack."

The silly little bastard walked back to the counter and handed the bag a money to Clem, and Clem choked it up real good with his left hand.

"Lay down on the floor," he said, and the little feller disappeared back behind the counter. Clem come a-hustling toward the door, and I jerked it open and stepped aside. He went out, and I follered him. Ever'thing outside looked quiet. Giving quick glances up and down the street, Clem headed acrost toward the horses and Arny with Bo right by his side. Me, I had dropped back a couple a steps a purpose. Them two Dawsons was about in the middle a the street whenever the sheriff come outa the front door a the general store a pointing a Henry rifle.

"Hold it right there," he called out. "You're under arrest."

Clem and Bo hesitated, a-looking like as if they was a-thinking about going for their guns, but just then ole Dick Cherry stepped out from in front a the eating place.

"Don't try it," he said.

Clem tried it. He went for his six-gun and yelled out at the same time, "Let's take them."

I shot the hat offa his head. "Throw down your guns, boys," I yelled.

Well, it come on them then what they was for real up against, but instead a doing the smart thing, Clem, he pulled his iron anyhow and snapped off a shot at the sheriff. The sheriff ducked back into the doorway. In the meantime, Arny and Bo had both hauled out their shooters, and Bo was taking aim at ole Cherry. I dropped Bo easy. Arny whirled on me, and ole Dick Cherry dropped him. Clem had by that time run to the horses, and he had ducked on down betwixt them. He tuck off like a pony express rider a-lurking down by the side a his horse. I figgered I could take him on down anyhow, but just as I was fixing to do that there little thing, damned if Bo didn't raise up from where I had thunk he was a laying dead.

"Look out, Kid," Cherry yelled, on accounta he didn't have no clear shot at Bo, and I whirled around and sent another slug into poor ole Bo. He dropped dead that time for sure.

"Clem's getting away with the money," I hollered, and the sheriff come outa hiding and raised that Henry up to his shoulder. He tuck a keerful aim and snapped off a shot, and I seed ole Clem give a flinch, and I seed that money sack go a-flying. Clem kept on a-riding. I run acrost the street and jumped on Ole Horse and tuck after Clem. Dick and the sheriff was right behind me. Whenever I come on that money sack, I just kept on a-going. I was after Clem, and I was a-wondering where all a the money from the Fosterville bank was at—what was left of it. Well, Ole Horse done a admirable job, but Clem and his nag had too much of a start on us. I had to give it up. I turned around and rid slow back to where Cherry and the sheriff was a-gathering up the sack and some money what had spilt out of it whenever Clem had dropped it.

"He's got too much of a start on me," I said.

"We can catch up to him later," Cherry said, and I seed something wild in his eyes as he was a stuffing some bills into the sack what the sheriff was a-holding.

"At least we recovered the money," the sheriff said, "and we got two of them."

"They's another five hunnerd riding out yonder away from us," I said, remarking, a course, on the reeward money on the Dawsons' heads.

"We'll catch up with him," Cherry said, kindly exasperated-like.

Well, them two got that sack stuffed back full, and the three of us rid back into town. Someone had done laid out the two dead Dawsons side by side on the sidewalk, and a man with one a them damn camera things was a-taking their dead poses with their guns a-laid acrost their chests and their dead eyes a-staring straight up. I had kilt me some men as you all know, but I hadn't never seed no one take their portraits like that, and it kindly made me want to puke, but I never.

"I want me a drink," I said, early as it was.

"I'll be along," Cherry said.

I went on over to the saloon and ordered me up a shot a good brown whiskey, and I drunk it down fast. I usually sip at it, you know. Then I called for a second one, and I did just kindly sip at that one. By and by, Cherry come in and bellied up to the bar beside me.

"What's wrong, Kid?" he said.

"Ain't nothing wrong," I said, a-lying to him. "It ain't the first time I kilt a man."

He laid out five hunnerd on the bar.

"That's your share for the two Dawsons," he said. Then he counted out five more a them big bills. "The bank president gave us a thousand for saving his money."

"That was right big a him," I said. I was thinking a the ten percent what ole Throne had promised. 'Course, ole Chastain had kindly prodded him into making it that much. He had offered five the first time.

"Say," I said to Cherry, "what about the Fosterville money?"

"I asked the sheriff. He's checking the pockets and the saddle bags of the dead men. Of course, if Clem has any of it, it's gone along with him."

"We have to go after him, Dick," I said. "I promised—"

"I know. You promised your lawman friend. Besides, there's another five hundred on his head, and there's the rest of the Fosterville bank money—almost for sure. We'll get on his trail right away. But for now, let's wait for the sheriff to clean up the mess in town."

I tuck me another sip a whiskey, and then I realized just where I was a-heading myself, and I said to Cherry, a-changing my tone somewhat, "I reckon in the morning'll do just fine."

Then, 'stead a ordering me another shot, I called for the bottle. Cherry got hisself a glass, and me and him went to set down at a table.

"Well, Kid," Dick said to me, "what do you think of the bounty-hunting business now?"

"I reckon they's always a-plenty a work," I said.

Ole Cherry laughed at that. "That's the truth," he said. "There's always another outlaw with a price on his head. And we did all right here this morning. A thousand dollars apiece. That's not bad for a morning's work. Right?"

I give a shrug. I was a-thinking that it was a might easier than panning for gold, and it sure did pay a hell of a lot more than chasing cows. A course, it could be dangerous, but then I was just cocky enough to believe that I was a bit more dangerous than most men what I had run up against, anyhow. I didn't say none a that to ole Cherry, though. Instead I just tuck me another sip a whiskey. My head was a-getting warmish. Just then I heared a feller up at the bar a-talking to the barkeep.

"Who'd they say brought down those two outlaws?"

"Fella named Cherry," the barkeep said, "and his partner. The one they call Kid Parmlee. That's them right over there."

"Kid Parmlee," the other feller said. "That's what I thought I heard."

I looked up then, and I seed that feller. He had turned around and was a-looking in our direction. I didn't think I had ever seed him before, but somehow, he had a kindly familiar look about him, and it was one that I didn't like none, neither. He seed me a-looking back at him, and he hitched his britches and come a-walking at me with a ugly sneer on his already ugly face. He was a good sized bastard, too. He come within a few paces of me and stopped still.

"You Kid Parmlee?"

"I get called that," I said. "Who might you be?"

"I figured I'd run across your trail some day," he said. "I guess this is my lucky day."

Well, I ain't dumb. I could see that he was trouble a-coming at me, and I was just already some woozy from the drinks I had drunk so early in the day. I scooted back my chair, and I stood up, and I felt my legs a-rubbery under me. I also felt like I was a-weaving some.

"So you run acrost my trail," I said. "So what?"

"I got it in my head to kill you, Kid," he said.

Well, hell, I had heard that before, and so it didn't skeer me none. "Any pertikler reason?" I asked him. "Or just for fun?"

"It'll be fun, all right," he said, "but there is a reason."

"You gonna let me in on it?"

"Yeah," he said. "I might as well. I think it's always a good policy to let a man know why he's about to die."

"And I kindly like knowing how come I'm a-fixing to kill a man," I said.

"My name's Chesley Hook," he said.

I kindly groaned out loud.

"That bother you?"

"I done kilt me a-right smart a your family," I said. "Whyn't you just let it be? I don't need to kill me no more Hookses nor Piggses. And besides that, ain't there no end to you? I figgered I'd done kilt the whole damn bunch 'cept for maybe wimmen and childern."

"You ain't funny, Kid," he said. "I mean to kill you right now. Go for your gun."

"You're a-starting this thing," I said. "Go for yours."

To tell you the gospel truth a the matter, there was a little something inside a me just then that told me I might very well be a-fixing to be dead, on accounta I weren't near at my level best. Whiskey always did impair my doings more than somewhat. Still, I weren't about to back down from no Hook, even if it did might mean my own killing. Then the next thing what happened, I didn't hardly know it till it was did.

I seed ole Hook a-reaching for his iron, and I went for mine, and usual the next thing woulda been, I'd a-shot him dead. But I never. I heared a roar from off to my left side, and my own trusty Colt weren't even clear a leather, and I seed a splotch a red on the chest of ole Hook, and I seed the stupid look come on his face. I seed his fingers kindly relax and let that there six-gun slip loose and fall to the floor. I watched him stand there a-swaying and a-looking at me with major surprise writ big on his ugly face. Then, I seed his eyes go kindly blank, and he pitched forward and landed hard on his face right smack there in fronta me. I looked over to my side, and there was ole Dick Cherry a-standing there with his shooter in his hand.

"I didn't mean to horn in, Kid," he said.

"If you hadn't a-horned, I'd be dead," I said. "He was faster'n me."

"Aw, you'd have probably beat him," Cherry said.

"Ain't no way," I said. "He was a-leveling on me when you shot. I hadn't even cleared leather. He'd a kilt me sure."

I set down heavy back in my seat and poured me another drink. The sheriff come a-running in then, and he seed the dead Hook and he seed me and ole Cherry. The barkeep told him what had tuck place there, and the sheriff, he accepted the story. He didn't even ask no questions. He said he'd send someone to take out the carcass by and by, and then he went on out again. I drank down my whiskey and poured another, and I could feel a serious drunk a-coming on me. But I was a-doing me some heavy thinking, too.

"Dick," I said, "you saved my worthless life."

"Ah, Kid—"

"No," I said. "You did. You for real did. I've faced me a bunch a men, and I've kilt all of them what I didn't skeer outa drawing. He had me cold. I know it. I seed it. You saved my ass, ole pard. You done it. I won't never forget it neither. I promise you that, Dick. I won't never forget it what you done."

Well, I reckon by that, ole Cherry had got tired a my drunken blubbering, on accounta he interrupted me right then and changed the subject kinda.

"What was that about his family?" he asked me, and so I had to go and tell the whole long and complicated tale a me

and the Piggses and the Hookses, and how it was the killing
of a Pigg, ole Joe to be exact, what had first set me out on
the fugitive's trail whenever I was just only a snot-nosed kid
a the tender age a sixteen years. I told Dick how come me
to kill a man at that ripe age, on accounta he had kilt my ole
dog Farty, and how my old man had did the first nice thing
he had ever did for me by giving me his old sway-backed
horse and ten dollars and telling me to get the hell outa
Texas. I told him from there how I come to learn cowboying
and gunfighting from ole Rod and Tex and the rest a the
boys at the Boxwood, and then I told him about how it
seemed like as if ever'time I turned around they was one
more a that Goddamned family a-coming at me.

"You know, they might be a-coming after you, too, now,"
I said.

"We'll worry about that when it happens," he said.

"Yeah," I said, "I seed you take that one there. I reckon
for sure you can handle yourself all right."

"Don't worry about it."

"Another damn Hook," I said. And then it come to me
that whenever I had first off met up with ole Cherry, he had
drawed on me, and I had beat him square, and he had friz
up, and I never shot him. I begun to wonder then if he had
did that a purpose, a-faking me out to make me think I was
faster than what he was. If he had did that, then I wondered
how come he had did it, but I went and shoved that there
nagging thought outa my head. They was just one thing what
was sure for certain, and that was that he had outdrawed both
me and that latest Hook, and he had saved my ass.

"Kid," Cherry said, "I think you've had enough. I think
you ought to go upstairs and sleep it off. What do you say?"

"Yeah," I said. "All right. I'm a-going. Hey, Dick?"

"What is it?"

"Send me that little ole gal on up, will you? What was her name?"

"You mean Sparky?"

"Yeah. Send Sparky on up to me."

Chapter 7

Well, somehow or 'nother I got my ass upstairs and into the bed in my room, and I guess I just went on over to it and flopped down just like I was, with my gunbelt and my boots and ever'thing still on me and not even a-bothering to shut the damn door, much less to lock it, and that's about the last thing I recall till I come awake way later in the day. Damned if I weren't nekkid as hell and ole Sparky a-laying there beside a me in the same gen'ral condition. Well, you might recall, I had been caught thataway once before, and I didn't like the outcome a that incident not one damn bit. I come up outa that bed real quick and run over to check the door, but ole Sparky, she knowed. She had bolted it good from the inside, so ever'thing was all right.

I headed back for the bed, and Sparky come awake just then. She set up and looked at me, a-rubbing her eyes, and she smiled. I crawled back in beside of her and tuck her plumb nekkidness into my arms and hugged her real good. "You tuck good keer a me, darlin'," I said. "I thank you for that."

"It was nothing compared to the way I'm fixing to take care of you," she said.

And Lord Godamighty did she ever mean what she said. She tuck keer a me all right. More than all right. She tuck wondrous keer a me. She give me one a the most magnificentest times I ever had in my life. She used ever'thing she had on ever'thing I had, and I won't never forget none of it, not a minute, for as long as I live if I was to get as old as ole Zeb and my ole paw put together, and their years all added up to a hunnerd and forty-seven or whatever it might come out to be. When she was all did with me, I couldn't move. I didn't want to neither. I just laid there like a whipped dog a-breathing slow and deep.

Well, final she got up and got a bowl a water and a sponge and washed me all off real good and her own self too, and then she went to getting herself dressed. "I've got to go now, Kid," she said. "Is it all right?" I knowed I weren't the onliest thing in her life what she had to deal with, and I told her that it was just fine, and I understood. I watched her till she got all dressed and left the room. Then I mustered up all a my strength, what weren't much just then, and got up to bolt the door back. I rolled myself a cigareet and lit it, and then I poured myself a drink a that whiskey and tuck me a sip. I was setting on the edge a the bed like that whenever I heared a knock at the door. I looked around real quick-like and seed where ole Sparky had hung my gunbelt on a chair back. I grabbed out my Colt and went over to the door. "Who's there?" I asked.

"It's Dick Cherry, Kid. Open up."

I did, and he come in and seed me all nekkid like that with a cigareet in my mouth and a gun in my hand. I bolted the door back and went back over to the bed and set again.

"Looks like you've turned your nights and days around," he said.

"I reckon so," I agreed, and I picked up the glass and tuck me another sip. "What the hell're you up to?"

"Mostly killing time," he said. "Waiting for you to come back around. I did do some investigating."

"Of what?"

"Well," he said, "Clem Dawson and his brothers didn't spend too much money here, and we didn't find too much on his brothers, so he must have most of that Fosterville bank money still on him."

"That's good," I said.

"But maybe not for long. He rode out of here heading south."

"I told you he was a-thinking about going to Houston."

"Yeah. But just about a two day ride south of here is a place called Devil's Roost. It looks like any other frontier town. Even has a sheriff's office and a jail. But it's an outlaw hangout. A safe haven for men on the run. The only thing is, it costs them to lay over there. If Dawson decides to stop over in Devil's Roost, he could use up that bank money in a short while."

"We got to get him first, then," I said. "That's all."

Ole Dick, he shuck his head. "It's too late for that. We've already wasted a day. There's no way we can catch him before he gets there."

"Well, maybe we can ketch him in that there town and get his ass afore he's spent too much a the money."

"What do you think he'll do if he sees you riding into Devil's Roost?"

"Well, I—"

"Outlaws are the law in Devil's Roost. They'll take his side. Especially if he's paying."

"So what're we going to do?" I asked him. "Just give up on it?"

"No. I mean to help you keep your promise to your favorite sheriff, and I mean to split the reward with you for the return of that money."

"But how in the hell're we going to get his ass outa that there Devil's town a outlaws?"

"I don't think he ever got a good look at me," Dick said. "We'll ride on down there and make us a camp just outside of Devil's Roost. You'll stay there, and I'll go into town. I'll try to find a way to lead him out in your direction. We'll take him out there."

"How you going to get him outa town?"

"I don't know yet. I'll have to think about it. We have a long ride ahead of us. There'll be plenty of time for thinking."

As late in the day as it was, we packed up and tuck to riding south. It seemed to me like I'd been on a trail like that most a my growed life, and I was a-getting kindly tired of it, but I never grumbled none about it to ole Cherry. We rid along for miles without saying nary word to one another, but just ever' now and then, one of us would say something. We was a-going along like that whenever ole Cherry, he said, "I know. I'll tell Dawson that I heard about you getting his brothers. I was there in Snake Creek. I'll get his interest that way."

"And if he don't kill you dead, you'll know that he never seed you during the shooting."

"That's right. And then I'll say that I know you're still on his trail, and I know where you're camped, but I'll say that I won't lead him to you unless he comes with me alone. I'll tell him you got the reward money for his brothers on you, and I don't want to split it too many ways. How's that sound?"

"It might could work like that," I said.

We didn't talk no more till we found us a place to camp for the night, and then we fixed us up a place to sleep and a place to cook. We looked to our horses, and then we et. We set up and talked over ole Cherry's plan some more before we went off to sleep. The next morning, we was up early. We whomped us up a breakfast, and I thunk about ole Zeb and his good biscuit, and I sure did wish that he was along with us just then. Them biscuit sure woulda hit the spot all right. Then I wondered what ole Zeb would a thunk about me having another new pard, and I figgered he wouldn't take to it none too kindly. Anyhow, we finished up and cleaned up and hit the trail again.

Wasn't much happened the rest a that day other than us a-moving south, but 'cept I tuck note a the fact that whenever we had left outa Snake Crick, we had been riding along over flat, dry prairie, and then the closer we come to that there Devil's place, the more greener things was a-getting and then a little more rollery, and along toward evening we was actual in some little green hills and valleys with some clumps a trees around here and there. It was a actual kindly pretty place, and I thunk about it being like that and at the same time a-hiding a outlaw town. By and by we seed it.

We come on top of a hill, and there it was all nestled down in a little valley real snug-like. It didn't look like no outlaw town, just only a ordinary town is all. "There it is, Kid," ole Dick said. "Now we got to find you a spot for a camp."

Well, we come acrost a nice one. It was about halfway up the hill there a-looking down on that there Devil's thing, and it were kindly set back in the hillside. It weren't no cave nor nothing like that. Just a place where the side a the hill kindly sunk back in on itself. I could rest easy and have me a view a the whole town. I could see anyone a-coming or a-going from in or out a there. We fixed up a camp, and then ole Cherry, he decided that he was a-going on in.

"You ain't a-going to wait till morning?" I asked him.

"Evening's better," he said. "Dawson's more likely to be up, probably drinking in the saloon. If I ride in there in the morning, I might have to wait half the day before I set eyes on him."

I reckoned that he was right about that, and so I didn't argue none with him. I just let him go on. Then I fixed my own self a meal and et it, and it weren't hardly no good for nothing but just to fill up my belly was all. I drunk me some coffee, and then I wrapped my ass up in my blanket and kindly snuggled back against the side a the hill where I could be real comfy but still watch the town down yonder below me. I guess I dropped off to sleep like that.

Well, I come awake with a start sometime in the night. It were dark all right. My little bitty fire was just only some red ashes, so I got up and throwed some sticks on it. The night was some cool. Then I got to thinking about old Cherry a-bringing that Dawson up the hill and him with the thought in his mind a-killing me dead on accounta his two brothers. I tried to think what was I a-going to do. Me and ole Cherry, we had talked all about him a-going into the town and tricking Dawson into coming out to my camp and all that, but we hadn't never even thunk about my end a the deal.

Final I come up with a idee, and I went and got a extry shirt outa my saddlebag, and I tuck to stuffing it with grass and leaves and such. I was glad then that I was so skinny, 'cause it didn't take too much stuffing. I propped that shirt up right there where I had been a-sleeping, and I set my hat on top of it. Then I throwed the blanket up like as if it was a-covering up my legs and feet. I walked way off back from it and tuck a look, and I was kindly proud a my work what I had did. I figgered it oughta fool him long enough. 'Course I didn't have no way a knowing how long it would be afore ole Cherry was to talk Dawson into coming up there with him, and what that meant was that I didn't have no idee how long I was a-going to have to lurk around a-watching and waiting. I was glad, though, that I had me such a good view a the town down yonder.

I went on ahead and boiled me up some more coffee, and I rolled me a cigareet and poured me out a cup a coffee and set my ass down on the other side a the fire from that there dummy I had fashioned up. I set down to smoke and sip coffee and wait. I tell you what, I surely did get bored a-setting there. I drunked up all a the coffee I had made, and I smoked up several cigareets. I had to get up twice to take a leak. I kept a-watching down at that town, and no one was a-coming. I had me a good view, too, like I told you. Hell, I could see ole Dick's horse there where he had tied it in front a the saloon.

I was a-feeling some drowsy again when I noticed that it were damn near daylight. Well, I guess it was long about dawn. I figgered that ole Dawson for sure and maybe even old Dick was a-sleeping it off by that. I was considering letting my own self drop back off. Then I seed ole Dick come outa the saloon down yonder. I could tell him by his black clothes, and he had someone with him, too. I reckoned it had to be ole Dawson. Dick clumb up on his horse, and that other feller what I was kindly sure must be ole Dawson, he mounted up on a horse, too, and they turned to ride outa town coming on out in my direction. I tensed up ready for action off to a side in the kindly dim shadders and waited. I didn't really think that I'd need to, but I went and drawed out my ole Colt anyhow and I cocked it. I was ready to kill.

I lost sight a Dawson and Cherry for just a bit whenever they come right to the bottom a the hill, but I could hear them a-talking, and I could hear their horses a-clomping along on the way up to my little ole camp. By and by, I seed them again, and they was real close that time. They was right on top a the camp, and they stopped. I could see ole Dawson a 'looking at that there dummy I had made.

"Kid," he said, and he didn't sound none to glad to see me. "Kid, get your ass up outa there." 'Course, I never moved. I mean that there dummy never. I seed Dawson give ole Cherry a somewhat puzzled kinda look, and then he looked back towards that dummy. "Wake up, Kid, damn it." I never and then he hauled out his shooter and fired a shot into the dirt just beside the dummy. It was meant to skeer me awake a course. Dawson looked at Cherry again. "What the hell's wrong with him?"

Cherry give a shrug. "He must be a sound sleeper."

"Say," said Dawson, "what're you trying to pull?"

He shot that dummy then, and he shot it twice again. I was a-counting. He had three shots left. Two if he only loaded five for reasons a safety, but I figgered ole Clem Dawson for a kinda careless feller, so I told myself he had three left. He turned the shooter on Cherry then.

"Drop your gun real easy," he said.

Cherry done what he was told, and then Dawson made him get offa his horse and walk over to stand beside the dummy. He told Cherry to pull the hat offa the dummy and Cherry done it. Then Dawson seed that dummy for what it for real was, and he looked all around hisself real quick and nervous-like.

"Where the hell's the Kid?" he said.

"The last I saw him, he was right here," said ole Cherry.

"Your scheming something up against me with the Kid."

"I told you the truth," Cherry said. "I saw the Kid here in this camp, and he told me he was coming after you. He had reward money in his pockets that he got for your brothers."

I thunk it was kindly clever of ole Cherry to tell just only the truth the way he done. 'Course, he left out some things in the telling, but what he told was the truth.

"I think I'll just kill you," Dawson said.

I stood up and stepped out, and my shooter was pointed right straight at ole Dawson. "You might want to kill me first," I said.

He turned quick, but he never shot. He faced me, and his shooter was a-pointed at me. Now here was a new kinda gunfight, all right. There we was a-standing and facing each other, both of us with our guns out and pointed and cocked. It weren't going to make no difference who was the fastest one on the draw, 'cause both guns was done drawed. It didn't make no difference how good a shot a feller was neither, on accounta at that there distance, hell, ole Sparky couldn't a-missed.

"What're we a-fixing to do, Clem," I said. "Kill each other?"

"What'd you come here for, you skinny little son of a bitch?"

"I come to take you back to jail or else to kill you in the trying," I said. "Whyn't you just toss that there gun down and come along peaceful?"

"What do you care?"

"I rid outa Fosterville with the posse after you robbed the bank there," I told him. "Jim Chastain's a friend a mine."

"Chastain? The sheriff?"

"That's right."

"Damn you. You killed my brothers."

"You're at least half right about that," I said. "You going to give it up?"

"No."

Just then ole Cherry moved, and Dawson spun around to see what he was a-doing. Cherry put his hands up in the air, and Dawson spun back towards me, and I pulled the trigger. My bullet smashed into his chest, and he jerked and twitched some, and then he fell over backwards and slud down the hillside a little ways. I went down there after him to make sure that he was deader'n hell, and I went through his pockets but I never come up with nothing more than pocket change. I tuck it anyhow. Then I went on back up to the camp and ole Cherry was just a-picking up his shooter from off the ground.

"He's dead," I said. "He didn't have no money to speak of on him, neither."

I reckon the two of us had the same idee at the same time then, on accounta both of us walked straight over to ole Dawson's horse, me on one side and Cherry on t'other, and we each opened up a flap a them saddlebags and shoved our hands down in them. The both of us come up empty, and we stood there a-staring across that horse's ass at each other for a minute without saying nothing. "You want some coffee?" I said.

We went over to the fire and I set on some more coffee to boil. Then we set acrost from each other. "Well," Cherry said, "that was the last of the Dawsons."

"Yeah, but where the hell's that bank money?"

"Dawson had him a room down in Devil's Roost. It could be in there."

"We're going to have to get our ass in there somehow and search for it," I said.

"That won't be easy. Not in that den of renegades. And if they find out that he's dead, they'll be searching his room themselves."

"Then we got to search it first and afore they find out that he ain't nothing but a corpus no more," I said. "How we going to go about it?"

"Hell, Kid, I don't know."

I poured us up some coffee and handed a cup to ole Dick. I tuck a sup outa mine, and it were hot all right. It was a good time a morning for it, though. I got to craving some eggs and ham and stuff. Special some a ole Zeb's biscuit.

"Look," Dick said, "now that Dawson's dead, no one down there knows you. Right?"

"I s'pose that's right," I said. "But then, I don't know who's all down there. There could be someone what knows me. Them Goddamned Hookses and Piggses seem to show up ever'where, and they always knows me. But I guess it wouldn't matter if they was to know me. I ain't a wanted man right now, but I been one a couple a times in my life."

"All right," Cherry said. "Let's just ride on down in there together and get us rooms for the night. We can get us a good breakfast, and then we can sort of snoop around. Find out where Dawson's room is and look for a chance to sneak in there and search it."

Well, I couldn't think a no better idee, and the thought of a real breakfast did sound good to me. I stood up and commenced to kicking dirt all over the fire.

"All right," I said. "Let's do her."

Chapter 8

Well, now, I reminded myself that me and ole Cherry was a-riding into that there Devil's Pit like a couple a wanted outlaws, you know, pretending to be such, that is, and so I went and put on my meanest look as we rid in on the main street. I narrered my eyes down to just slits, and I never looked one way nor t'other, just only straight on ahead, but then, if there was to be anything suspicious-like a-going on around me, why, I could still catch a glimpse of it outa the corner a my eyeballs. Now, we done like any respectable outlaws would a did just a-coming into any ole town. We stopped our horses right there in front a the saloon, what was called Devil's Hangout, and we tied up there at the hitch rail and went on inside, still not a-bothering to look to one side nor t'other.

As we walked on into that there saloon, though, I could tell that folks was a-eyeballing us all right. They was a-looking at us from ever' direction. Well, we acted like as if we never noticed nothing about it, though, and we just bellied right on up to the bar and called out for whiskey. We got it brung to us pretty quick, too. We paid for the bottle, and the barkeep said, "You're strangers in town."

It weren't no question, so I never bothered giving out with no answer, but ole Dick Cherry, he popped up and said, "I was in here last night. I met up with ole Clem Dawson right in here. I thought you might've noticed."

"Oh, yeah," the barkeep said. "Now that you mention it, I did see you with Dawson. Say, where is ole Clem?"

"We rode out to meet up with the Kid here, me and Clem, that is," Cherry said, "but when we found him, Dawson said he had other business. He wouldn't tell us what it was. He just rode on off headed north. Said he'd be back late tonight. He said it would be all right if we were to bunk down in his room here till he gets back. Maybe you could tell us where that would be."

"I don't know about that," the barkeep said. "Letting someone into another man's room. You'll have to talk to Wheeler about that."

"Oh? Where will we find this Wheeler?"

"You boys are strangers, ain't you? Mr. Wheeler's right over yonder having a drink with those two boys in the Montana peak hats."

Me and ole Cherry both looked over where the barkeep was a-indicating, and we seed the two Montana peaks, all right. There was a feller a-setting at the same table with them what had to be Wheeler. He was wearing a black suit with a white shirt and a vest and a black string tie. He was a stocky feller, and he wore a handlebar mustache. His front hairline was well back on top a his head, and he was a smoking a ceegar, just a-clouding up the air all around him. He had the look of a gambler to me, or maybe a lawyer.

"You said 'the Kid,' " the barkeep popped up.

"What?" Cherry said.

"You called your pard here, the Kid. What Kid might that be?"

"Is they more than one?" I said, and I said it in my coldest tone a voice with my eyeballs slitted way down narrer.

"Well, sure. I've heard of Billy the Kid, the Verdigris Kid, the Sundance Kid, the Apache Kid, Kid Curry. If I was to think on it real hard, I bet you I could come up with a few more."

"Well, you missed one," I said.

"You?"

"Yeah. I sure ain't none a them you named."

"Well?"

"This here is Kid Parmlee," Cherry said.

"Oh yeah," said the barkeep. "I heard a him all right. They call him a regular Billy the Kid."

"They'd call that other'n a regular Kid Parmlee if only he was good enough," I said. I was sure sick a hearing that comparison made about me and that back-shooting other and more famouser kid. Hell, I kilt more'n him, and I didn't even keep count. I never heared that he ever shot no ears off, neither.

"Yeah," the barkeep said, "well, uh, I'll just see if Mr. Wheeler is busy over there."

He walked around the far end a the bar and went out amongst the customers at the tables, and he come up to one side and kindly behind that Wheeler, and he leaned over and mouthed something into Wheeler's right ear. Ole Wheeler give him a look, and then he give another one to me and ole Dick Cherry from over there acrost the room. Then he whispered something on back to the barkeep. The barkeep looked up at us, and then he come back around behind the bar and on down to where me and ole Dick was a-waiting on him. In the meantime, I seed Wheeler say something to the two Montana peaks, and they got their ass up and went on over to another table to plop down and set, a-leaving Wheeler there all by his lonesome.

"Go on over and join him," the barkeep said to us.

"You never said who this here Wheeler is," I said.

"Why, he owns this place. He damn near owns the whole town. I thought everyone knew that. Go on. He's waiting for you."

We picked up our glasses and bottle and ambled on over to Wheeler where he was a-waiting on us. He looked up and smiled, and I thunk at the time that his smile was fakey and kindly slick-like. Kindly like a ole boy what's a-trying to sell you a jaded horse, you know? He's a-trying to cover up something with that there phony smile a-spreaded all acrost his face. I didn't like him none right off from the start.

"Sit down," he said. "I'm Jared Wheeler."

"I'm Dick Cherry," my pard said, "and this is Kid Parmlee."

Ole Wheeler stuck out his clammy hand, and me and Cherry both shuck it. Then we set down acrost from him.

"Kid Parmlee," Wheeler said. "I've heard that you're—"

"I'd ruther you not to say it," I told him. I still had my eyeballs slitted way down, and I was a-keeping my voice cold. I was kindly astonished once again, though, to find out just how far my reputation had spread out.

"Well," Wheeler said, "I guess I don't blame you. I've heard about you. We'll let it go at that. What can I do for you boys?"

"I came in last night," Cherry said, "to meet up with Clem Dawson."

"Did you?"

"What?"

"Did you meet up with Dawson?"

"Yeah. Me and the Kid here were supposed to meet him, but the Kid is suspicious. Real cautious. He didn't want to ride into town till we'd talked with Clem about it. So Clem rode out with me last night to where the Kid was camped. We had us a long talk. We were planning a—well, some business together. Clem told us he had a room here in town, and he said we could share it with him. Then he said he had some other business, private business, up north. He told us to ride on in and wait for him in his room. Said he'd be back here tonight. The bartender said that we ought to talk to you about that, uh, about moving into Clem's room, you know."

"Are you two on the lam?"

"Why, I—"

"You're safe from the law here. Are you on the lam?"

"I've had a lawman on my trail," I said, a-recalling how ole Cherry had lied by not telling the whole truth that time. Wheeler looked at Cherry.

"Well," Dick said, "I was sort of run out of town by the local sheriff back down the road."

"I see," said Wheeler. "Now, just what kind of business were you talking over with Dawson last night?"

Cherry give me a look, and I give one right back to him.

"It's all right," Wheeler said. "You know what kind of town this is, don't you?"

"It looks pretty much like any other town to me," I said.

"I've, uh, heard some things," said Cherry.

"Just so we'll all understand one another," Wheeler said, "I'll explain it to you real clear. Devil's Roost is a refuge for outlaws, for men on the run. That's why Dawson came here. He has a price on his head, and he knew that this is a safe haven. No lawman will dare set foot in Devil's Roost. The last four that did never rode out again. We take good care of our guests. Devil's Roost is a place where you can get yourself a safe, quiet room, have a good time, ride out when you want and take care of your business, and ride right back in again. We have everything you could want here, everything you need. And you're safe. And we don't ask for too much."

"Yeah?" I said. "How much is that?"

"One hundred dollars a night, and that's cheap for all you get. You don't have to keep looking over your shoulder all the time. You buy your eats and drinks. If you ride out of here to pull a job, when you ride back in, I get ten percent. That's the whole deal."

It seemed to me that I'd been a-hearing a lot a that percent stuff lately, and I hadn't never heared much about it atall during the whole rest a my life. 'Course, I was still a young-

ster. "A hunnerd dollars is awful steep for just only a room,"
I said.

"A room where you can sleep quiet and undisturbed,"
Wheeler said. "And that's a hundred each, even if you're
sharing a room. We provide a service, and you pay for it.
It's your choice. You can stay or ride on through to somewhere else."

Me and Cherry give each other a look then, and I give
him a nod. 'Course, if we meant to track down that there
stole bank money, we didn't have much choice in the matter.
Me and ole Cherry, we had done figgered that it just had to
be somewheres in this here town, most likely right in ole
Dawson's room what he was a-paying a hunnerd bucks a
night for. That is, a hunnerd bucks a the Fosterville bank's
money, and that there was a-cutting down on my percentage
ever' night the bastard stayed.

"Can we get into Clem's room?" Cherry asked.

"I don't see why not," said Wheeler. "You say he told
you to wait for him there. If you prefer to stay three in a
room instead of having a room each, it's all the same to me.
The price is the same."

We each of us, me and ole Dick, digged down into our
pockets, then, and come up with the bucks and laid them on
the table. Wheeler counted it out real keerful and stuffed it
into his own pocket. Then he reached into another pocket
and brung out two skeleton keys what he tossed on the table
in front of us. "Dawson's room is number twelve," he said.
"Top of the stairs and down the hall on your right."

I picked up my key. Cherry said, "Thanks," and tuck up
the other'n. Then we stood up to go check out the room.

"Stable's down at the end of the street," Wheeler said.
"Prices are reasonable. We don't figure the horses are wanted
by the law."

"Thanks again," Cherry said. Then he turned to me.
"We'd best take care of the horses first, Kid."

"Yeah," I said, still acting sullen as I knowed how. I was a-thinking that it sure woulda been nice and handy to have them horses waiting just right where we had left them, so that whenever we come up with that money, we could high-tail it outa town right fast. But Cherry was right. If we was to make Wheeler believe that we was planning to stay the night, we needed to take keer a the horses. 'Special since Wheeler was the one what had thunk of it. We turned to walk out, but ole Wheeler stopped us.

"By the way, boys, when Dawson gets back, and the three of you ride out to conduct your business, don't forget about my ten percent."

"We never forget a percent," I said.

We tuck our horses to the stable, and then we walked back to the saloon and went straight through to the stairway. We went on up and found ole Dawson's room all right. Inside, we lit us a oil lamp what was a-setting there on a table, and we commenced to looking around. We like to a tore the place apart, but we never found no money.

"Damn," I said. "I woulda had to a kilt the son of a bitch before we could make him tell us where he had hid the loot at."

"What could he have done with it?" Cherry said.

"Dog shit if I know," I said.

"Do you suppose this town has a bank?"

"A town fulla bank robbers?"

"Yeah. Well, neither of his brothers had it on them. It wasn't anywhere in the room they were sharing. He didn't have it on him either, and it's not here in his room. He hid it somewhere or stashed it somewhere here in town."

"Would you leave anything what was worth anything with that sleazy ole bastard Wheeler?" I asked.

"No, I wouldn't," Dick said, "but Dawson had to do something with that cash."

"What are we a going to do?" I said. "Search the whole damn town?"

"Hell, we were lucky to get to search Dawson's room. I'm a little surprised that Wheeler bought that story so easy."

The door come open just then, and them two Montana peaks stepped in a holding shotguns what was done cocked. Even if I coulda kilt the both of them, a twitch a either one a their trigger fingers woulda splashed me and ole Cherry both all over the damn room. They come on in and kindly stepped away from each other, and then ole Wheeler come a walking in betwixt them with a wide grin on his shitty face.

"I did buy that story pretty easy, didn't I?" he said.

"What is this?" Cherry asked.

"You didn't tell me the truth," said Wheeler. "And you called me a sleazy bastard. Tell me the whole truth right now, and if I like it all right, and if I believe you, then I won't hold it against you that you didn't tell me up front."

I didn't have no idee what ole Cherry was a thinking nor what he might say if I was to wait for him to say it, but I sure didn't like them two greeners cocked in the same room with me, and then a idee popped right quick into my usual slow head, and so I just went and blurted it on out. It seemed like the only thing to do at the time.

"You're right, Mr. Wheeler," I said. "Ole Dawson, he weren't our pardner atall. Matter a fact, we hardly knowed him. Only thing we knowed was that him and his brothers robbed the bank back at a place called Fosterville. They run from a posse, and they hadn't hardly had no time to spend the money, so we figgered they still had it. Then ole Clem's two brothers got theirselfs kilt, and we was kindly hanging around a-listening to folks talk, and we heared that they didn't have no money on them and that no one found none in their room neither. Well, me and my pard here, we figgered that ole Clem must still have that there bank money on him."

"And you figured to take it away from him and keep it for yourselves."

"That's about the size of it," I said.

"If Dawson didn't know you, how'd you get him to ride out of town with you?"

"I lied to him," Cherry said. He had caught onto my line a bullshit and jumped right in. "I told him that the Kid was out there and that he was the one who had killed his brothers."

"Who did kill them?"

"The sheriff and some town folks caught them coming out of the bank," Cherry said.

"So you two just watched it all develop and decided to horn in on it?"

"That's right."

"I thought it was something like that," Wheeler said.

"What made you suspicious of us in the first place?" Cherry asked him.

"I talked with Dawson. He told me about his brothers, and he never mentioned any other partners. Tell me, did you kill him?"

I give Cherry a look.

"Look, uh, Mr. Wheeler," Cherry said, "if we take off our gunbelts, would you tell these two to put away those shotguns? They're making me awful nervous."

"Drop them on the floor," Wheeler said. Me and ole Cherry, we done that. Then Wheeler give a nod to them two Montana peaks, and they eased the hammers down on them shotguns and went on out in the hall. Wheeler nodded over toward the bed, and me and Dick walked over and set on the edge of it.

"Is that better?" Wheeler said.

"Considerable," I said.

"Now," he said, "did you kill Dawson?"

"I did," I said. "I kilt him. He was a-throwing down on me, though. I ain't never kilt a man what weren't trying to kill me. I shot a couple a ears off without giving no warning, but I never kilt a man thataway."

"Now, I'm going to save you boys a whole lot of trouble," Wheeler said. "You can stop looking for Dawson's bank loot. I got it myself. Somehow, I didn't think he was coming back."

"What would you a did if he hada come back?" I asked.

"Oh, I'd have returned it to him. We have a reputation here. You and your belongings are safe—as long as you pay."

"Yeah, well, that might be a problem for us after tonight," said Cherry. "I don't think we can afford your town. We were kind of counting on, well, you know."

"There's a place across the street where you can get a good breakfast in the morning," Wheeler said. "I'll tell them to take care of you. After you've had your breakfast, come back over here. I'll be in my office downstairs. Maybe we can work something out."

He didn't say nothing more, not a good night nor bye-bye. He just turned around and walked out and left us there in that room. Me and ole Cherry, we just kindly stared at each other for a minute. I was used to being hassled by law-men, but I hadn't never been hassled like that by the boss of a town what was a kind of a outlaw hisself. I didn't have no idee what ole Dick might a been thinking.

"What the hell do you make a all that?" I asked him.

"I don't know," he said, "except that Wheeler was one step ahead of us on that bank money. It makes me nervous, though."

"It makes me more curiouser than nervous," I said. "He's up to something. He's a-fixing to make us some kinda proposition in the morning. Otherwise, he'd a had them two Montanas go on and kill us dead."

"You're probably right about that."

"Sure, I am. And I'll tell you two things right now."

"What?"

"I mean to find out what he's up to."

"And?"

"I ain't aiming to leave outa this here Devil's Hole without that there bank money."

Chapter 9

Well, we done one better than what that damned ole Jared Wheeler said. We went and actual caught up with him in time for breakfast in the morning, and I tell you what, I et till I couldn't hardly stand it no more, on accounta the pure and simple fact that he was a-paying for it all, and I wanted to make damn sure I got ever'thing outa him I could get. I et flapjacks, fried eggs, ham, taters, bacon, biscuit, gravy, and I drunk coffee, lots and lots of it. I tried my bestest to run his bill way on up there, but, hell, I'm sure paying for it never hurt him none. Not the way he was collecting money offa all a them fugitives ever' damn day a the week, and him owning the saloon and the hotel rooms and all. Besides, I reckoned that he likely owned the damned eating place along with ever'thing else.

Well, he never talked much atall as long as we was all eating like that, but whenever we final was all did stuffing ourselfs, and it was me what was the last one of all to quit, skinny as I was, well then he went and got real serious on us. He put a kinda scowl on his ugly ole face, and he went and wrinkled his brow on up like as if he was a-thinking on something real hard. "Boys," he said, "I recall you told me that you couldn't afford much more of my hospitality. Is that right? Am I remembering what you said correctly?"

"That's about the truth of it," I said. 'Course I was a-telling him a ball faced lie. Me and ole Cherry, we both had us plenty a money in our pockets to last us for a while, even at Wheeler's puffed up prices.

"If you could afford it, would you stay longer?"

I give a look to ole Dick Cherry, and he give me a nod.

"I believe we would, Mr. Wheeler," he said.

"It is a comfort to know that the law ain't a-going to slip up on a feller's back," I said. "But only that there was a big 'if' what you said," I added.

"It was that," said Dick.

"I have a proposition for you," said Wheeler. "You interested?"

"That all depends on what's the deal," I said. "I never agree on nothing up front what I don't know what it is before I go and agree to it. That there's a policy a mine what I always sticks to."

"The deal is that you stay here, and you pay me after the job is done. You pay me what you would've paid even without the job. You just pay later instead of up front. The loot you get from the job is yours, all except my ten percent."

There come that percent again. I was a-starting in to feel like a big shot businessman a some kind or 'nother just a-listening to that kinda talk so much all of a sudden.

"How much loot we talking about?" I asked him.

"It's a payroll shipment," Wheeler said. "A quarter of a million dollars."

I didn't rightly know how much money that meant in real numbers, but I never let on about my ignorance. Lucky for me ole Cherry spelled it out.

"That's two hundred and fifty thousand," he said. "Ten percent would be twenty-five thousand dollars. That would leave me and the kid with two hundred and twenty-five thousand."

Wheeler grinned. "That's right," he said.

I give Cherry a look and asked him, "How much is that split in two?"

"One hundred and twelve thousand, five hundred dollars for you, and the same for me," he said.

"A hunnerd and twelve thousand and five hunnerd dollars." I said. Then I looked back at Wheeler. "How come you to be so generous in the splitting up of all that much money?" I asked.

"It's not being generous. It's my standard rate. I get twenty-five thousand from you, ten thousand from someone else, and so on. I'm doing all right. I also get your hundred a night for the room."

"And you own the whole damn town, too," I said. "The saloon. How about this here eatery?"

"It's mine," he said, and he were still grinning. "Well, what do you say? It's entirely up to you. You can take the job, or you can ride on out of town. I can always find someone else."

I reckoned that was for sure and him with a whole town full a outlaws paying him more than a hunnerd dollars a day. Hell, they had to come up with some way a-paying the bills or else get on outa there and take their chances with the law.

"We'll take it," I said. "What is it?"

"Not here. Like I told you last night," he said, "we'll talk about it in my office. Let's go."

We follered Wheeler outa the eating place and across the street to the saloon. His office was through the big main room and back behind the back wall. He unlocked the door and went on in, and me and ole Dick follered along. As Wheeler was a-going back behind a big desk to settle his ass, he told us to set ourselfs down. We set in two chairs what was direct acrost the desk from Wheeler. He opened up a box a ceegars and offered them around, and pretty soon the three of us had that there little office all filled up with gray-blue smoke. They was good ceegars too. Not cheap.

"Well?" Dick said. "What's the job?"

"Just hold on a bit," Wheeler said. "You'll find out all about it soon enough."

I hadn't said nothing, but I was a-taking the time to look around the office kindly casual-like, you know, and I seed a safe over against the wall to my left. I was a-wondering then if that was where the Fosterville bank money, what was left of it, was stashed away at. I figgered it likely it was. The problem was how to get at it. I sure weren't no safe cracker. I had heared about robbers a-blowing up safes, a course, but I wouldn't a-knowed how much dynamite to use, and really, I didn't want to use none a that stuff neither. I sure didn't want to go waking up a whole town full a outlaws. Besides, I heared once about a outlaw what tried to rob a safe by blowing it up thataway, and the dumb son of a bitch blowed his own ass right smack through the roof a the place. I figgered I'd just tell ole Cherry after a while what it was I was a-thinking on, and then maybe the two of us could think up some way to deal with the situation. Just then the door come open and damned if them two Montana peaks didn't come ambling on into the room and grab theirselfs a couple a chairs and set.

" 'Morning, boys," Wheeler said.

They mumbled good mornings back at him, give us cold stares, and then Wheeler told them who we was. Then he said, "This is Spike Dutton and his brother, Haw. You'll be riding with them on this job. Spike, Haw, the kid here will be in charge."

"I thought we was in charge a this job," Spike said.

"I never said that. There just wasn't anyone else involved until now. The kid'll take over."

"How come?" Spike said. "We was in on it first. We know the whole set up. Him and his pal there come in at the last minute, a couple a Johnny-come-latelys, and you want them to just take it on over?"

"That's right. In the first place," Wheeler said, "Kid Parmlee has struck fear in hearts for hundreds of miles around. He's a dead shot, and he's fast. Hell, he just killed all three Dawson brothers."

That there weren't true, a course, but I never corrected him none. I just let him go on and let them all believe that there tale. At the time, it seemed like as if it might be to our benefit for them to think thataway.

"In the second place, you two put together aren't smart enough to skin a cat. That's the reason I've been looking for someone else to help you out. I was thinking about Dawson, but the kid killed him. Besides, Dawson was just one man. The kid's got a partner."

"And he's just only a smidgen slower than me," I said. "He can part your hair all right and not even scratch your scalp."

"I'm slow compared to the Kid," Cherry said.

"Well, I don't like it," said Haw. "I don't think he looks so tough, neither. He ain't nothing but a snot-nosed kid is all."

Well, I stood right up then, and I slitted my eyes down some and backed away a ways a-looking hard at that there Haw Dutton.

"Mr. Wheeler," I said, without taking my eyes offa Haw a course, "you want us to go outside to settle this, or you want me to just take him down right here in your office?"

"There's no need to go outside and make a public show," Wheeler said.

"All right then, stand up, Dutton," I said. "Hell, both of you if you want. It don't make no difference to me. Dick will stay out of it. I don't need no help to kill the both of you. Stand on up."

Haw Dutton stood up kindly slow, and he stared at me.

"Keep your seat, Spike," he said.

"Mr. Wheeler thinks we needs four for this job," I said, "so on second thought, I won't kill you after all. Which ear you want to keep on your head?"

"What?" Haw asked, wrinkling up his face like as if he couldn't quite believe what it was I had just said at him. I decided to explain it to him a little more fuller then.

"I'm a-fixing to shoot off a ear offa you. Which one you want to keep?"

"You ain't going to do no such a thing," ole Haw said, and he give a nervous laugh. "I'm fixing to kill you."

"Mr. Wheeler," I said, "which one a his ears you want me to shoot offa this weasly-faced bastard?"

"Take off his right one, Kid."

I mighta knowed he'd a said that. I thunk then that I shouldn't oughta have pushed it quite so damn far. I shoulda just been happy to say that I'd shoot off a ear and not went to calling which one. You know, it's a mite tougher for a right handed shooter to take off a right ear than a left one. But it was too late. I had done asked him, and he had told me, so I had to shoot Haw's right ear off without doing no worse damage to him than just that. I stared at him and never moved.

"Go on," he yelled at me.

"I'm a-waiting for you," I said. "You're going to need a head start on me."

Ole Spike, he got up outa his chair real slow-like, and he moved a good ways off from his brother. I seed that my current pard, ole Dick Cherry, were keeping his eye sharp on Spike just in case he was to decide to give his brother a little help on the side, you know. I was glad a that, 'cause thataway, you see, I didn't have to concentrate on nothing but just only Haw's right ear what I was a-meaning to knock right offa the side a his head or at the least tear a big hole outa the thing.

"You want to take back what you said and sit down,

Haw?" Wheeler asked. "It's not too late. There won't be any hard feelings, will there, Kid?"

"No hard feelings," I agreed.

"I ain't backing down," Haw shouted, and at the same time he went for his shooter. I jerked mine out and blasted, all in one smooth move. Haw's gun was out all right, but it weren't yet so much as leveled up at me whenever the hot lead a my bullet tore his right ear. Blood went a-flying, and Haw, he yelped something fierce and dropped his gun. His right hand went up to the side a his head, and that there ear blood was a-running free, just a-pulsing through his fingers and running down his arm to drip offa his elbone and puddle up on the floor a ole Wheeler's nice fancy office room.

"Ow, ow, ow," Haw yellered out. "I'm a-bleeding to death here."

"You won't bleed to death from no tore ear," I told him. "You will bleed considerable though. Kindly like a stuck pig. I oughta know. I've shot off a few."

"You son of a bitch."

"How come you to go calling me names thataway?" I said. "Hell, I coulda just as easy a-missed the mark a wee little bit and kilt you deader'n a flat toad, but I never. You'd oughta appreciate little favors like that."

"Calm down, Haw," Wheeler said. "He's right. Besides, you asked for it." He pulled open a desk drawer and dragged out a bar towel what he throwed over at ole Haw. "Use this," he said. He tossed a second one at ole Spike. "Mop the floor."

Haw went to dancing around, still giving out with little yelps. I seed that neither Haw nor his brother wasn't about to do nothing more, so I went and holstered my Colt and set my ass back down in my chair.

"That was good shooting, Kid," Wheeler said. "Good thinking, too. You Dutton boys see now why the Kid's in charge?"

"I see, Mr. Wheeler," Spike said.

"My head hurts," said Haw, "and I'm bleeding bad."

Spike jabbed a elbone into Haw's side, and Haw jumped and real fast said, "Yeah. Yeah, I see."

I give a narrer-eyed look at ole Wheeler then, and I said, "Now you going to tell me and ole Dick here just what this job is?"

"That payroll I mentioned will be on the stagecoach at noon tomorrow on the road from Victorville to a place called End of the Line. It'll be headed south. There's a good spot for an ambush about halfway between the two towns. Spike knows where it is. If you get there by noon tomorrow, you'll be ahead of the stage. The four of you can take it easy. Get the payroll and come straight back here with it. That's all."

"How long a ride is it to over yonder from here?" I asked.

"If you leave Devil's Roost at first light in the morning, you'll be there in plenty of time," Wheeler said.

"A quarter of a million?" Dick said.

"A quarter of a million," said Wheeler. "Well, is it a deal?"

"We'll be a wanting a real early breakfast," I said. "Men can't do that kinda robbing on a empty stomach."

"It'll be ready."

When me and ole Dick turned to leave Wheeler's office, I give a motion a my hand to the Dutton boys, and they both got up fast to foller me. I reckon that me and Wheeler together had done convinced them that I was the boss all right. That Haw, he kept up his whimpering and whining, but he done what I said him to do. I led the way to the stable, and I made them show me their horses. They was good enough. Then we went to the general store, and I made sure that we all four of us had a-plenty a ammunition and even some trail grub. I told ever'one to check their canteens and make sure they was full a water.

Well, we had us a full day a rest to look forward to, and I told them boys to not be getting their ass drunk and to get them a good long rest and a good night's sleep. I told them what time to meet up with us for breakfast, and then I sent them off on their way. "Come on," I said to ole Dick, and I led him back to our own room, what had once been the room a ole Clem Dawson. I shut the door and locked it up, even though I weren't none too sure that locking a door in Jared Wheeler's Devil Town would do no good if Wheeler was to want to come through it. Ole Dick, he throwed hisself down on the bed, and me, I tuck myself a chair and leaned it back on two legs against the wall.

"With four of us in on the deal," Dick said, "our cut's only going to be fifty-six thousand, two hundred and fifty dollars."

I kindly muttered something. I weren't really paying no attention to what he was a-saying.

"Unless we kill those two Duttons."

"You notice that there safe in Wheeler's office?" I asked.

"Yeah."

"You reckon that there Fosterville money is in there?"

"Probably so."

"You got any idee how we might could get it out?"

"I've never robbed a safe in my life," Cherry said.

"Me neither," I said, "but we got to figger out just how to rob that one."

"What for?"

"The Fosterville bank money," I said.

"Come on, Kid," Dick said. "We're going after a quarter of a million in the morning. What do we care about the Fosterville bank's money?"

I kindly lifted up one ear at that there comment what come from ole Dick. I weren't quite sure for certain that I had heared him right, or if I had, that I had for real understood just what the hell he was a-getting at.

"What do you mean by that?" I asked him.

He set up and give me a hard stare.

"It's plain enough," he said. "If we have a quarter of a million dollars, we won't need however much the Dawsons got out of the bank at Fosterville. Likely it's only a few thousand. What do we care? We'll have enough to live like kings. We'll be set up for life."

"We come after them Dawsons for the reeward money," I said, "and for a percentage of the returned bank money. And on accounta I promised that I'd get that there bank money back to the bank. This here stagecoach job, the only reason we're a-going along with it is 'cause we ain't yet figgered out how to get our hands on the Fosterville money yet. Whenever we get that payroll and get it back here, we'll have to get to where Wheeler stashes his loot, take the payroll and the Fosterville money, and return it all to where it belongs. Then we'll collect our reewards and go on our ways."

Well, ole Dick, he looked like as if he really wanted to say something to me then, but instead a doing that, why, he just heaved out a heavy sigh and give a shrug. "All right, Kid," he said, "whatever you say. Like Wheeler said, you're the boss."

"I don't necessary want to be no boss," I said. "I just only want to do what it was we set out to do. That's all."

"All right."

"I'm a-thinking," I said, "when we come back here to this Devil's Pot with all that cash, and we take it on in there to ole Wheeler's office, why, he'll likely open up that there safe. We'll watch him real good and sly, and maybe we can tell just how it is he does it."

"Yeah? Then what? You thinking about pulling off a robbery in this place? Devil's Roost? A town full of desperate outlaws?"

"It's the only way I can think of to get the money back."

"You're crazy."

"You got a better idee? I'm a-listening."

"No. I don't."

"Well, then, quit your bellyaching about it. Unless you come up with a better way a doing it, we'll do it the way I said."

"Yeah," ole Dick said. "I hope they give us a decent burial in this owlhoot's nest. That's all I have to say."

Chapter 10

The rest a that there day weren't nothing much to talk about. I did go into the saloon and ketch them two Duttons after they'd had them each about three or four drinks, and I told them to cut it out and go to bed. Whenever they whined a bit at that thought, I told them they had three more ears I could shoot at. They went to their room all right. Then whenever I felt reasonable sure they was a-going to stay there till morning, I tuck me and ole Dick Cherry off to our room. I wanted us all up early, well rested and raring to go.

In the morning I was up first, and I kicked the side a the bed to wake up ole Cherry. He come up without no problems. Soon as we was dressed and ready to go, we walked over to the room where the Duttons was a-staying, and I banged on their door till they come awake. Then me and Dick went in and waited till they was ready. The four of us went downstairs, outside and acrost the street to the eating place together. We found us a table inside, which weren't no trouble on accounta it was so early, and we set down and ordered us each up a big breakfast. I told that man there what tuck our orders that ole Wheeler were a-putting it on the cuff for me, and he never argued with me none. Pretty soon we had et and drunk our fill, and we left that place and walked to the stable. We saddled up our horses and headed on out.

I had noticed since we first went into the Duttons's room, and all the way through breakfast and even afterwards that ole Haw Dutton would ever' now and then rub his ear scab and give me a hard look. I knowed that he wouldn't dare to face me and try anything, but I was pretty damn sure that if he ever got hisself a good chance, he would most for sure try to kill me by backshooting or some other such cowardly way a doing the deed. I didn't figger on giving him a chance.

We never talked a whole hell of a lot on the way over to that there stage coach road what was west a the Devil's Spot and a running north and south. There weren't a lot to say. We all knowed what it was we was a-fixing to pull off, and we knowed how much it was worth. What we didn't know was just exact how we was a-fixing to do it, on accounta it was me what was calling the shots, and I hadn't never seed the place where it was we was a-fixing to hold up the stage. I had to get us there plenty early so I could look over the lay a the land and figger that out.

Well, we made it early enough, and sure enough, the road tuck a sharp turn around a high-up wall a rock on the right. Just around the curve it went to climbing uphill. It was a place where the driver would for sure have to slow it down considerable, and what's more, he wouldn't be able to see what was in the road around the bend. The ground on the left side a the road, that was the east side, it were might near flat, but it did have a few clumps a brush spotted here and there, enough for a man or two to crouch down behind and hide his ass.

I rid along north and south real slow-like, a-looking at both sides a the road and up toward the top a that there sheer wall a rock, studying real hard on the situation. The other three was a-getting kindly impatient with me, I could tell. Final I looked at ole Spike Dutton, and I asked him, "Can you get up there on top a that there wall, you reckon?"

"Yeah," he said. "I know the way."

"How far north along this road can you see from up there?"

He give a shrug. "I don't know. Several miles, I'd say."

"If you're up there on top, and you see that stage a-coming, would you have time to get back down here and tell me, and it not be a-getting too close to us yet?"

"Sure. I'd have plenty a time."

"All right," I said. "You go on up there then. Soon as you see the stage coming, get back down here and tell me. Then we'll get ready for it."

"I'll just go up there with you," Haw said to Spike.

"He won't need no help up there," I said. "You stay here."

I tell you what, ole Haw give me a mean devil look at that, but he never said nothing. To tell you the truth a the matter, I wanted to keep them two brothers separated as much as I could on accounta I figgered that Haw's cowardness would take more charge a his senses if he was alone from his brother. Anyhow, Spike rid south a-headed for the place where he knowed he could get on up on top fairly easy. Haw stayed with me and Cherry, a-frowning something fierce.

I went and set behind a rock on the north a the curve and west a the road and studied, trying to picture a stagecoach a-coming and then rolling on around that there curve. I satisfied myself that I could be hid real good there, and whenever the stage went on past me, I could stand up and throw down on them from the rear end. Then I walked across the road and got down behind one a them clumps a brush what I done told you about. I studied from there too and come to the same conclusion as I had did on the first spot. I figgered I'd put Haw behind the rock and Dick behind the brush. Then I went hunting some more places.

Just around the curve I figgered to put my own self, and then acrost the road and up a ways was another clump where I decided to have Spike hide out. Here's the way I schemed it up. Soon as that stage come a-rolling in sight around the bend, Spike would show hisself and call out to them to halt.

He'd be a holding a rifle gun. Almost immediate after that, I would come outa my hidey hole and repeat his orders. He'd be ahead of them, and I'd be just a little bit behind. Then the two behindest, Haw and Dick would show theirselfs. The driver and shotgun rider and anyone inside the stage what might be a possible defender a the right would know that they was surrounded, having armed men at all four corners. Likely they'd give it up without a fight, which was what I was a-hoping for, on accounta I didn't want no one to get kilt in the doing a this here deed. Please remember that I ain't really no outlaw. I was still involved in the process a trying to recover some stole bank loot, and I meant to return that there payroll, too, just as soon as it was possible for me to get it did.

Well 'bout as soon as I had it all figgered out, here come ole Spike a-hauling ass down the road towards me and a-waving his hat. He come to a quick stop just a few feet away from me, and he said, "I seen it. It's a-coming."

"All right," I said. "Get the rest a the horses and take them all down thataway out a sight. Then hurry on back here."

Well, Spike done that, and when he come back, I gethered them all around me and told them what my plan a action was. "If we all do it right," I said, "there won't even have to be no shooting. I don't want no shooting if we can possible help it. You all got that? I mean it now. If any one a you shoots anyone, I mean to shoot off his ear, and you know I can do it."

Ole Haw give me a hell of a look and stroked his ear scab, but no one argued with me none, and so I showed them their places. I explained to Spike that just as soon as the driver and shotgun rider come into his view he was to show hisself and call a halt. He said he understood all right, and so we all hid our ass and waited. It seemed like a hell of a long wait too, but final I heared the coach a-coming. I heared it come close, and then I could even tell whenever it slowed down to make that curve. Then they was horses a snorting and pounding their hoofs right alongside a me, and then the coach come in view. It was so close that if the driver had spitted off the side a the coach, it coulda went in my eye. Then I heared Spike, right on schedule.

"Hold it up there."

I stepped out with my Colt in my hand and cocked. "You heared him. Stop them horses."

Well, the driver, he stopped them all right, but that there shotgun looked a mite hesitant.

"They's two more behind you," I said. "Sneak a look."

The driver and the shotgun looked back, and I reckon they seed Dick and Haw back there. Both of them seemed like as if they was a mite more convinced a the realness a their predicament.

"Throw them guns down," I said, and they did. "You got passengers?"

"No passengers," the driver said.

I walked over and looked, and he never lied to me. This was just all too easy.

"You're a carrying a payroll," I said. "Toss it down."

"It's inside," said the driver.

I opened the door and seed a saddlebags a-laying on the floor. I reached in and opened a side and pulled out a wad a bills, big ones, too. I checked both flaps and the bags was stuffed full. I had expected a strongbox a some kind, but here it was, all that money in saddlebags. I closed the flaps back and jerked the bags out, tossing them over my left shoulder.

"All right," I said. "Roll on outa here."

The driver whipped up the team and the coach started in to lumbering up the steep road. I stood a-watching it go, and the other three come out and gethered around me. "Go get the horses," I said to Spike, and he run and grabbed onto the back end a the stage to take hisself a ride up to where he had hid our mounts. Haw and Dick was both a-staring at the saddlebags on my shoulder.

"Well, let's see it," Dick said, and his eyes was greedy.

"Just hold on," I said. "We'll see it soon enough."

Spike come back with the horses, and I clumb onto the back a Ole Horse. "Let's get outa here," I said, and the others mounted up and follered me. I figgered they'd be a belly-aching real soon to take a look at all that money, so I rid over to the side of a little crick and stopped and dismounted. I throwed them saddlebags down in the dirt. It was well past noon, and I was some hungry.

"Go on," I said. "Take your look. Then let's have us a little fire and some coffee and grub."

Did they ever have theirselfs a time over all a that money! They held handfuls of it and kissed it and rubbed their cheeks with it and throwed it into the air. Final, they actual set and counted it, and ole Wheeler had been right, by God, about how much money was in that there payroll. It were all there. While they was all a-acting fools like that, I had built a pot a coffee, and when it was all boiled up real good, I made them stuff all that money back and come and set and drink some coffee. We didn't have no real cook amongst us, but we had brung along some hardtack and some jerky, so we et that and washed it down with coffee. Ole Spike, he went over to the edge a the crick and got down to wash his face in it. He was still there whenever Haw went down to join him. I didn't think nothing of it at first, but whenever they had been there together like that for a few minutes, I come suspicious.

"Dick," I said, and I jerked my head towards them brothers, "I don't like that."

"What?" he said.

"Them brothers hoovering together like that. They just might be scheming up some way a knocking us off and getting off with all a this money."

"You want to kill them?"

"Naw. Not just like that. You oughta know me better'n that. I'm just suspicious is all. I think we best keep our eyes on them two."

"Better yet," Dick said, "why don't I wander down there and see if I can tell what they're up to?"

I thunk on that for a minute. I didn't rightly think they'd let ole Dick in on anything, seeing as he was my partner and all that, but then on the other hand, it was me what they was a-hating, 'special that Haw. They might let ole Dick in on something. It was worth a try, and it couldn't hurt nothing. If nothing else, if they was a-scheming on us, why, when Dick got hisself in amongst them, they'd have to stop their scheming.

"Give it a try," I said.

Dick stood up kindly casual-like and tuck his canteen over to the crick. Whenever he kneeled down to refill it, he were right close to the Dutton boys. They clammed up and stared at him. Haw looked over at me. I reached for the coffee pot like as if I didn't have no idee that nothing was a-going on. By and by I could hear them a-talking again in hushed tones. Dick were a-talking with them. I sipped coffee and waited. They talked on and on. Final I decided they'd had enough time. If they had talked up something, well, let them try it. If they hadn't had enough time that was okay, too.

"Let's pack it up and hit the trail," I said. "We hustle our ass on along we might make it back to the Devil's Shit place before dark."

We put out the fire and straightened up that little camp site pretty quick on accounta we hadn't did much there, and then them Duttons was the first ones over to the horses, but only they never mounted up. Instead, they turned back to face me, a-standing side by side. I give them a curious look.

"Dick?" I said.

"I'm right behind you, Kid."

"What do you reckon them two's got on their furry brains?"

"They don't want to take the money back to Wheeler," Dick said. "And they don't want to split it four ways, either."

"They actual think they can take us?"

"I guess they mean to try."

"Haw," I said, "you know what happened last time you tried to go against me. You want your ears to be a-matching? Is that what you want?"

He never said nothing. "Spike," I said, "you seed me nick your brother's ear. You think you can take me? You think even the two a you together can stand up to me?"

"You never know, Kid," said Spike. "One of us might get lucky."

"I reckon it'd have to be luck," I said. "Now unbuckle your gunbelts and let them drop before I decide to get mad and start in to shooting. Go on, now. Do what I say."

"We might get lucky," Haw said, and he was damn near drooling at the thought a killing me. It was beginning to look like I was a-going to have to kill them two boys. I decided to try once more to talk them out of it.

"Drop your gunbelts, like I said, and this'll stay just with the four of us here. I won't say nothing to Wheeler. Your only other choice is, I'll just kill the both of you. I won't take no time to go shooting ears nor nothing like that. I'll just kill you with one shot each. What do you say?"

"Kid?" ole Dick said from behind me.

"What?"

I didn't bother turning to look at him. I was too busy keeping both eyes on them Duttons what seemed like as if they had lost alla their brains, what wasn't none too many in the first place.

"Like they said, they might get lucky."

Then I felt a sudden blow to the top a my head, and I seed red stars a-bursting and a-popping in front a me, and then I seed black all around with different colors a things a-hopping and a-dancing around, and I sudden lost my balance and fell over on my face. I felt like as if my head had been splitted wide open, and I couldn't see nothing but that black with them dancing things in it, and the world seemed to be a-spinning around and a-tilting from one side to t'other, back and forth. I heared voices, though. They was real vague like they was far off, but I heared them.

"Let me kill the son of a bitch."

"No. I told you. And you agreed. Just take his Colt. We'll take his horse, too. He won't get far like that. I think I busted his skull anyway. He'll likely die right here."

"It'll be slower and more painfuller like that, too, Haw."

"Oh, hell, all right."

I could feel it whenever someone jerked the Colt outa my holster, and then I could for sure feel it whenever someone give me a swift kick in the ribs.

"Cut it out. Let's go."

"All right. All right. Son of a bitch."

"Which way?"

"South. To Mexico."

I laid there and I listened to them horses' hoofs a-pounding as them three assholes runned off a-leaving me there to die a slow and painful death. I can tell you one thing for sure. I weren't dead, but I was sure a-feeling that painful part. My head hurt like hell, and after that kick to the side, so did my ribs. I reckon I rolled around some then and done some out-loud moaning and groaning. I figgered that I might for sure die a horrible and agonizing death right there in the dirt just a few feet away from that there crick water. Well, thinking along them lines reminded me a that crick, and I decided that I would crawl on over to it and at least dunk my hurting head in them soothing waters, but only whenever I went and tried to crawl, I just couldn't hardly make no progress, it hurt so bad. I don't know if it really did or not, but it sure as hell seemed like as if it tuck me a hour at least to get over there and drop my head down in the crick. And it was some soothing, but only I had to come up for air now and then, and the coming up hurted me all over again.

Final I drunk me some a that water, and then a little while later I managed to roll over so that I could lay there almost on my back with the back a my head laying in the edge a the crick, so that I could take advantage a the soothinness a the waters and still breathe. I got me enough relief thataway that I was able to start to think a little, and I was a-thinking that I was plumb helpless. Even if I coulda got up onto my feet, which I couldn't, it was a hell of a long walk to the Devil's Den. Them bastards had tuck Ole Horse with them. I was kindly sad thinking that likely I had seed the last of Ole Horse. Then I got to thinking about who all else I had seed the last of: ole Zeb, and Red, and even Jim Chastain. Hell, even my ole paw and maw come to mind then.

I wished for a time there that I had been a praying kind, 'cause I figgered that I was a-fixing to meet my Maker, and I was pretty damn sure that he'd be a-sending me straight down to hell if what them preachers said was true. Then my head was clear enough, in spite of how much it was paining me, to ask itself a question, what was, what the hell happened? The answer come real easy. Ole Dick, whenever he went down to the crick to try to find out what them Duttons was up to, he had conspired with them. Then, whenever I was a-facing them two and him behind me, he had whopped me on the head with his shooter. He had double-crossed me. I had knowed that he was greedy for that money. He hadn't made no secret a that fact. But he was my pardner. I never figgered him to do me like he done. Whop me on top a the head from behind for the sake a money. And him my pardner. I made up my mind right then that I weren't gonna lay there and die after all. No sir. I meant to live long enough to kill ole Dick Cherry.

Chapter 11

Well, sir, I laid there like that for most a the rest a that day before I tried to move atall, and whenever I did final try to move, why, I can tell you, it hurt me like blue-blazing hell. I rolled my head over somewhat, and I kindly rolled over onto my belly so that I could get me up onto my hands and knees, but only my head throbbed and sharp pains went a-shooting through my ribcage. I ain't never hurted like that there, not even whenever I got myself shot through.

Now the reason I was a-putting myself through so damn much agony is that I had to get myself up to go and answer the call a nature if you get my meaning plain enough. I sure didn't want to just lay there and do it in my britches. If I was a-going to die right there, why, I didn't want no one coming along later and finding my body in that embarrassing state, and if by some miracle a the Lord I was to live, why, there was even more reason to keep my pants clean. So that's how come me to be a-suffering all that misery and wretchedness in order to get my ass up from there.

Well, I done it all right, and then I went right back to where I had come from, and I set my ass back down there beside a the crick. I knowed for sure that I never had the strength to start in walking back to the Devil's Town. It hurt too damn bad to walk for one thing. And then too, I didn't have no idee how long I had been a-laying there in misery 'cept only the sun were getting low in the western sky, so I reckon it had done been most a the whole rest a the day.

My head weren't yet quite clear, but I started in trying to think anyhow. I wanted to figger out what the hell I had oughta be a-doing about my miserable predicament. There I was all alone miles and miles from any kinda civilization on foot without no food nor no gun, and on top a all a that I was hurt some. My head was splitted and my ribs was caved in. I started into feeling hungry, too. All I could do was to just drink water outa that there crick, and I was thankful for that one blessing that I was there at a crick. I figgered I could live on water for a while, but sooner or later I was a going to have to have some vittles.

Trouble was I didn't have no idee on how I might could take keer a my problems. I didn't have no way a looking at my own head to see how bad it was splitted, and it was a-hurting me too much to reach up and touch it and feel around, and not only that, but if I was to a tried to reach up to it, why my ribs hurt real bad whenever I raised up my arm. And it was my right arm, too. 'Course, I didn't have no gun nohow. And about them ribs, all I knowed that anyone, even a doctor, could do about busted-in ribs was to just wrap something real tight around them, and I didn't have nothing to wrap them with, nor I couldn't a did the job myself if I had a had something. The more I thunk the more I figgered I was just going to lay there and die.

Well, the lastest and furtherest kinda thought I had ever had was that I would die like that. It had come to me that I might could get my ass blowed away one a these days. You know, someone might slip up behind me and shoot me in the back, or I might get my ass involved again in one a them big general shootouts where it didn't make no difference how good a man was, they was so many bullets a-flying you could ketch one total by accident. Or I might be off in them mountains with ole Zeb and fall offa the side and wind up down in China. Or maybe a whore might get mad at me and slice me up with a hide-out knife or bang me hard over the head with a whiskey bottle. Or some lawman like ole Chastain might cut me in half with a shotgun blast. All a them kinda things had crossed my mind before at one time or another, but never just a-laying hurt beside a crick without no food nor horse nor gun.

Well, with the sun a-going down, I figgered I might just as well get me some sleep, and I was a-hoping that I might wake up the next morning feeling a whole lot better. It tuck some doing, but I found me a spot on the ground what weren't too damned uncomfortable where I could lay myself out with the least amount a pain, and I settled in there for the night. I couldn't sleep, though, on accounta all a them thoughts kept a-swirling around in my head. Them thoughts and others, like I was a thinking on ole Zeb and ole Red and ole Chastain. All a my friends. I even thunk on ole Churkee and wondered how he found the Churkee Nation and did he like it as good as Californy.

I thunk a lot about ole Dick Cherry too and how I had thunk that he was my pardner and then him to do me what he done. I thunk about finding him and killing him. I wanted to do it a-facing him. I wanted him to know it was me and to know how come he was a-fixing to die. I wanted to see the desperation in his eyeballs whenever he final reached for his shooter a-hoping for a miracle just before I blasted his ass away.

I was a-thinking all a them thoughts, but mostly of all my belly was complaining to me something awful. There wasn't nothing nowhere around to eat, and I was powerful hungry. You ever try to get some sleep whenever your belly's a-growling at you? I tell you what, it's damn near a impossible thing to do. If I'd a been somewhere in a town and a-feeling that hungry and not be able to sleep thataway, why, I'd a got my ass up and gone to find some food and maybe some company. But that there was a big if and it didn't make no matter nohow.

Somehow, some time in the middle a the night by some mercy I drifted off. And I musta slept a good many hours too. I might not a ever waked up again but only I felt a sharp pain in my side, and then I felt something like as if they was something stepping on me, and I opened up my eyes, and the sun was already up a ways. It were daylight, and I squinted my eyeballs in that bright sunlight, and then I seed that damn buzzard a-walking on my belly. Well, I couldn't help myself none. I screamed. And I slapped at him with both a my arms, and it hurt my ribs like hell, but I kept on a-slapping anyhow, and he hopped on me and spread out his wings and moved over a few feet away to look at me.

He figgered I was near dead, and he meant to be the first one there whenever I give up the ghost. Well, I tell you, his attitude pissed me off. "You nasty son of a bitch," I yelled at him. "You ain't eating my ass." I picked up a fist sized rock and heaved it at him, but I missed, the pain in my side was a-messing with my aim. It didn't hardly even skeer him none. He just only kindly side-stepped. I hunted up another rock, and this time I meant to get him no matter how bad it hurt.

I planned my throw real good, and I figgered on the pain and swore that I would endure it. Then I heaved, and damned if I didn't splat that rock right into that nasty bird's head. Buzzard blood flew, and he fell over and flapped around for a bit, and then he croaked right there with me a-watching. Well, I looked at him. He was kinda fat. But then I told myself that I didn't really want to eat no buzzard. I weren't yet that desperate. I told myself that over and over, but still I kept a-staring at him. I knowed I could pluck him. I had my penknife in my pocket, and it weren't the best for the job, but I could gut him and cut him up.

Only the mainest thing was, I didn't know if there was any way in hell I could get a fire started. I felt in my pocket for my makings and my matches, and I did have some. They hadn't got wet neither whenever I dunked my head in that crick. That give some hope, and I started in to looking around for something to build a fire with. Well, it tuck me some time and a lot a pain, but I final had gethered up a small pile a sticks and brush and dried weeds and such, and I did manage to get a small fire a going.

It skeered me though that it would all burn up real fast before I was ready to put any a that nasty bird on to cook, so I went around some more a-gethering more fuel. When I final felt safe, I went over to that dead buzzard, and I went to plucking. I tell you what, if I'd a had anything in me to puke up, I'd a did it. It like to made me sick to death. It were a stinking, nasty thing. I damn near give it up a time or two, but I never. I kept on a-going, and when I final had it all plucked, it kindly looked like a turkey to me or a fat chicken, and I tried to make me believe that it really was one a them things and not what it actual were.

Well, I busted off its wings and legs and I broke its carcass in half, and I throwed them pieces a meat onto my little fire, and while it was a-starting to sizzle, I made my way back over to the edge a the crick and washed off some a the blood and black feathers from my hands. I had buzzard blood all over the front a my shirt, too, but there weren't nothing I could do about that.

By and by, I et that bird's leg. And you know what? It weren't too bad. I et the other'n. Then I et the two wings, and then I weren't suffering so much no more. I pulled the rest a the carcass outa the fire figgering that I'd likely get hungry again before the day was did, and I'd best save me something. Well, that damn bird what had frighted me so on accounta it thunk that I was a meal had turned out to be a life-saving meal for me. I set there feeling some triumphant.

My head weren't hurting as bad as it had did before. My ribs was still paining me a-plenty, though.

I wondered what ole Red woulda said if I was to ever told her I'd kept me alive by eating a buzzard, and I decided that she didn't never need to know. Maybe no one would ever know. Eating buzzard might be one a them things a feller had ought to keep secret, like shitting in his pants or something. Well, anyhow, my belly being full, I got to thinking some clearer, and it come to me that there just might be something to eat in that there crick. I went back over and went to studying on it.

First off, I tuck myself another drink to help to wash down that buzzard meat, and then I set back and stared at that crick water a-flowing by. I didn't see no fishes right off, but I figgered they was in there all right. Only thing was I didn't have no way a-ketching me no fish. I wondered then about crawdads. They was fit to eat, better'n buzzard, but it'd take a pile a the critters to make a meal, and they can move pretty fast. First thing I had to figger was they even any of them in there.

I looked up and down, and I seed some big flat rocks off to my right, so I moved on down there. I got down on my hands and knees, groaning some all the time, and then I reached out to get a holt on one a them flat rocks, and it did hurt some in the reaching. Then I went and flipped it over, and I damn near yelled whenever I done that, but I did see some crawdads a-scurrying off. I went to craving them.

Well, I had to figger me a way to ketch me some a them. I knowed I couldn't never just reach out and grab me some. Even if I could glom onto one or two thataway, I couldn't never ketch enough to make a meal. Now, I knowed that them little backwards-walking devils was meat eaters, and I got to thinking about that there buzzard meat what I had left over. But only what if I was to use the buzzard meat as bait and then not ketch me enough crawdads to be of any real use? I'd a wasted the meat too. Then what? Well, I had to think on that for a spell.

I went back over close to my little fire and studied on what was left a my earlier meal, and I hated the thought a tossing any of it out into the crick for crawdad bait. Then it come to me that crawdads might crave guts as much as meat. I could use the guts what I had cleaned outa that buzzard for bait. But I didn't have no string nor no net nor nothing. I knowed, or at least I was pretty sure, that if I was to toss in some a them buzzard guts them crawdads would crawl all over it. But then I would have to have some way a pulling it back outa the water, crawdads and all, and I couldn't think what that could be. I knowed my buzzard meat weren't gonna last me too much longer. One or two more meals was all.

It wouldn't do me no good atall to throw away a meal a buzzard for a maybe meal a crawdads. But I did want them crawdads since I had actual saw them in there in that crick water. Then my brain went and spinned a dirty trick on me. I thunk about them slimy little critters a-crawling around in that there water, and it come to me that they done ever'thing in there. They et and they shat and they pissed. They went and made more crawdads on each other. Then there was the fishes. They done it all in there, too. And I was a-drinking that water. It come to me that if I didn't die from some other thing, I might die a fish and crawdad shit poisoning. I went to craving a drink a water too.

Well, the craving got the best a them other thoughts, and I went and had me another drink a water, but I done it up-stream a where I had saw them crawdads. One thing them ugly thoughts done for me was they made me more deter-mined than ever to get them little bastards. Then it come to me. I knowed I couldn't hurt my ole shirt no more than what it was already ruint what with buzzard blood and all splat-tered all over it. I tuck it off, and the taking off of it sure did hurt, 'special the pulling a my arms outa the sleeves. I got it off though, and I went and kindly spreaded it out in the water close to the edge a the crick right close to them flat rocks. Then I went and tuck up some a them buzzard guts, and I went back to the crick and throwed them right in the middle a my shirt. Then I set and waited.

By God, I was right. I sure felt clever. It weren't long atall and them crawdads was a-crawling all over them buzzard guts. Then they was so many a the little devils, they was a-crawling all over theirselfs, and I couldn't even see the bait no more. I left them alone for a spell like that, letting them get real good and involved in what they was a doing, and then I slipped out into the water a ways real easy-like, and I bent over, gritting teeth, and I tuck my shirt up by two different sides, and then I hauled it outa the water all at once a-bringing crawdads and all with it. I hurried on over to my fire, and I laid that shirt down there.

Then I went to popping heads offa crawdads as fast as ever I could. They was a-trying like hell to scurry back towards the crick, so I had to grab them up, stop them, and then pop off their heads. You know, if you do it just right, whenever you pop the head off a crawdad, you pulls out his gut at the same time, all in one stroke, and he's cleaned and ready to cook. Well, by God, I got them all. Ever' one. I had me a good pile a crawdads there. A meal's worth. By then I was hungry again, too, so I just tossed them in the fire. I tell you what. They wasn't bad eating.

I et up all a them crawdads, and later on in the day, I et the rest a that there buzzard, and then I knowed that I was in trouble again. I didn't figger that no buzzard was going to come and perch on my belly again, and I was all outa crawdad bait. But at least I wouldn't go to sleep hungry again. I rolled me a smoke and smoked it, and that were kindly relaxing under the troubling circumstances. It come to me that there I was without the barest necessaries but I had me a luxury. I had me the makings. Long about when the sun started in getting low, I decided to sleep again. My nasty shirt had might near dried out again, and I spread it out so I wouldn't be a-laying my nekkid skin on the pebbly ground. I went to sleep without near so much trouble as what I'd had the night before.

Come morning, I were well rested, but I was terrible hungry. I was thinking on ham and eggs and biscuit and gravy. And coffee. I sure was a-craving some hot coffee. I tuck keer a nature's calls, and then I drunk me some crick water, and I thunk about them crawdads and fishes a-doing all that there nasty stuff in that water, but I drunk it anyhow. My head were feeling some more better, only throbbing now and then, and my sides was still a-aching pretty bad, but only I had done figgered out how to move around with the pain. I picked up my ole shirt and flipped it around trying to dust it off some, and nasty as it was, I put it back on. I didn't want to get my back blistered in the sun on top a all my other ailments.

Well, I went to walking around and a-looking off towards Devil's Place even though I knowed I could never walk that distance, but I was a-wondering what the hell I might could do about the situation I was in. I was a-asking myself questions, but I wasn't coming up with no answers. I was all outa buzzard and crawdad and crawdad bait. I was back where all I had was water what fishes and crawdads had been nastying up on a regular basis, and I didn't have no way a killing or ketching me any food. I even went to looking around to see if there might maybe be some kinda plant I could pull up and chaw on, but I never seed nothing a the kind. 'Course, I weren't too smart about that kinda stuff. Zeb had showed me a few things, but I never seed none a them things there around that crick.

I thunk hard about starting out to walk toward Devil's Ass. Just setting there at the crick seemed like as if I was

a-giving up, and that didn't seem right. On the other hand,
if I was to start in walking, I would get my ass out there
somewhere without even water to drink. So it seemed to me
like as if I was better off there at the crick. At least I had
water. Maybe someone would come along before I was to
die a starvation.

Then it come to me. What if Cherry and them Duttons
was to come back? I would be total helpless. I didn't have
no gun. Even if I hadn't a been hurt, I wouldn't a been no
use without a gun. I was skinny and scrawny, and I couldn't
a-fit nothing with just only my bare hands and my feet to
kick with. Why, if they was to come back, they could kill
me dead with their fists or with a rock or they could just
shoot me dead. I wouldn't be able to do nothing but just only
stand there and wait for it.

But then, why would they come back? They had all that
there payroll money, and they would have Wheeler and all
the outlaws a Devil's House after their ass. I figgered that
had been a stupid thought I'd had and all because I was there
in such a vulnerable state a being. I went to studying up on
the pros and cons a staying or going again, but I weren't
getting nowhere with them thoughts. Then I heared a horse
a-coming. It was off a ways yet, and at first I weren't total
sure. I thunk that I might just be a-hearing what I wanted to
hear, but I stood still and listened real keerful. It were a horse
a-coming all right.

At first I thunk that I had been saved. Then it come to
me that I didn't have no idee who it might be on that horse,
and they was a-plenty out there what would just love to find
me in that there helpless state what I was in. I looked around
for someplace to hide my ass, but I couldn't find nothing.
Whoever it was that was a-coming was a-going to find me
for sure. I didn't know what the hell to do. And the horse
was a-getting closer. I could tell. I looked around, and real
desperate-like, I picked me up a rock. I had kilt me a buzzard

with a rock. Maybe I could hit a man before he drawed on me. It was better'n nothing.

Then I seed the horse in the distance. Not clear, though. It was kindly shimmering-like as it moved on towards me. I stood a-waiting for whatever it was that was a-coming at me. And it come closer. Then I got a real surprise. I seed that the horse didn't have no rider. A wild mustang? A runaway? I got to wondering what it would do when it seed me. I hoped that I would be able to talk it into coming to me, but that weren't none too easy with a strange horse. I tossed aside the rock I had picked up and stared at that horse, still coming right at me.

"Come on," I said. "Come on." And he kept a-coming. Then I seed that it was for real and actual Ole Horse. My Ole Horse. Somehow he had broke loose from Cherry and them and come a-running back to me. I swear to God, I hadn't had nothing in my whole entire life that loyal to me since my poor ole dog Farty had been kilt by that damned Joe Pigg what I had then kilt and run off, and that had started me on this whole life a gunfighting and such.

I hadn't never been so happy to see no one in my whole life as what I was to see Ole Horse a-coming at me. I let him get some closer, and then I yelled out, "Come on, Ole Horse. Come on." He come a-running up to me and then he stopped, and I hugged him and kissed him and talked to him, and then I led him over to the crick to get him a drink. Oh, my, but I was happy.

When I got over my initial excitedness, I looked Ole Horse over. He were still saddled, and my saddlebags was still a-hanging on behind. I opened up the flaps and checked inside. They wasn't nothing there. My first inclination was to jump on Ole Horse's back and ride on out, but then I told myself that I didn't rightly know how long he had been a-running. I decided to let him rest up some, so I pulled the saddle offa his back and throwed it on the ground. It hurt me some in the doing. Then I rolled me a smoke and lit it and laid back and just enjoyed the sight a Ole Horse a-grazing and a-drinking nasty crick water. I figgered in just a bit I'd saddle him back up, and we'd head out.

Chapter 12

Well, I thunk that I'd had some pain from my bashed-in head and them caved-in ribs and all, but I hadn't felt the half of it, I can tell you. Whenever I felt like Ole Horse had rested up and grazed and drunk nasty crick water for long enough, I decided it was time to head on back towards the Devil's Den, and whenever I went and swung that there saddle back up onto his back it damn near kilt me, the pain was so terrible. I like to a blacked out from it. I come dizzy, and I had to set on the ground for a spell. Ole Horse musta wondered what the hell was wrong with me. Anyhow, in a bit I was up to standing up and moving on ahead, and so I got myself to my feet and I cinched up the saddle right smart. That hurt some, too, the pulling and all, but nothing like what it had did whenever I throwed that saddle up on his back.

I made sure my little bitty fire was all out real good, and I couldn't see that I had no other cleaning up to do, so I figgered it was time. I walked over to Old Horse's side, and I reached up with both a my hands to get a holt a the saddle horn. That even hurt some, just the reaching up like that. I knowed the next step weren't going to be no pleasant task neither. I lifted up my left leg and put my foot in the stirrup. Then I just stood there like that for a few seconds, and I tuck me a few deep breaths a-getting myself ready for the next real big move. Final I figgered I had done put it off long enough, and I give a hellacious hard shove with my right leg, and I pulled as hard as I could with my two hands, and I swung my ass right up into the saddle. Oh God, it hurt. It hurt a-going up, and it hurt again whenever I set down.

I set still there a-trying to recover from the pain and the effort and waiting for the stars to cut out their dancing in front a my eyeballs. Final I said, "Let's go, Ole Horse," and I give him a little nudge, and he started off, but I held him to a slow walk. I figgered that was all I could stand a the jarring and jouncing what comes with riding a horse. Again, I thunk that Ole Horse was prob'ly a-wondering what the hell was wrong with me, a-riding him so slow like that. Not that I ordinary tuck off with him like a bat outa hell, 'cause I never, only 'cept in dire emergencies, but ordinary I would likely a trotted him along a bit more livelier than what I was doing just then.

Well, it were a slow ride back to that Wheeler's Devil Town. I stopped along the way a time or two whenever I seed some good grass and water for Ole Horse, but since I didn't have no food nor no way a-ketching me any, I sure didn't have no need a stopping for my own meals. I just kept a-plugging away, and even whenever I stopped for Ole Horse, I never got down outa the saddle. The reason being was that I didn't want to go through that painful ordeal a getting back up there again.

It were nightfall whenever I final rid on into hell. I hadn't met up with no one along the trail, but there in town, they was outlaws all over the place. I put Ole Horse in the stable and went a-hobbling on over to ole Wheeler's office. Ever'one in the saloon give me stares as I walked through, I was so beat up and dirty looking. 'Course, I was also the only son of a bitch in the place without a six-gun strapped on me. Just as I come to the door to Wheeler's office room, I wondered if he would believe my story or would he just kill me dead on accounta me losing all that payroll money from him. I tuck me a breath and rapped on the door.

"Come on in."

I opened the door up and stepped on inside, and ole Wheeler, he looked up at me from behind his big, slick desk, and when he got hisself a good look, his eyeballs popped wide open. "What the hell happened to you, Kid?" he said.

"It's a kind of a long story," I said.

"Well, sit down." He got up and went over to a cabinet what stood against one wall and got a bottle and a glass and poured me a glass a whiskey. I set in a chair there by his desk, and he brung me the drink. I tuck it with thanks and tuck me a sip. Oh my, but it was good after what all I had been through.

"You was right about that there payroll," I said. "And we tuck it too without no trouble atall." I tuck me another sip.

"Well?"

"Well, we was on our way here with the payroll, and them two owlhoots what you stuck me with decided that they didn't need to bring that money back here and share none of it with you. They stood ready to face me down, and I was ready to take them both on and kill the both of them, too. I've tuck more than two before, and I knowed I could do it. Then damned if my own pard, ole Dick Cherry, didn't crack open my skull from behind me. He double-crossed me and tuck up with them Duttons. They tuck the money, all the food, my horse, and my gun, and they left me a-laying there to die slow and miserable. Lucky for me, Ole Horse, he musta got away from them somehow, on accounta he come back to me. That's the only reason I'm here to tell it."

"So the Duttons and Dick Cherry turned on you and me both."

"They damn sure did."

"I can't let them get away with this."

"Hell, me neither. I mean to kill them all, 'special ole Dick for turning on me, and him my pardner. Only thing is,

Mr. Wheeler, here I am not just only busted up, but busted. I ain't got no way to pay you for a room nor nothing."

"You're on my payroll," he said, "starting right now. There's no charge for your room, your meals, your drinks, the stable—nothing. Here."

He hauled some bills outa his pocket and shoved them at me. I tuck them and shoved them down into my own pocket. I stood up then with a groan.

"I'll get on their trail just as soon as I can heal up some," I said.

"How bad is it?"

"My cracked head ain't too bad," I said. "It don't hurt too much by now. Not 'lessen I touch it. What's bad is they kicked in my ribs, and I can't hardly do nothing without it hurts like blazes."

"Go on up to your room and take it easy," Wheeler said. "I'll have a hot bath brought up to you, and I'll send Doc to see you. Take that bottle and glass along with you, too. You might need them."

I thanked him and left his office. Then I clumb the stairs up to the room what had been mine and Cherry's and before that had been the Dawson boys's room. I tuck off my hat and boots and that there nasty shirt I had been a-wearing, and then I had me another drink before I fell back onto the bed. The falling back hurted my rib cage. I was about drifted off to sleep whenever I heared a knock at my door.

"Who is it?" I said.

"Your bath."

"Oh. Well, come on in."

Well, a whole damn crew come in. Two of them lugged a tub in, and the rest of them was toting buckets a hot water what they poured into the tub. They come back several more times before they had that tub all filled up, and then one of them dumped some kinda soap powders in there and sudsied it all up. Ever'one left the room but just only one last man, and he pulled a table over to the side a the tub, and laid out a big towel and a rag and a brush on the table. Then he put a ashtray on it with a ceegar beside of it and some matches. He set my bottle on it, too.

"Anything else?" he asked me.

"I reckon not," I said, and he left. Well, I stood up and studied that there hot and sudsy water, and I finished my drink and stripped my ass the rest a the way off nekkid and stepped into that hot water. It tuck a bit for me to ease my whole self on down in there, but once I was in it up to my chin, it sure did feel good. I got to thinking just how dirty I for real was, what with dirt and sweat, my own blood, and buzzard blood and guts, and nasty crick water. A good cleaning had oughta do me a world a good, I thunk. Then I heared another knock.

"Who's there?"

"It's Doc."

Well, that plumb puzzled me on accounta, I knowed that ole Wheeler had said he was a going to send a doc up to see me, leastways someone he called Doc and I had figgered must be a real doc, but that there voice what I had just then heared was a little sweet voice like a woman's voice.

"Doc?" I said.

"That's right. Mr. Wheeler sent me up."

"Well, come on in."

The door opened up and one a the most beautifullest ladies what I had ever saw come a-sweeping into the room. She had kinda auburn hair, I think they calls it, and it was all put up on top a her head, and she was a wearing a white blouse with lacy stuff around her wrists and her neck, and she had on a long black skirt. She was a-carrying a black bag what looked like a doctoring bag all right. My face went plumb red, leastways I think it did 'cause it sure het up some. I could feel it.

"They call you Kid?" she asked me.

"Yes'm," I said. I hadn't been expecting no lady to come in on my bath like that, and I were some embarrassed.

"Mr. Wheeler said you might have some broken ribs. I thought you might need some help scrubbing."

"Uh, yes'm."

She put aside her doctoring bag and got down on her knees beside the tub and tuck up the brush and went after me. It was real nice, I can tell you. Then she went to washing my head, and whenever she seed all that scabby blood messed up in my hair and all, she went to feeling around in there and a-looking and studying on it. It was some tender to even her touch, but I didn't mind none.

"Mmm," she said. "That's bad. I'll just clean it up first."

She washed my whole head and cleaned up that there wound, and then she went and got some kinda salve outa her bag and daubed some on it, and it felt cool and nice. Once she had tuck keer a that, she went back to washing up the rest a me, and I do mean the whole, entire rest a me. She washed me all over real thorough-like, and I got to feeling like I wanted something more outa her, and the evidence a my wanting was right down there underneath that sudsy water. She knowed it, too. She had run into it with her scrubbing hand. She never said nothing, though, and neither did I. Whenever she had final finished up with all a her washing, she stood up, picked up the towel and held it up, and said, "All right. You can get out now."

I didn't want to on accounta several things, but then the way she was a-holding that towel up, I figgered she wouldn't be a-looking at me you know where, so I stood on up, and she wrapped that towel around me and went to giving me a real brisk rub-down and drying off. Whenever she dried on my ribs I winced some to let her know they was a-hurting me. All did, she wrapped that towel around my waist and tucked it in so it would stay there, so my embarrassment was mostly hid.

She had me go over to the bed and set down on the edge of it, and then she got some long bandages outa her black bag, and she went to wrapping me all around real tight. "That's about all we can do for broken ribs," she said. "It'll just take some time for them to mend. You'll be just fine."

"Say," I said, "are you for real a real doc?"

"Yes," she said. "I am."

"Well, how—"

"Not many places were willing to let a woman doctor set up practice in their town," she said. "Mr. Wheeler wasn't so particular."

"But you're here in a whole town full a just only outlaws," I said. "Don't that skeer you none? You being a lady and all?"

"Mr. Wheeler assured me that I would be safe here," she said. "Once a rowdy did try to attack me, but Mr. Wheeler had him quickly subdued and thrown out of town. I've had no more problems."

"Well, are you and ole Wheeler, uh—"

"Ours is strictly a business relationship, I assure you."

"Oh."

"Now what about you? You're awfully young to be an outlaw, aren't you?"

Well, I come wide open. I went and told her the whole tale a that Joe Pigg a-killing my poor ole dog Farty, and then me a-killing Joe Pigg, and me only thirteen year old. I told her my whole sad story, about how Paw give me ten dollars and a sway-backed horse and told me to get outa Texas, and then how I went to cowboying and gunfighting. I might near told her that I weren't really no outlaw but was just only pretending to be one so I could get back some stole money and return it to the bank, but I stopped myself just in time. Hell. For all I knowed, sweet as she looked, she mighta blabbed the whole thing on to ole Wheeler, and I sure couldn't have none a that. No, sir.

She set down beside a me then and put a arm around me and give me a hug, and it sure did give me a thrill. I reckon my sad story kindly brung out the mothering instinct in her, and it didn't hurt none that I was skinny and scrawny and young and even some beat up. Whenever she done that, why, I just kindly laid my head over on her shoulder, and I were a-looking down at the pretty shape a her tits under that there white lacy blouse. It was all I could do to keep my hands down. I was a-wanting her something fierce.

"You don't belong here with these men," she said. "There has to be a better life for you than this."

"Well, what about you?" I said. "I don't rightly believe that you belong here neither. Why, you're a real lady."

And I meant that, too. She was just about the only woman I had ever knowed besides my own ole maw who weren't a whore. Well, I had sorta knowed Mrs. O back at the first cowboying job I had ever had, but then she was older than my maw or at least just as old.

"I told you why I'm here," she said.

"Well then, I reckon I done the same for you. Say, what do I call you? Doc?"

"Everyone here does. Doc will do just fine."

I lifted up my head, and I had on my most pitifullest lost-kid look I could muster up, and I looked her right in her big, lovely brown eyes, and her face was just right there close to mine, and I got bold as hell and just went and give her a kiss right on her lips. I was afraid she might jump away or maybe even slap my face or something, but she never. She just kissed me back, long and luscious. I'd a thunk I was in heaven but only my rib cage was a-hurting, and I figgered folks in heaven didn't never hurt no more.

Well, damned if she didn't lay me back on that bed and take that towel off from around me, and then she straightened herself up and stripped right off. She clumb into bed with me then, and I ain't gonna talk about no more details a that wonderful time what we had then, but it was most lovely, I'll tell you that much. She weren't no whore, but she was as good as any I ever had. No. Hell. She was better.

The next few days, Doc come around to see me right regular, and she checked my head, and she checked my ribs and rewrapped them, and then we'd have us a right nice romp together. I come to look real forward to her visits. Slowly, my ribs got better, like she said they would, and pretty soon I could lift my arms up. I decided it was time to find out could I still draw and shoot, and so I made my way down and out and over to the hardware store, where I bought myself a new Colt and gunbelt. I tuck Doc with me with a picnic basket, and we went a ways outa town.

We had us a good time together, and I tried out my shooting arm, and I was damn near as good as ever. I knowed I'd be back in prime shape in just another few days. Whenever we went back into town, Doc went on to her office, and I went to see ole Wheeler.

"How are you feeling?" he asked me.

"I'm a feeling like a free loader," I said. "I think it's nigh onto time for me to get after ole Cherry and them Duttons."

"I can get a couple of boys to ride with you."

"I'd ruther not if you don't mind."

"You're thinking of the Duttons."

"And Cherry. I can trust my own self. I don't know about no one else."

"There's three of them."

"And I can take them. The mostest trouble will be in the finding a the bastards."

"How will you go about it?"

"I'll head south. I got good reason to believe they was headed for Mexico."

"That's a long ways."

"They won't be that far, yet. Leastways, I don't think they will. But however far they've got, I'll find them, and I'll kill them."

Wheeler poured me a drink and handed me a ceegar and a match. Then he leaned back in his big soft chair and give me a look.

"And me?" he said. "Will I ever see you again?"

"You're a-thinking on that big payroll."

"You're right."

"I'll be back. I don't want that payroll for myself."

I didn't lie to him, neither. I wanted to return the payroll, and what's more I meant to get back the Fosterville bank money and return it as well. So I never lied. I just failed to tell ole Wheeler the whole and total truth a the matter was all. I was also a-thinking on ole Doc, and I sure didn't want to ride away from that Devil's Hole and not never see her no more. What I did want was I wanted to get her to ride outa there with me and see if I couldn't maybe get her set up in a better life somewheres. Me having friends in Fosterville, maybe they'd listen to me and let a lady doc set up there and even go to see her with their ailments and hurts and woes and stuff. The only thing about that was that I was having me a good ole time with the doc, and ole Red was back there in Fosterville, and that there might bring on some complications what I didn't feel like as if I needed in my young life. I knowed I'd have to think on it some more.

"When will you start?" Wheeler said.

"First thing in the morning."

"Get anything you need in the general store," he said. "Write it down on my tab."

Chapter 13

I moved out early the next morning, all right, a-headed southwest. I coulda went right back to where them three bastards had left me laying to die and likely a-picked up their trail from there, but that woulda meant heading west and then turning south. I figgered it'd be quicker to just head kindly southwest and hope to pick up the trail thataway. They had done had a good head start on me, and to tell the whole truth a the matter, they coulda gone anywheres, but I had it in my head that they was aiming for Mexico. They weren't too big a surplus a towns down along that way, so I figgered I had me a pretty good chance a coming acrost them. The other thing was, they wouldn't be a-looking for me. They figgered I was dead, or damn near.

I rid till noon, and then I stopped and had myself a meal and rested Ole Horse. I drunk me a right smart a coffee too, and I rolled a smoke and puffed it all up. Then I put the saddle back on Ole Horse and started in again. But I had me a funny kinda feeling. There weren't no good reason for it. I just had it, that's all. It was one a them kinda feelings what makes a man keep on a-watching over his shoulder and looking around in all directions so he won't be caught by surprise. That's the kinda feeling I was a-having.

"Keep your ears pricked up and your eyeballs peeled, Ole Horse," I said. "I got me a sensation."

Ole Horse, he blowed some air like as if he was a giving me a answer to what it was I had just said to him. Sometimes whenever I was off on a trail like that by my own self, why, I would talk to Ole Horse just only to hear my own self talk. Just sorta to make the time pass, you know. But other times, and this here was one of them, I swear, I thunk that I was really a-talking to him. I mean, I thunk that he could not only hear my voice but that he were a-comprehending the meanings a my words, and just then I tuck that there blow noise a his as a real and actual honest-to-God answer to what I had said. I felt a little better a-knowing that there was now two sets a eyes and two sets a ears at work paying attention to my surroundings.

"Ole Horse," I said, "I reckon you're just about the bestest companion and pard a feller could possible have. Why, hell, you saved my life whenever you got yourself aloose from them outlaws and come back after me. You're ever' bit as good as ole Zeb, or Churkee, and a sight better than Paw. I ain't even a-counting that Goddamned Dick Cherry no more.

"No one hardly comes close to you, and that's the truth. 'Course, ole Farty, he woulda if he'd a still been around. You'd a liked Farty, Ole Horse. The three of us woulda got on great. I sure do wish you coulda knowed him."

Now if anyone had a been around to hear me what I was a-saying and to see how it was I was a-talking to a horse like that, well, I'm sure they'd a believed with all their minds that I was plumb crazy and had ought be put away somewheres where I couldn't hurt myself nor no one else neither. But, hell, when a feller's off by his lonesome like that, why, if he didn't have no horse to talk to, he'd talk to his own self or even to rocks and trees and such. It's just a way a dealing with the lonesomeness a the situation. Just then Ole Horse give out with a little nicker, and then I thunk, now damn it, it's more'n that. Ole Horse is a-talking to me, and I just ain't smart enough to understand his lingo. I reckon he understood mine pretty good, though. You reckon horses is smarter than men? I wonder about them kinda deep thoughts now and then.

Well, I tell you what, that there country was some a the most desolatest land I had ever saw. I rid the rest a that day like that a-talking now and then with Ole Horse, and a-paying keen attention to my surroundings, and I never seed nor heared nothing. Not a damn thing. Whenever the sun got low in the sky, I hunted us up a good camping spot, and I unsaddled Ole Horse.

"Thanks, Ole Horse," I said. "We had us a good day a traveling."

Ole Horse blowed at me, and I be damned for a rooster if I didn't understand him to say, "That's all right, Kid."

Ole Horse went to grazing, and I went to gethering up sticks to build me a fire with, and by and by, we was real well settled in for the night. But I still had that uneasy feeling about me, and I thunk that I could tell that Ole Horse, he did, too. He seemed to me like as if he was extry special alert, you know. I cooked and et and drunk some coffee and smoked, and Ole Horse, he grazed and drunk his fill a water, and final I went on to sleep.

I slept good that night. Too good, I thunk whenever I come awake the next morning. It come into my head that someone coulda walked right up to me a-sleeping like that and cut my throat to wake me up. Then I had one a the most enlightening experiences a my whole entire life. You ain't a going to believe it when I tell you, neither. I ain't never told it before on accounta I didn't want no one a-making fun a me nor making light a the onliest real religious experience a my life. What I discovered was that not only could Ole Horse understand my talking out loud, he could read my thoughts. I know that on accounta I was thinking along them lines what I done told you, that I slept too sound, you know. Then Ole Horse nickered at me, and I understood him.

"It's all right, Kid," he said. "I was watching over you."

Well, tears actual come into my eyes. I walked right over to Ole Horse and I hugged his neck, and I give him a kiss on the end a his nose. "Thanks, Ole Horse," I said. "Thanks, best buddy."

I fixed me up some breakfast and coffee, and in a little while I cleaned up my camp site and saddled Ole Horse. We was off again, and the sun just barely a-peeking out over the eastern horizon. I figgered we'd oughta cut the trail a them three I was a-tracking along about noon, and I asked Ole Horse for his opinion on that matter, and he agreed with me. We rid on for a spell, then, without talking. Then I said, "Ole Horse, am I just being jumpy, or is there for real someone out there somewheres?" He told me that he had the self-same feeling as what I had. We stayed alert. With the sun high overhead, I went to looking for us another camping site.

Whenever I final stopped at a likely place, the sun were almost direct overhead. I done like before. I unsaddled Ole Horse and built up a small fire. Then I went to cooking me up some food. I was busy paying attention to my cooking, on accounta I was some hungry, and Ole Horse give out a loud whinny. I looked up at him right quick.

"What is it?" I asked him. He blowed, and I could see where he was a-looking. I turned my head to look thataway too, and then I seed what it was a-bothering him. It were a fair distance off to our northeast, but it looked to be right smack on our back trail, and it were a thin wisp a smoke a rising up and then fading away in the sky. A camp fire. Like mine, prob'ly, a cooking fire for a noon meal.

"Yeah. I see it now, Ole Horse," I said. "Someone's on our trail, all right. They're far enough back that we ain't got to worry about them none for a little while, but sooner or later we're gonna have to do something about them."

Ole Horse nickered at me.

"Me too," I said. "I wonder just who the bastards might could be. Well, hell, we'll find out. Maybe a little later on this afternoon."

I finished up the cooking a my meal, and then I et it and drunk me some coffee. I asked Ole Horse if he had et and drunk his fill and were well rested, and he said that he was ready to go, all right, so I throwed the saddle back on him and, after cleaning up my mess, clumb up on his back. "Let's go then," I said. I was real happy to notice that my ribs weren't killing me no more whenever I tossed the saddle up onto Ole Horse.

It was just a little ways on whenever we come onto the north and south running road, and they was tracks a-plenty on that son of a bitch. I told Ole Horse, "I reckon they likely tuck this road." He blowed at me, and we turned south. By and by, we come acrost a wagon a-headed north. The wagon driver stopped, and so did I. He was a freighter a-hauling some kinda goods up north to the gold fields. We made a little small talk, and then I said, "Say, I'm a-hunting three friends a mine what tuck this road south ahead a me. You mighta passed them by. Ole Dick Cherry is one. Dick usual dresses up in black and tries to look like a bad gunfighter, but he's just a phony is all. He's really a nice kinda feller. The two he was with, last I knowed, is a coupla brothers name a Dutton. I don't know how come ole Cherry to pardner up with them. They ain't too bright, but anyhow, did you maybe run acrost anyone what looked like them three?"

"Night before last," he said, surprising the hell outa me. "A little town called End of the Line straight south of here. Right on this road. You can't miss it. I overnighted in a hotel there and picked up some more freight the next morning. Saw them at breakfast. Anyhow, I saw three men that looked like what you said."

I thanked that feller right kindly, and we went on our both ways. A few more miles on down the road, I seed where a

outcropping a boulders and such riz up on the right side a
the road. Ole Horse nickered, and I said, "You thinking what
I'm a thinking?" and he damned sure was, too. We rid on
down there, and then we hunted us a way around behind that
outcropping. They was good grass there. I pulled the saddle
offa Ole Horse's back.

"This could take a while," I said. "I'm fixing to lay up in
them rocks and just wait it out. So you just relax down here
and nibble away on this good grass. Don't worry none. When
I'm done up there, I'll be right on back."

He blowed a answer, and I went to crawling up the backside a them boulders like a skinny scorpion. I clumb around
for a while till I found my way might near the top. Then I
kindly worked around to the front side. I checked out two
or three different locations in there till I found me a spot
what was comfortable enough and at the same time give me
a good view a the road down below and a good hiding place.
I settled down to wait. I couldn't yet see no one coming
from up the road, so I rolled me a smoke and lit it. I set
there a-smoking and thinking on the wonderful ways a the
world around me.

I was a thinking how I had sure enough had me a good
many conversations in my time with folks like Rod and Tex
and the other hands at the Boxwood Ranch, and with ole
Zeb, and ole Jim Chastain, and Churkee and ole Red, but
just at that very minute, I couldn't think a no one I'd had
any more profounder discussions with than what I'd had with
Ole Horse. And the thought what come right after that was
that I sure must have a thick skull for it to have tuck me so
long to figger out that I could talk with Ole Horse.

Then I got to thinking about ole Farty again, and I was
a-thinking that if only ole Farty coulda lived to be around,
why, me and him and Ole Horse coulda had some real good
serious talks, the three of us: a man and a dog and a horse.
There weren't no better pards on earth than that. I almost got

me a tear in my left eye recalling ole Farty and a-thinking about that there now impossible scene.

It weren't too long after that I seed three riders a-coming down the road from the north. I slipped out my Colt and cocked her and got ready for action. They could be the ones what me and Ole Horse had detected on our trail. I waited till they was kindly close, and then I called out, "Hold up there."

They stopped all right, and they looked around like as if they was a-trying to figger what was best to do. Two of them had their right hands out like as if they might draw, but they never. They give looks to each other, but they never said nothing, neither. I reckon they all of them decided that the best thing to do was to just set still and wait.

"Take out your shooters with only two fingers and drop them," I said.

They was kindly slow in the doing of it, but they done it.

"Now," I said, "you can tell me how come you to be on my trail."

The two on the outside looked in at the one in the middle like as if they had chose him to do the talking, so he went on ahead and spoke up.

"What makes you think we're on your trail?" he said. "We're just riding south on this road is all. Headed for the little town of End of the Line."

"You got business there?" I asked him. "What kind a business you in?"

"Why, no. That is, we're what you might call between jobs. We got a little cash among us. Heard that End of the Line's a nice little town. We just thought to hang out there for a while. That's all."

I stood up to show myself.

"Do you know me?"

"Why, no. How could I? We?"

"You're a lying son of a bitch," I said. "I'm Kid Parmlee, and you three been a dogging my trail ever since I left outa Devil's Knob or whatever the hell's the name a that town. I wanta know how come."

"We don't know what you're talking about."

"Listen here," I said. "I've kilt me some men, and I've shot off some ears just for fun. I'm a-fixing to do one or t'other to you if you don't start in to giving out with some straight answers. I ain't decided yet which I'll do."

"Look, mister, we just come down from straight north of here. We're looking to have us some fun down in End of the Line. That's all. You've got us mistaken for someone else."

"I'm fixing to start shooting," I said, "and I ain't going to give no warning neither. What I'm a-fixing to do is this. I'm a-fixing to kill one of you, and I'm gonna shoot the ears offa the other two. I ain't saying which one is gonna get kilt."

"Ace," said the feller on the right, the one clostest to me, "we better tell him."

"Shut up," said that there Ace.

"Get yourself killed if you want," the man said, "but I ain't getting killed or shot up for Wheeler."

"I knowed you come outa Devil's Hole after me," I said. "Tell me the rest. How come you to be follering me?"

"Wheeler sent us," Ace said. "He thought you might need some help when you catch up with those other three."

"What three?" I said.

"You know."

"You tell me."

"All right. Dick Cherry and the Dutton boys. You and them stole a payroll, and then they took off with it. You're on their trail. Wheeler didn't like the odds, so he sent us to keep an eye on things and help out if need be."

"Truth a the matter is," I said, "Wheeler don't trust me. He sent you three along in case I was to get that there payroll back and then hightail it. Ain't that right?"

"He did mention that as a thing to watch out for."

"Now listen good to me," I said. "You're a-going straight back to Wheeler. You tell him that I don't need no help, and I don't need no watching. I mean to get them three bastards, and when I do, I mean to take that there payroll back to Devil's Ass. Tell him I said that, and tell him I said to not send no one else after me. Anyone else comes after me, I'll kill them without asking no questions. You got all that?"

"I got it," Ace said, "but we ain't turning back. We got our orders from Wheeler. Now that you know who we are, why don't we all just ride along together?"

"Two reasons," I said. "Number one, I don't need no help, and you'd just get in my way. And the other'n is that I don't like you. Now turn around and head back."

"I told you we can't do that."

I fired a quick shot without no warning, and my hot lead tore a hole through ole Ace's left ear. He yelled out something awful and slapped a hand to the side a his head. The other two stuck their hands up in the air right fast. Blood run thick betwixt Ace's fingers. He moaned.

"You son of a bitch," he said.

"I see you met up with my ole maw," I said. "Now, you two get down and pick up your-all shooters and holster them." I waited while they done that, and they done it real keerful too, so as to make sure that I knowed they wasn't fixing to try to shoot me. When they had did it, I said, "Now mount back up," and they did. "Turn around and ride."

I didn't get no more argument outa Ace. Them three Wheeler pups rid back towards the Devil's House at a right smart clip. I watched till they was near outa sight. Then I put my shooter away and worked my way back acrost that outcropping and down the backside to where I had left Ole

Horse. When I come in sight, he looked up and give me a
knowing look and a whinny.

"Yeah, pard," I said. "We was right about them bastards,
but it's okay now. They're a-hightailing it back home to their
boss. One of them's got a clipped ear."

Ole Horse give a nicker then that I could tell was really
a horse laugh. Someone else might not a been able to tell,
but I could. He was a-laughing about that Ace's ear. Well, I
laughed with him, and then I went and saddled him back up
and mounted, and we went back on around to the road and
turned south.

"We're a headed for a place called End a the Line," I
said, "and you know what I bet? I bet it's just like any other
town out here in these parts. It's got a hotel. I know that on
accounta that freighter back yonder said so. It's got a saloon
and a eating place and likely a stable. I bet there's whores
there. It might have a doc for patching up bullet holes, but
I bet you it ain't got a doc to match what ole Wheeler's got
back there in the Devil's Pit. No sir. There ain't a doc like
Doc nowhere else in the whole world. Not clean down to
China there ain't."

I got to thinking then about ole Doc again, and how she
was the only woman what weren't no whore what I had, you
know, got close to. I went to wondering again just what I
was going to do about her whenever I had tuck keer a all
this business I was involved in. That made me think again
about what all it was I did have to take keer of. I had tuck
out original to get the Dawsons and take back the Fosterville
bank money. Well, I had got the Dawsons all right, but I
weren't even close to getting the money back.

Then, in trying to get closer to the bank money, I had
agreed to help rob that payroll offa the stage. I had thunk,
maybe foolishly, that if I was to take stole money to Wheeler,
he might just slip up and show me where he kept such truck.
Well, the payroll had been stole from me before I could get

it back to him. So now I had me three more men to kill and more money to get back.

Now, I thunk, whenever I ketch up to Cherry and them Duttons and kill their ass and get that payroll back, I got to take it back to Wheeler at Devil's Toenail, and just right then is when I'm a-gonna come up to the toughest part a the whole deal. Right smack in the middle of a whole den a outlaws without no law and all by my lonesome, I'm gonna have to steal all that stole money and get the hell outa there alive in order to return all the money to where it belongs. And in the doing of it, I gotta get ole Doc outa there, too, so I can get her someplace to a decent town where she can do her doctoring work.

I tell you what, I had got myself into a right smart pickle. I sure had. Ole Horse, he musta been reading my mind again, on accounta just then he blowed, and what it said was, "You sure have, ole pard. You sure have."

Chapter 14

We was riding on along towards End a the Line when Ole Horse, he give a kind of a snort, and the meaning a that there rude sound he made was clear to me.

"Damn it, Ole Horse," I said, "you're right about that."

And he was, too. You see, my problem was that I weren't thinking far enough ahead. What I shoulda did was I shoulda kilt them three back there in the road. I shoulda kilt them even though they chickened out and didn't want to fight with me. I shoulda kilt them on accounta before this mess was all over and did with, I was a-gonna have to deal with Wheeler and his whole damn town full a outlaws, and if I hada gone on ahead and kilt them three, why, there'd a been three less to worry over whenever that time come around. Well, there weren't no use in worrying about it. I had done let the chance pass me by. But Ole Horse, he knowed. I can tell you, I was some embarrassed about that, and I was glad that I was a-setting on his back so that I didn't have to look him in the face.

Well now, I rid that road for two full days, camping along the way at nights, and I did see some travelers along the way. The ones I jawed with, like that there freighter, some a them thunk that they had seed the men I described to them, and others said they never, but other than that there really ain't nothing much to talk about. It were near the end a my second day a riding, and from what folks had told me on the road I figgered I was might near to End a the Line. Being as how I was in a country what was all new to me, though, I didn't rightly want to keep riding at night, so I stopped again beside a the road, and I unsaddled Ole Horse and built me a little fire. I hadn't talked too much with Ole Horse for a spell, and I decided that had to come to a end.

"Ole Horse," I said, "we got to stop acting like this."

He blowed at me.

"I made a little mistake back yonder, and we both knows it. Hell, ever'one makes one now and then. Ain't you never made a mistake?"

He nickered as how he couldn't recall one just then.

"Well, all right. If you ain't you ain't, and so I did, but you got to put that there thought outa your mind and not go on a-dwelling on it like you been. I'll try my damnedest not to make no more. All right?"

He allowed as how he'd go along with that, and I said, "I reckon I sure am a lucky feller all right to be partnered up with someone like you what ain't never made no mistakes." And he agreed with me on that one for sure.

We settled in for the night and was up early and ready to go. I didn't bother making myself no breakfast and coffee on accounta I thunk I was that close to End a the Line, and I'd just wait. Some farther down the road, I got to wishing that I hadn't decided to wait for End a the Line. I was craving some food and coffee. I was a-thinking that I had already made me another mistake, and I wondered if Ole Horse was a-reading my mind again. If he was to ketch me in too many mistakes like that, he might get to where he was ashamed a being rid by me. Just about then, though, I seed a town up ahead, and that sure did set my mind to ease.

The first thing I done was I found the stable, and I tuck Ole Horse in there. I told the man to take real good keer a him and feed him real good on oats, and Ole Horse, he nickered me a thanks for that. I walked on out and found a eating place where I really put on the feedbag. I was a-keeping my eyes peeled for any sight a my former pardner and them Duttons. After I et and paid for my food, I went to asking around had anyone seed them three. The man in the place said that he had saw them all right, but they hadn't come in that morning.

I went outside and walked the street a looking in places and asking more folks. Some knowed who I was a-talking about and others didn't have no idee. I figgered that I was a-fixing to spend the whole day in that town and so I might as well have me a room, so I went into the hotel, and I got me a room for that coming night, and I asked again about Cherry and the Duttons.

"That sounds like three who're staying here," the clerk said, "only that ain't the names they're using. They call themselves John and Joe and Jim Carter."

"Has they gone out yet this morning?"

"I don't think so. I ain't seen them."

He give me a key and room number, and he even told me the number a the room them "Carters" was staying in. I went upstairs and checked the two room numbers. Them "Carters" was just down the hall from me. I unlocked my room and went inside. I left the door open just a crack, and I put a chair where I could set and look out that crack, and I would see whenever them three left outa their room. I knowed it could be a pretty good long wait depending on how late they had stayed up the night before and how much they had drunk and whored, so I rolled myself a cigareet and lit it. I set there a-smoking and a-watching and a-waiting.

I was just damn near ready to give it up from being bored to death, and I was even thinking about yelling out "fire" to skeer them outa the room, whenever their door come open and they walked out. My heart kindly thrilled in my chest and I went for my Colt, but then I stopped myself. That there weren't the right place for me to go killing. I sure did want to, though. Instead I just set and watched while they filed outa the room and headed for the stairs. I let them go, and then I had me a thought.

When they was all well down the stairs, I went out in the hall and over to their door, and I tried my room key in it. It was just only a skeleton key, and likely all the keys was the same. I was right. It unlocked the door. I looked up and down the hallway to make sure no one was a-watching me, and then I opened up the door and went inside. It didn't take too much looking around before I seed that there saddlebags what we had stoled from offa the stagecoach. I jerked them up and throwed them on the bed and opened the flaps, and sure enough, they was still stuffed full with money. I didn't bother to go counting it. I didn't want to stay in their room long enough for that, and besides I likely couldn't a counted that high nohow. I figgered they was at least some pocket money pulled outa there for each one a them three, though.

I tuck the saddlebags down the hall to my own room, and I locked the door and set there a-staring at them. I weren't thinking about running off with all that money, if that's what you're a-thinking. I was trying to figger out just what the hell to do now that I had got my hands on it again. I surely did want to kill them three for what they had did to me. I 'special wanted to kill ole Cherry for double-crossing a pardner. But it come to me that the money was more important just then than the killing, and if I was to take time for the killing, why, it might just interfere with the getting a the money back where it belonged to be.

I made me a quick decision. I tuck that there payroll and headed back for the stable. I got Ole Horse saddled up, and I throwed that extry saddlebag on him, and I headed outa town going back the way I had come in. I never seed them three on the way out. Well, I moved along lickety-split for a ways a-wanting to get some space betwixt me and them others. I told Ole Horse how come me to be a-running him like that, and he understood all right. He didn't mind. In a while I slowed him down.

"Well, Ole Horse," I said, "did I make another mistake here, or did I do the right and smart thing for a change? I tuck the money, and I didn't even face them three. I didn't want to take no chance on not getting outa there with all that money."

He said I done all right. He weren't about to heap no praises on me, though. We rid on till noon, and I kept a-looking back behind me to see were I follered, but I never seed no one a-coming. I stopped to rest Ole Horse with that sun direct over my head. I had me a smoke, but I never built no fire. I et a cold, hard biscuit and washed it down with water outa my canteen. Pretty quick I mounted up again and we rid on.

Now the trip back was just about like the trip down. I seed some travelers along the way, but I never seed no pursuit after me, although I was constant nervous a bit and always on guard, you know. I come on back to the Devil's Place about how I had come on End a the Line. It was late and dark night, and I still had me a little ways to go. I decided to go on and make me a camp for the night, and I built me a fire and cooked me a meal. It weren't much. Some bacon and beans what I et with a cold biscuit, but I did brew me some coffee and drunk me a few cups. Then I slept, but I was still some nervous. I told Ole Horse, and he promised me that he would stay alert to anyone a-trying to slip up on me.

You see, he had let hisself get caught and tuck away by them three that time, but I hadn't never said nothing to him about that. Anyhow, I figgered that he weren't about to let that happen again, 'special since he had bragged about not never having made no mistakes. I slept all right, considering the circumstances what I was in, and I was up early the next morning. I told Ole Horse we'd just go on in and get us some proper food for the morning. He agreed to that.

Whenever we rid into Devil Shit, and I was a-headed for the stable, the first feller I seed was that there Ace what I had shot his ear, and his ear was a-looking a mess, I can tell you. He give me a ugly look and headed for the saloon. I figgered he was a-going straight to ole Wheeler to tell him I was back. I tuck keer a Ole Horse, and then I walked on over to the eating place a-toting them saddlebag. I set down and ordered me up a big breakfast and lots a coffee. My plate had just only been laid there in front a me whenever ole Wheeler come in with Ace walking along behind him. Ace stared at me real sullen-like. Wheeler come and set down.

"Good morning, Kid," he said.

" 'Morning, Mr. Wheeler."

"You got something for me?"

"Right now I got me a breakfast to eat," I said. "It's been a long, wearisome trail."

He eyeballed them saddlebag, but he didn't say nothing. Instead he waved at the waiter feller and got hisself some coffee. Ace was still a-standing by the door and staring at me. I got myself busy eating and acted like I wasn't paying neither one a them no attention. I got to say, Wheeler showed me that he had a-plenty a patience. He waited till I was done with my food and set back to sip on one last cup a coffee.

"You ready to talk now, Kid?"

"Soon as I finish this here cup," I said, "let's go on over to your office."

"All right."

We finished up and I grabbed up them saddlebag, and we headed for the saloon, but I stopped. I looked back at Ace where he was a-follering along.

"I don't need ole Notch-ear a-walking along behind my back," I said.

Wheeler turned towards Ace. "It's all right, Ace," he said. "Run along. I don't need you."

We made our way on into the office. Wheeler went on around behind his desk, and then I tossed the saddlebag on top of it right there under his nose. He opened it up, and his eyeballs got big and round.

"Good," he said. "You did real good, Kid. I'll count this and take out my percentage and give the rest to you."

"If you don't mind to do it for me, Mr. Wheeler," I said, "I'd just as soon you put it all in a safe place for me. I'll ask you for it whenever I need it."

"Your money's safe in Devil's Roost," he said. "No one staying here would dare steal anything in this town."

"Men sometimes does funny things," I said. " 'Special for money. I'd feel better about it if you was to hold on to it for me."

He give a shrug. "All right," he said. Then he done just what I was a-hoping he would do. He got up and tuck the saddlebags over to his big safe, and he squatted down there in front a the thing, and he didn't even seem to notice or to keer that I was a-standing there a-watching over his shoulder while he dialed that there wheel on the front. I watched real keerful, and I was able to ketch the numbers he was a-dialing up. I said them over and over in my head. He pulled the door open and tossed that payroll in there. I got myself busy a-rolling a cigareet just as he turned back around.

"What about Cherry and the Duttons?" he asked me.

"They're still alive," I said, and I told him how I come by the money and how come me to not go on and kill them bastards. "What I'd like to do now is I'd like to go back just after them."

"Likely you won't have to go all the way back," Wheeler said. "I'd bet they're on your trail by now. Of course, they won't dare come back into Devil's Roost."

"I reckon you're right on both counts," I said. "If I was to turn around and head right back where I just come from, likely I'd run smack into them."

"You want any help?"

"No sir. I'd ruther not."

He grinned. "Especially not Ace."

"No. He wants to kill me worse than them other three."

"He's a bad *hombre*," Wheeler said. "And he's dangerous. He won't try anything here in town, though. He knows better than that. But when you ride out of here, if I was you, I'd watch my back trail."

"I always do, Mr. Wheeler," I said. "That's how come me to still be here."

That there was a kinda lie what I told. My ole paw and ole Zeb had both saved me from getting back-shot a time or two, and Ole Horse, he had kept watch over me, too. But I figgered it was best to let on to Wheeler, and anyone else for that matter, that I were a rangy lone wolf what tuck keer a my own self just fine.

"Well," Wheeler said, "have it your own way. When do you mean to go after them?"

"I figger I'll lay around today and rest up my own self and my Ole Horse," I said, "then get a early start tomorrer."

"All right," he said. "Anything you need, just let me know."

"Thanks," I said. "I will."

I went on out a there and up the stairs to my room, and I throwed myself on the bed. I was tired and sleepy from the trip. I hadn't lied to Wheeler about the resting up part. I was laying there a-thinking that Wheeler seemed to a tuck a liking to me. It come to me that I could stay right there in that town and live a right easy life if I was a mind to. Why, hell, I had all the money in the world, and I'd have the pertection a Wheeler's outlaw town. I had Doc, too. At least, I thunk I did. I considered getting up again and going to see Doc, but I was just too tuckered out. Pretty soon, I was asleep.

I didn't know what time it was whenever I come to, but it was in the middle a the day. I got up and left the room. I went back to that eating place and had me another meal. Then I walked over to Doc's office. She seemed real glad to see me, and I was sure tickled to see her.

"Kid," she said. "Oh, I'm so glad you're back safe. How're your ribs?"

"Oh, they've healed up all right. My head, too. 'Course, it's plenty hard. That's what my ole maw used to always say."

She throwed her arms around me and give me a real nice kiss, and that got me to hankering after more, but only right then in her office and in the middle a the day weren't the right time nor place for it, so we kindly made us a little promise to each other to get back together late in the evening. I made me some lame excuse then and left and walked on over to the saloon. I bellied up to the bar and ordered me a shot a whiskey, and then up in the big mirrer behind the bar, I seed that Ace a-glaring at me from a table way back behind me.

I knowed that ole Wheeler had said that Ace wouldn't try nothing right there in town, but still I didn't like him a-looking at my back like that. I paid for my shot, and then I picked it up in my left hand and turned my back to the bar. Sipping that whiskey, I stared right back at Ace. He didn't look away, neither. Final, I'd had all of it I needed. I sipped the last a my whiskey and put the glass on the bar. I hadn't tuck my eyes offa Ace.

"You wanting to start something, Ace?" I said.

It come real quiet then in the saloon. He didn't answer me right off. Final he said, "Not here in town. It ain't allowed."

"It ain't far outa town," I said. "You want to go out there? I'll go with you. That there ear a yours I nicked, hell, that coulda just been a lucky shot. For all you know, I coulda been aiming right betwixt your eyes."

Well, now I ask you, what was that Ace to do? There we was in the saloon with several men around a-listening to ever'thing we said, and they was all outlaws, hard cases, and I had called Ace right there in front of them. He didn't really have no choice. He stood up.

"Let's go," he said.

We walked out side by side and headed for the edge a town. Wheeler come outa his office and seed us a-leaving. "What's going on?" he said.

"He don't want to put it off no longer, Mr. Wheeler," I said. "We're going out a town."

Wheeler follered along, and then so did several others. We only had to walk past three or four buildings and then off a little farther to get past the sign with the name a the town on it, but it seemed like a longer walk than that, walking alongside that Ace what wanted so bad to kill me. I noticed that he had the advantage on me on accounta he was a-walking to my left. He coulda pulled his shooter and let me have it in the side, but if I was to pull mine, I'd a had to a turned before I could shoot him. As we walked down the street, I begun to moving to my right to put some space betwixt us.

"Whenever we get past that there sign," I said, "it's ever' man for hisself."

He never said nothing, but whenever we tuck a step acrost the line, he made his move. He went for his shooter, and I jumped to my right, and his shot went wild. I slipped my shooter out and shot off his other ear. He screamed out and shot a wild shot at me, and then I dropped him with one right in his heart.

Chapter 15

Well, no one seemed to give much of a damn about the fact that I had kilt ole Ace. I guess he didn't have no real friends in that there outlaw town. Instead folks marveled at how slick I had tuck him down, and on top a all a that, the word had done got around that the reason he was a-wanting to get me so bad was on accounta I had shot his ear deliberate, and that ain't no mean trick, I can tell you. So I got me a good many slaps on the back, and they was several a them outlaws a-wanting to buy me drinks that evening. I let them, too, but only I was keerful.

After all, it were a outlaw town, and no matter what it seemed like to me at the time, ole Ace just mighta had him one friend what had keered enough for him to slip up behind me and shoot me in the back. I weren't really too worried about that, though, on accounta three things. Like I done said, I didn't really think that ole Ace had a friend. Then after what they had done seed and heared about my shooting, I figgered they weren't many a them would wanta try me. Final, there was the rule a ole Wheeler's, that no one start no trouble in his town.

I had me another reason for not letting myself get too drunk though, and that was that I had made plans with Doc for us to get together that evening. Anyhow, there I was a-setting at a table with my back to the wall and all a them boys in the saloon just a-dying to buy me drinks. They was all a-talking about my fight with ole Ace, and how I had just real cool-like let him have the first shot, and then I had shotted his other ear and then kilt him. They was downright amazed.

"Hell, I heard about him before, all right," some feller said. "You know what they say? They say he's a regular Billy the Kid."

"Say," I said, "I'd like for someone to find that there Billy the Kid and bring him in here to see me. We'd find out who's a regular what. I ain't never heared a him shooting off no ears, just only killing folks from the back is all."

At that a feller shoved his way through the crowd and stood just acrost the table from me a-looking down at me.

"I rode with the Kid in New Mexico," he said, "during the Lincoln County War. He's no back-shooter, and he never wasted his time with fancy gun tricks."

"If he's standing behind someone's back," I said, "he wouldn't have no reason for no fancy tricks. The feller wouldn't a seed them no how."

"I wish you'd take that back about Billy."

"Well, I ain't a-gonna do it. For some time now folks has been a-saying that I'm a regular Billy the Kid, and I've got plumb sick a hearing it. Ever' time I hear it, I'm a-gonna say just what it is I think about it, and that's what you heared me say, and I ain't taking nothing back."

"Well, I ain't going to fight you. I ain't that stupid. I just wish you'd take it back, that's all. Hell, it ain't Billy's fault that folks're saying what they're saying. He might not like it, neither."

"Like I said, he can come and see me anytime he's a mind to."

Billy's buddy turned around and walked away, and the crowd got loud again. I watched that feller though. He was a-burning on accounta what I had said about his precious Billy. He said he weren't going to fight me, but I thunk that maybe he just might pull a Billy the Kid trick and try to shoot me in the back one a these fine days. I wished that I had asked him his name, but it was too late. I had done let the chance pass by. Then another feller tuck keer a that oversight for me.

"Kid, don't let what ole Tom said bother you none. He just likes to talk is all. Hell, I ain't for real sure that he ever really rode with the Kid or even fought in the Lincoln County War."

"You say his name is Tom?"

"That's right. Tom Grant."

"Well, as long as he minds his own business, I won't give it no other thought."

I checked the time, and then I had me one more drink. I ordered a bath sent up to my room on accounta I had been on the trail some, and I wanted to smell nice and pretty for Doc. I excused myself and went to the barber shop for a haircut and a shave and some smelly water. By the time I got back to my room, the bath was all ready for me. I was just getting ready to strip myself off nekkid when there come a little knock on my door. I give a cold hard look at the door and said, "Who is it?"

"It's just me," come a sweet little voice, and I went and opened up the door for the doc. She sure was pretty. Even more'n what I remembered.

"Come on in," I said, stepping off to one side to get outa her way. She come in, and I shut the door and bolted it. It did have a inside bolt. "I weren't expecting you so soon. I was just a fixing to have myself a bath."

She smiled and said, "Don't let me stop you."

Well, I stripped off and she did too, and we both of us got down in that there tub, and I tell you what, they weren't much room left in it for nothing else. But we went to scrubbing all over on each other real thorough, and it sure was

fun. By and by, we got out and got dried off and went to
the bed. We had us even more fun there.

After a while, we tuck us a break from all our rambunc-
tuousness, and Doc, she kindly propped herself up on one
elbow and looked down at me a-smiling. She run her free
hand through my hair.

"You're riding out again?" she said.

"Yeah. I got to."

"You will be careful?"

"Yeah. I will."

Laying there a-looking up at her like that, I couldn't hardly believe that she could be anything more than what she
said she was, and I couldn't believe there was no way in the
whole world that she could be anything special to Wheeler
or him to her. All she was was just a doc in that town. That
was all.

"Would you get outa this here outlaw town if you could?"
I asked her.

"I'm doing all right," she said, looking down at the sheet
past my eyeballs.

"I reckon you are at that," I said, "but just for the sake a
talking, if there was a way a getting you outa here and into
a regular town where they was women and kids and such
and they would let you set up your doctoring business, would
you want to do it?"

"It would be nice to see children. And to see other women
besides the—saloon girls. Why are you asking me this?"

"Oh, nothing," I said. "I just might know someplace you
could go, and I ain't a-going to be settling in this damn town
my own self. I'll be a-getting out a here one a these days. I
guess I been a-wondering if you want to go with me when
the time comes."

She didn't say nothing right off. She just stared like as if
she was in real deep thought, and then she said, "When the
time comes, I'll let you know."

* * *

Whenever I waked up the next morning and kindly rolled my head over, the first thing I seed was ole Doc. She was done up and about half dressed, and she seed me stir on the bed, and she looked down on me real sweet-like and smiled. Then she come to the bedside and leaned over and give me a good-morning kiss. Straightening herself up again, she said, "Kid, you be real careful. I don't want anything to happen to you."

"I'll be just fine," I said. "Don't worry none about me. But only, while I'm gone, will you think on what I asked you last night?"

I was a-referencing what I had said about her a-getting out a the Devil's Pot, and she knowed all right just what it was I meant.

"I'll think about it," she said.

Well, pretty soon she was gone outa the room, and it sure did seem empty in there where she had been just a little bit ago. That there was one a them things about life what made me ponder now and then. You know, how things what happens, once they've done happened they don't seem like they was really real atall. The only thing what seems real is just what's a going on right now this minute. A course, you remember what happened before, but when you're a-setting in a empty room with just only your own self, what happened before don't seem real no more.

Even whenever I had been all stove up out there on the prairie and left alone to die, as miserable as I was then, setting in that there hotel room, that there experience didn't hardly seem real no more. I had me a little bit a pain left from it was all. I s'pose that whatever happens whether it's good or bad, it's always gone soon enough.

Well, I'd had enough a that deep thinking, and I had me some things to do, so I got on up and got myself dressed and headed out. I had me a breakfast at the eating place and then went on down to the stable to saddle up Ole Horse. Right soon we was a-headed outa town. I had me a place in mind on that trail, and I was a-hoping that I wouldn't meet up with Cherry and them before I come to it. It was a place with a high hill on the side a the road where a man could set and watch over what was a-coming or going down below. And a horse could be hid back behind it without no trouble. I wanted to ketch them three by surprise.

It were a fair ride out to that place, but I come to it all right, and I hadn't seed no sign a them bastards. I put Ole Horse back out a sight, and I clumb up to the top. I snuggled my ass down in a kinda hole where I could see both ways on the road down there, and I rolled me a cigareet and lit it. Then I made up my mind that I was in for a long wait.

It come to me that I might could wait forever. I didn't really have no way a knowing that they would be a-trailing me. They might believe that I was done dead. The way they had left me, I shoulda been, that's for sure. But then, on the other hand, whenever they found out that they had been robbed a that stole money, they'd just about have to think that it was me what done it. Unless they had been a-blabbing like three fools, there weren't no one else who knowed they had it.

So if they figgered it was me, the next thing they'd figger is that I was a-headed back to Hell Hole with it to turn over a share to ole Wheeler like we had promised to do in the first place. They had tried to get me to take it with them, and I had turned them down, so they knowed what my mind was on that subject. Having mulled all a that over, I figgered they was after me all right.

Well, I smoked that cigareet, and I dozed off a bit, and then I come awake, and I rolled and smoked another cigareet. It sure was boring just a-setting there like that. I got all ex-cited whenever I seed some riders a-coming, but then they come closter, and it weren't the ones I was a-waiting for. I tell you what, I be damned if I didn't set there the whole rest a that day and they never come along. Well, I was hungry, and I was a-going to have to spend the night out there and watch some more the next day. Come near dark, I went back down the back side to Ole Horse, and I fixed me up a little camp and cooked up some beans and coffee. I explained things to Ole Horse, put out the fire and went back up to my perch for the night. I tuck me a blanket along.

I was snugging down for the night when I heared the horses a-coming. I waited kindly tense-like. They was three of them. Damned if they didn't stop right down below me. That weren't really no good camping spot, but then, them three weren't the smartest I had ever knowed. They went and set up their camp. They built up a fire, bigger than what they needed. It was ole Zeb what learned me that you don't need no big fire at a camp site, and ever since then I didn't think too much a someone what built one up too big like that. But only I was kinda glad they did, on accounta whenever they had it all built up, why, I could see them plain. It was them all right. Dick Cherry and them two dumb Duttons.

I had them right where I wanted them. Sort of. If I was to go scooting down the side a that hill, they'd hear me sure. I had to get over to their little camp quiet-like. In case you might be a-wondering how come me not to just shoot them from where I was at, they's two reasons for that. First off, it was too far for a revolver shot, even for someone as good as me. And then I didn't want to kill them without they was a-knowing who it was a-doing the killing. I wanted to face them so they'd see me.

So I was a-thinking that I'd best go down the back way and then walk the long way around, but while I was a thinking on that, another thought come intruding into my head. What was I a-going to do after I had kilt them, I asked myself, and my answer was that I was going back into town and tell ole Wheeler what it was I had did. And then what?

Why, hell, I'd be right back where I was at before, just only me against a whole town a outlaws. I had to get all that money outa ole Wheeler's safe, you know.

I done a powerful lot a thinking on my way down the backside a that there hill, and then I went over to Ole Horse, and I tuck his reins. "Ole Horse," I said in a nearly whisper, "them three what I want is over on the other side a the hill and the other side a the road. We got to walk around there, and we got to be real quiet in the doing of it. I need to sneak up close on them. You understand me?"

Well, he blowed kindly soft a-telling me that he did, so I started walking and a-leading Ole Horse along. We walked on around the westernest end a that hill, and then I told Ole Horse to wait for me there. I went on alone. I got up kindly close to the camp before anyone in there heared a thing. Then I reckon ole Dick musta heared me step on something, on accounta he stiffened up and pulled out his shooter, and he said, "What was that?"

"I didn't hear nothing," said Haw.

Spike jumped up and said, "What? What you hear?"

"Shut up," said Dick. "Listen."

Well, I figgered I was close enough then. "You all a-looking for me?" I said out loud.

Both Duttons pulled their shooters out, and all three a them owlhoots was a-looking this way and that in the dark a-trying to spot me.

"Kid?" said Dick. "Is that you?"

"It ain't Billy the Kid," I said.

"Damn," said Spike.

"I told you we shoulda finished him off," Haw said.

"Shut up," Dick said. "Kid? What do you want? You mean to kill us?"

"Ain't that how come you to be here?" I said. "To kill me?"

"Now, wait, Kid—"

"Ain't nothing else woulda brung you back thisaway. Not after what you done."

"Kid, let's talk about it. Can we talk?"

"Funny thing," I said. "That there's just what I want to do. Talk. If you'll put away them shooters, I'll come on in to the light a your fire, and we'll set and talk. You got coffee on?"

"All right, Kid," said Dick. "Come on in."

He put away his shooter. "It's a trick," said Haw. "I don't trust him."

"Put it away, Haw," Dick said. "It's no trick. He could drop us all three from out there in the dark if that's what he meant to do. Put it away."

Both Duttons holstered their guns, and I walked on in. I tell you what, I ain't never seed three nervouser sons a bitches than what them three was. They all knowed that if we was to have a stand-up gunfight, I could likely drop all three. Even if I couldn't, I could drop two before the third one could get a shot into me. They was just a-standing there a-looking at me come in.

"What about that coffee?" I said.

"Get it going," Dick said to Haw, and Haw went to fixing it. "Shall we sit?" said Dick.

Dick and Spike set down on the ground side by side, and I set direct acrost the fire from them. We didn't say nothing, yet. We waited for Haw to get the pot on the fire to boil. Then he set beside a his brother.

"I reckon you know I'm a-wanting to kill you real bad for what you done to me," I said, "and I know damn well you come back thisaway to kill me for a-taking that there payroll away from you."

"I'd say that's clear enough on both sides," said Dick. "So why the talk?"

"It won't do you no good to kill me, on accounta I done tuck that payroll to ole Wheeler, and he's got it all locked up tight. I know where it is, though, and I know how to get it. I let him have it 'cause I wanted to know for sure where he put all his loot. I want that Fosterville bank money."

"You got a one track mind, Kid," Cherry said.

"Once I gets on a trail, I keeps on it," I said, "if that's what you mean."

"Yeah."

"Anyhow, I need you three alive to help me get all that money back from ole Wheeler. Four of us against that whole town, that's bad enough odds, but me all by my lonesome, well, I wouldn't have no chance atall. So what do you say? Do we set aside our grudges long enough to get all that money away from Wheeler?"

"If we get the money and come out alive," Dick said, "what then?"

"I know what you want, and you know what I want. We'll deal with that whenever the time comes. Right now, we ain't even got nothing to fight over."

Dick Cherry looked acrost the fire at me for a bit, and then he looked at them Duttons.

"What do you say, boys?" he said. "It'll be four of us against all of Devil's Roost, and then three of us against Kid Parmlee."

"I don't like the odds," Spike said, "either way."

"The stakes are high," Cherry said.

"That's for sure," said Haw. He looked at his brother eager-like.

"Hell," said Spike, "let's do her."

"All right," I said. "Now listen here. Ever' gang has got to have a leader, and I name my own self leader a this here gang. Anyone object to that?" I waited a bit and didn't hear no objections, so I went on. "We got to make us a plan if we want to come outa this alive and with the money. We can't just go charging in there."

"Where's the money, Kid?" Cherry asked.

"In Wheeler's office safe," I said. "I can open it."

"How?"

"Never mind. I just can."

"Then why can't you just sneak in there and get it and sneak out again?"

"You see a winder in that back room?" I asked.

"Well, no, I guess not, come to think of it."

"The only way in there is right smack through the big main room a the saloon, and it's the only way out again. We're going to have to come up with something besides just only sneaking."

Chapter 16

Well, we went to talking then about how in the world could the three of us take on that whole town and get the job did and get out a there alive.

"It seems to me," Cherry said, "the whole trick is going to be to find a way to get the Kid here into Wheeler's office so he can get the money out of the safe."

"And then get me out again," I added.

"There's damn near always someone in that saloon," Spike said. "What if we was to start some kind of commotion across the street or something like that?"

"That there's the idee, all right," I said, "but what we got to figger is just what kinda commotion and when's the best time to do it. You three can't just ride into town. You'd be shot on sight. If I go back in, Wheeler's going to want to know did I get you."

"We'd ought to go in after dark," Haw said.

"That saloon's jumping till the wee hours," his brother said.

"The bestest time might be just before sunup," I said. "Might near the whole town's asleep long about then."

"I think you're right," Cherry said. "We'd have a better chance of getting in and out without being seen."

"Yeah."

We all come quiet at once then. Didn't no one seem to have nothing more to say. I tuck out my makings and rolled me a cigareet. I didn't offer them over to no one else. They wasn't no friends a mine. We was a-working together out a necessity. That's all.

"So when do we go?" asked ole Dick.

"Daybreak," I said.

"Tomorrow?"

"Why put it off?"

"I guess you're right," Dick said. "We might as well get in there and get it done."

"Well, but just what is it we're gonna do?" Haw asked.

"How about this here?" I said. "I'll just go riding straight into town like there ain't nothing wrong. I'll stop in front a the saloon and go in. Likely there won't be no one around, and I'll get into ole Wheeler's office somehow. Then I'll open that safe, get the money, and get on out."

"That sounds too easy," said Spike. "What the hell you want us in on this for?"

"It is too easy," I said. "There might easy could be someone in that saloon. Ole Wheeler might even be in his office. I might have to go shooting someone, and if I was to have to do that, why, hell, it could bring ever' outlaw in town down on me. So just in case a the worstest, here's what I want from you all. When I ride in on the main street, I want the three a you to ride in on the backside a the buildings on t'other side. 'Bout the time I tie up Ole Horse at the rail out front a the saloon, I want you to start a fire on the back wall a the eating place. By the time I get that there money, the whole town had ought to be busy with the fire."

"Why don't we set two or three buildings while we're at it?" said Haw.

"Sure," I said. "The more the better. Soon as you get them blazes a-going, work your ways around some building or other to where you can see me when I come out to mount up on Ole Horse. That's just in case our diversion don't work and someone gets to shooting at me. You see me get up on

Ole Horse and take lickety-split outa town, you mount up and get out, too. We'll meet up right there where me and Dick made a camp whenever we first come here. You show them where that's at, Dick."

"Yeah."

"Well," I said, "how's it sound?"

"Sounds good to me," Cherry said. "You're the one in trouble if anything goes wrong. You'll be a target right out there on the main street. No one's likely to see us three out behind the burning buildings."

"They's one other thing," I said. "It just could be that someone'll ketch on, and they might could be some pursuit and some fighting. We got to agree to agree till we ain't got no more worries 'bout Devil's Tooth. Then we can agree to start in disagreeing. But no back-shooting nor sneaking off nor nothing till then. Till then, we're a-working together. What do you say?"

"I agree," Cherry said.

Them two dumb Duttons looked at each other and nodded.

"We agree," said Spike.

"All right, then. Let's check our weapons, and you all figger out how you're a going to start them fires, and then let's get our ass all ready for daylight."

We had us a little bit of a ride before we would get on over to Devil's Den, but we had time to make it there before daybreak in the morning. When I went back down the road to get Ole Horse, I was away from them three for a space. I come up to Ole Horse. "Well," I said, "I made me some plans, and it means trusting them three again, but just for a short time." I told him the plans, and he kindly shuck his head like as if to say something like I wouldn't never learn. I explained to him how they was a-going to have to trust me too if they wanted to get their hands on that money, and how we was all going to be too busy with that whole town a outlaws to be fighting each other, at least for a while. He give me a kinda grudging okay on that.

Well now at the same time as I was a-talking to Ole Horse, them three was able to talk amongst theirselfs with me outa the way, and I wondered if they was already scheming against me again. I figgered though that they'd have to play along with me till we had either got plumb away from Wheeler and his town or else put the whole son of a bitch outa commission. When that time come, I didn't really think for a minute that them boys would wait till we'd had our discussion that we had agreed to have. No sir. Soon as they seed they didn't have no more need for me, why, they'd try to plug me. 'Special if they was behind me.

I made up my mind that I would not let any one a them three get behind me no matter what the hell was a-going on. And just as soon as the time come when we had bested Wheeler and his bunch, I would be a-watching them bastards like a hawk watches a mouse in the field. It was going to come to a killing—or three. I meant to see that it was them three and not me what done the dying.

We come onto Devil Snot just before daybreak. My guess on the timing had been real close, and I was glad, too. I didn't want no time for just setting around and thinking. I wanted to get right at it. Me and Dick showed them Duttons our meeting place, that there spot where I had camped and waited for Dick the first night we come on Devil Shit, and we reminded them that would be where we would all come a-running to if things was to get hot or whenever we got did with the job. Either way.

"I'm a going in," I said, and I headed Ole Horse for the main street.

"Let's go, boys," Dick said. Them three headed in their own right direction.

I was some nervous riding right down the middle a the street like that, knowing what it was I was a-fixing to pull and knowing what the hell would happen to me if I was to get ketched. I was a-hoping mainly that I wouldn't run onto ole Wheeler hisself. If I was to, why, he would ask me had I kilt them three and if not what the hell was I a-doing back in town. I weren't right sure just what I would tell him if it should come to that.

The town was pretty well asleep, all right. I seed one drunk bastard a-staggering along the sidewalk and one ole mangy dog went to barking at Ole Horse. There weren't no other horses out on the street atall. I pulled up in front a the saloon just like I had planned, and I got offa Ole Horse and lapped his reins real loose around the hitch rail.

"I shouldn't be in there too awful long, Ole Horse," I said. "Whenever you see me a-coming out, be ready to move outa here fast."

He give me a understanding snort, and I walked on into the saloon. The ole boy what they called Nick was behind the bar a-mopping things up, and they was two drunken out-laws a-setting at a table with a bottle half full a whiskey a-setting right betwixt them. Their heads was a-wobbling loose on their shoulders, and I don't think they even noticed me a-coming in. I made a quick study and walked over to the bar.

"What can I do for you, Kid?" Nick said.

"Is Mr. Wheeler in there?" I asked, nodding towards his office room.

"He went home to bed hours ago."

"In that case," I said, slipping out my Colt, "you can walk back there to that office with me and unlock the door."

"I don't have a key to that room."

"You'd best shit one," I said, "or else we'll just have to break it down with your head. Go on."

Nick headed for the office door, walking along behind the bar. I watched him real close to make sure he didn't come up with no scattergun or nothing. When he come out from the other end a the bar and headed for the office door, and I seed that he didn't have no gun, I walked over to them two outlaws. They still didn't hardly notice me. I put my Colt away and then I put a hand on each a their heads and shoved their heads real hard down onto the table. I knocked them both out cold. Then I tuck out my Colt again and joined up with Nick there by the office door.

"Open it up," I said.

"You won't get out of this town alive, Kid."

"Open the door."

He tuck a key outa his pocket and unlocked it. Then he opened it and swung the door wide.

"After you," I said, and he walked on in. I looked at that safe, and then I looked at Nick. "Do you know how to open that thing?" I asked him.

"No one knows the combination but Mr. Wheeler," he said.

"That's too bad," I said, "on accounta I know it, but only if I gets busy a-opening that safe, I won't be able to keep a eye on you. I'll have to knock you in the head or kill you or something. If you was able to open it up, why, I wouldn't have to do that to you. Oh well."

I went like I was a-fixing to shoot him dead, and he said, "Wait a minute." Then he hurried over to that safe and dropped down on his knees and went to twirling that there little wheel on its door. Just then I heared some hollering out in the street, and I heared one thing clear enough. I heared someone yell out, "Fire." Well, the boys had did their job all right. So far.

"Hurry it up," I said to Nick.

"Don't make me nervous. I'll have to start all over again."

"You take too long, I'll just kill you and do it my own self."

Just then he turned the handle and pulled the door, and it come open.

"Get ever'thing outa there," I said, and he went to pulling stuff out. I seed the saddlebags, and then I seed a sack about half full a something. I figgered it was money. "Stuff ever'thing else into that there sack," I said, and he done what I told him to do. "Now get back away from there."

Nick stood up and backed away, and I went over there and tuck me a quick look inside the safe to make sure he had emptied it all. He had.

"All right, Nick," I said, "I don't wanta have to kill you, but if I have to, I will. You do what I tell you to do, and you won't get kilt. Now just lay down there on the floor on your belly. Stay there and don't move. Don't yell. Don't do nothing."

"All right. All right." He got down on all fours, and then he stretched hisself out on his belly.

"Don't move," I said.

I picked up the saddlebags and the sack both in my left hand, and I headed for the front door. The two outlaws I had knocked silly was still out cold. I hurried on through that room to the front door and went outside. Ole Horse was anxious to get going. I could tell. Out on the street they was all kinda fellers running around. Some was in nightshirts and some was near nekkid. Most was barefooted. A few of them had done got buckets a water and was a-running toward the eating place, but only the flames was still mostly in the back. They was getting high though, and some a the flames had done licked their way to the two next-door buildings. Ever'one seemed to be a-hollering orders at ever'one else and all that same time, too.

I jerked Ole Horse's reins aloose and was about to climb up on his back when I seed ole Wheeler a-coming down the sidewalk. He looked right at me. That caught me by surprise, and I hesitated just a second or two.

"Kid?" he said.

I swung my ass on up into the saddle.

"Kid, what're you doing? What have you got there?"

Nick stepped into the doorway just then, and he said, "Boss. The Kid's robbed your safe."

I jerked out my Colt, and I shot Wheeler dead just as he was a-trying to pull a pocket pistol from outa his coat pocket. Then I turned my shooter on Nick, and I never seed no one look so skeert.

"Son of a bitch," I said. I put my Colt away on accounta to draw it out I had dropped the reins. My left hand was still fulla saddlebags and a money sack. I went to gethering up the reins, but my shot what had kilt Wheeler had also attracted some attention. I seed a man acrost the street aim a gun at me, but ole Dick Cherry come out from behind a building over there and shot the son of a bitch dead. I gethered up the reins and headed hell for leather outa town. Back behind me the Devil's Town had for real turned into a kinda hell right here on this earth. Three buildings was a-burning and gunshots was popping all around. Folks was yelling and running. I looked back over my shoulder once, and I seed two men drop dead in the street.

Then of a sudden, I heared and felt at the same time a ferocious boom. It made my ears ring, and it shuck the very ground. Even though it happened behind my back, I seed red in the sky in front a me, and Ole Horse stumbled and went down, and I went a-flying over his head. I hung on tight to the money bags, even when I hit the ground, and I hit head first. Lucky thing for me I kindly ducked my head just before hitting, and I went and rolled on my back and come up a-setting on my ass a-feeling silly. I looked back then, and I seed all kinds a trash and shit a-falling outa the sky.

Then come a second blast, and I was a-looking at it that time. I seed flames a-shooting up into the sky and more trash a-flying. Men was getting blowed over in the street, and I seed at least one man a-flying through the air. Ole Horse was a-getting to his feet again, and I sure was glad to see that he weren't hurt too bad. He snorted something at me what I tuck to mean something like, "Lord God A'mighty."

I went back to him and clumb back into the saddle.

"Come on," I said. "Let's get the hell outa here."

'Course, what I shoulda said was, let's get outa this hell, but anyhow, we hurried our way on up into them low hills where that one camp site was at. I didn't have no idee if Cherry nor either one a them Duttons was still alive after that there conflagration in hell, but if they was, I meant to meet up with them just like I had said I would. I had the money, all of it, leastways I thunk pretty sure that I did, and I coulda just kept on a-riding and been pretty sure a-getting the money back where it belonged to be. But I was that mad at them three that I wanted to see them all deader'n flat rocks before I left that country for good.

I made it to that camp site, what you might recall was up a ways on a hillside, and I looked down over that hell town, and one whole side a the town was on fire. It were plumb outa control. I seed men a-running to the stable to save their horses, and I even seed some men mount up and ride like hell toward the south. Them flames had somehow jumped clean acrost the street where they was a-ketching the rest a the town. Then I seed my three temporary companions a-coming in my direction. They had survived it all right.

I moved Ole Horse off to one side, and then I stepped into the shadders my own self to wait for them. I rolled myself a cigareet, but I never lit it. They come a-riding on up, and ole Cherry, he was the first one outa the saddle.

"Kid? You here?" he said.

"Right here," I said.

Them dumb Duttons was still in their saddles.

"Don't nobody try nothing stupid," I said. "Get on down, boys."

They swung down then. Well, there I was a-facing all three a the bastards. I knowed that I could do considerable damage before any one a them might take me down, and I might could even take all three a them and nary a scratch on me. They knowed it too.

"What the hell was all that blowing up down there?" I asked.

"Right next door to the eating place," Haw said. "It was the general store."

"There was a bunch of gunpowder in there," said his brother, "and dynamite."

"Well, it sure blowed that damn town off a the face a the world," I said. "And ever'one I seed leaving was a headed south. I don't believe anyone'll be a-coming after us from down there, do you?"

"I don't reckon so," Haw said. "Hell, ain't hardly no one left down there."

"I don't know," Spike said. "Wheeler can hold onto a grudge a long time."

"Not no more he can't," I said.

"What do you mean?" Cherry asked me.

"I kilt him."

"You mean—it's all over? We won?"

"It's all over and we won it," I said.

"You got the money?"

"I got it."

"Well, Kid," Cherry said, "listen. All we want is our share of the loot. There's no reason for us to fight each other. Why don't we just count out the shares right here, and then let's each go our own ways? What do you say? We got nothing against you. All we want is the money."

"That sounds pretty good, Dick," I said, "but you're a-forgetting one thing, ain't you?"

"What?"

"You're forgetting what it was you three done to me. You're forgetting that you left me afoot without no food nor gun. You knocked me in the head and kicked in my ribs and left me like that to die. And you 'special, Dick. You was my pard."

"I stopped them from killing you, Kid. Hell, I knew you wouldn't die. I knew you were too tough to die like that. Hell, Kid, you owe me your life."

Chapter 17

I knowed it were true what ole Dick had said. I had been conscious enough whenever that one Dutton had said he wanted to finish my ass off, and ole Dick had stopped him. Even so, it had been ole Dick what had banged me over the head in the first place whenever he coulda stood with me against them two and we coulda tuck them easy. Hell, if he'd a just got over a few feet outa the way where he was safe and stayed out of it, I coulda tuck both a them Duttons all by my lonesomeness. And besides all that, I coulda died easy out there just like he had said, so he mighta have saved my life all right but just only long enough to leave me to die slow. I'm sure I woulda if it hadn't a been for Ole Horse. So that there what he said didn't cut no ice with me. No, sir.

So there I was a-standing and facing them three with blood in my eyeballs for all of them, and ole Dick a trying to talk me out of it. Of a sudden I didn't know what the hell to do. I wanted to kill them for what they had did. That's true enough. Anyways, a part a me did. But there was another part a me what couldn't help a-thinking that it'd somehow be in bad taste or something to just kill them all dead just like that. I figgered that were a result a the bad influence on me a ole Jim Chastain, the sheriff, and that there Texas Ranger name a Rice I had rid with once.

"All right," I said, "drop your gunbelts, and be real keerful in the doing of it."

"If you're a fixing to kill us," said ole Haw Dutton, "at least give us a chance."

"Shut up, you fool," Dick said. "If he was fixing to kill us, he wouldn't tell us to drop our guns."

Dick dropped his, and then so did the two Duttons. I made them all back way up, and then I went over and gethered up all the guns. One of them was my own real personal Colt what the bastards had tuck whenever they abandoned me to the cruel elements the way they done. I was sure glad to have it back again. I didn't have time to check it over just then, so I just throwed the belt acrost my shoulder. Then I went and pulled the rifles outa the scabbards on the sides a their horses. I throwed them rifles down on the ground with the six-guns, and then I went and mounted Ole Horse. Then I said, "Mount up, you three."

They did, and I started us towards that there stagecoach road where we had robbed the payroll. It come to me then that I didn't have no idee what kinda payroll that there had been, nor where it come from nor where it had been a-going. I didn't want to let on to Cherry and them Duttons though, so I just kept a riding. Well, it weren't long before them dumb Duttons begin to bellyaching. They was hungry or they was thirsting or their ass was sore from all the riding.

"You two shut up," I said. "If you get to be too big a pain in the ass for me, I'll just kill you dead and leave you here for the buzzards to eat on."

Long about noon we stopped, and I made Cherry fix the grub while I watched from a safe distance off so he wouldn't have no chance to throw something hot at me. Whenever we was all did eating and drinking some coffee, I made them Duttons clean up our mess. Then we headed out again. When we was a-getting close to that stage road it were near dark, and so I found us a camp site. I done the same thing what I had did at noon, and after we had all et, I made ole Cherry tie them other two up for the night. Then I checked the knots 'cause I sure didn't trust him none to a did the job right. He musta figgered I'd do that, though, 'cause he had tied them real good all right.

Then I had me my biggest problem. I had to tie ole Dick. Now, ole Dick coulda easy whipped my ass, and I couldn't rightly figger how I could tie him without getting too close and giving him a chance to get his hands on me. I made him set acrost the fire from me while I studied on it, and damned if he didn't figger out what I was a worrying on.

"You can't tie me with a gun in one hand, can you, Kid?" he said, and he was a-grinning wide.

"Shut up," I said.

"You can't get me tied, can you? It'd take you both hands, and you'd be right up close to me. I don't think you could outwrestle me, Kid."

"I said shut up."

"What're you going to do? Kill me? You could have done that a while ago. I don't think you'll kill me." I didn't say nothing at that, and pretty soon, ole Dick, he went on. "About the only thing you can do, Kid, is to stay awake all night and watch me. It'd be like a gambling game. We'll see which one falls asleep first. If it's you, I don't know if I'd leave you alive again. There's too much money at stake, and you have too much integrity."

"I ain't neither," I said. 'Course, I didn't know what that there word meant, and I weren't paying too much attention to ole Dick nohow. I was a-thinking as hard as I knowed how on just how to deal with the situation what I was in. Then I got to looking at a tree just outside the ring a our camp. It was a good sized tree with a hefty low branch. It was a little too low for a good hanging branch, but it was higher than a man's reach all right, and it give me a idee.

"Go over there to your saddle," I told ole Dick, "and get your lariat off it."

"What for?"

"Just do it."

"Or you'll kill me?"

"I'll damn sure shoot a ear offa the side a your head."

He got up. "Yeah," he said. "You'd do that all right."

He went and got the rope. "What now?" he said.

"Toss it over that there branch." He done it. "Now throw the tail end of it over thisaway." He done that too, tossing the most a the coil at me. "All right," I said, "put your hands through the loop and pull it snug." He tuck up the loop end and snugged it on down and then stuck his hands through it like what I told him. I picked up the other end a the rope and went to pulling till I had pulled his both arms straight up over his head and pulled that there loop tight on his wrists. "Now set down," I told him. I give him just enough slack to let him set on the ground and lean his back against the tree trunk. Then I pulled that rope as tight as I could again, and I went and wrapped it around the trunk of another close-by tree.

"Ow, damn it," Cherry said. "You're tearing the skin off my wrists."

"It's better than killing, ain't it?"

I walked over to check his wrists, and the rope was snugged up on them all right. The only thing was, he coulda stood up and then loosened that rope from around his wrists. I hadn't thunk a that. I couldn't leave it go thataway. I went after another rope, and I looped that one around his both feet, and then I tied it tight to another tree trunk. I had him stretched where he couldn't do nothing.

"You expect me to sleep like this?" he said.

"I don't rightly keer if you get no sleep atall," I said. I went back over by the fire and poured myself out another cup a coffee, and I rolled me a cigareet, and I set back to relax, having all my prisoners all trussed up thataway.

"I'd like to have another cup a coffee," ole Haw said.

"You say even one more word," I said, "and I'll pour some over your head."

Well, they all quieted down, and it weren't long before them Duttons was both a-snoring. Cherry was quiet, but I don't think he was sleeping. Not yet. I got up and walked over to where Ole Horse was a-grazing. I walked up close to his ear on accounta I didn't want none a them prisoners a mine to hear me what I was fixing to say.

"Ole Horse," I said low in his big ear, "I gotta get me some shut-eye tonight. I think them three is all tied up good, but only I ain't too sure about ole Dick Cherry there. There might could be some way he could sneak aloose."

Ole Horse kindly fluttered his lips making what some folks would consider to be a rude noise, you know, but only I understood his meaning all right. What he told me was for me to relax and get me a good night's sleep. He said he'd keep his eyes on that Cherry, and if it looked like as if ole Cherry might be about to get aloose, why, he'd just walk over there and step on him. I thanked him quietly and went on over to my bedroll and stretched out for the night. I had my two Colts under the blanket with me.

In the morning whenever I woke up, ever'thing was all right, just like I had left it the night before. Them three mighta been uncomfortable, but they was all asleep and a-snoring. I thanked Ole Horse again, and then I went and built up the fire. I cooked up a breakfast a beans and bacon and boiled some coffee. Then I went and loosed ole Cherry's feet. I kicked him on the bottom a his left boot, and he come awake.

"Get your ass up," I said.

He struggled up to his feet and loosened up the rope around his wrists and tuck his wrists out and went to rubbing on them.

"Go over yonder and dish out a plate for ole Haw," I said. "Untie him and give it to him. Then do the same for his brother, and then get them each a cup a coffee. Then you can do the same for yourself."

I kept my distance and watched him real keerful while he done all that. Then I tuck keer a my own self. When we was all done eating and drinking coffee, I made them three clean ever'thing up and saddle the horses. I checked the cinch on Ole Horse to make sure that no one was trying to play me any tricks, and then I mounted us all up and headed us for the stagecoach road. It was damn near noon whenever we got there, and I found the same place we had set and waited to rob that stage. I had our horses back behind that hill, and I made them three stay down on the road. I got up higher and watched. By and by, I seed that stage a-coming.

"You three down there," I called out. "Lay back against the rock outa sight. When I yell, step out in the road in front a the stage."

I waited till the stage had slowed for the curve, and then I hollered, "Now!" The Duttons and ole Cherry all stepped out in front a the team, and the lead horses balked some, and the driver pulled back on the reins.

"Whoa. Whoa. What the hell's this all about?"

I reckon he were puzzled on accounta being stopped by three unarmed men. The shotgun guard raised up his greener and helt it ready.

"What do you men want?" the driver asked.

"I can tell you that," I called down to him. "Them's the three men what robbed your stage a that payroll a while back."

"What?"

"I suggest you tie them all up real good and tight so you can take them on in and turn them over to the law."

"Say, who are you and what's this all about? How do I know these are the men?"

"It's them all right," I said, "and here's what they tuck."

I stood up and tossed that saddlebag over the edge and it landed with a whump on top a the stage. The driver turned around and grabbed it quick and opened up the flaps and dug in there. He give the guard a look.

"He's right, by God."

"That's the payroll?" the guard said.

"Looks to be all here, too."

"Well, I'll be damned."

"Keep that gun on them while I get down and tie them up."

I watched from my perch while the driver clumb down and went and tied each one a them three. A passenger come outa the stage to see what was a-going on. He was a man what looked like he could handle hisself all right.

"I'm putting these three inside with you," the driver said. "Keep your eye on them."

"You got them tied real good?" the passenger asked.

"I tied them good, but you can check the knots if you've a mind."

They went to shoving them three into the stage, and I stood up and showed myself. The driver looked up at me.

"Who might you be?" he asked.

"I'm knowed as Kid Parmlee."

"I sure do thank you for catching those three and returning the money."

"He helped us steal it," ole Haw shouted from inside the stage.

The guard turned his shotgun barrel in my direction, and him and the driver and that there passenger all looked up at me.

"That don't even make sense, now do it?" I said. "How come would I help these bastards to steal all that money and then come and give it right back to you?"

"Well, Kid Parmlee," the driver said, "I'll tell the sheriff how we got this money back and who it was that done it.

There'll be a whole bunch a folks grateful to you for what you done."

"Glad to do it," I said. "Now I'm going to go down the backside a this hill, and then I'll come on around with their horses and tie them on behind the stage."

"All right."

Pretty quick I done that, and then I shuck hands all around, but not, a course, with the prisoners. Whenever I walked by the stage, they glared out at me through the winders. Once again, I could see that they sure was a-wanting to kill me, and once again, I asked myself how come I had not just gone on ahead and kilt them. But I had did what I had did, and there weren't no going back on it. I was just a-going to have to live with it. I got to hoping that the law would put the three a them away for a long time. I sure didn't want to see any of them again. I was done sick a the sight of them.

I set on the back a Ole Horse and watched that stagecoach roll on down the road with the recovered payroll and the three robbers in it. I felt like as if I had did a real good deed, and I figgered ole Jim Chastain would be right proud a me for the doing of it. Ole Rice too. And Red, and Doc. Doc? Damn. I had forgot all about ole Doc. I wondered had she got herself blowed all to hell back yonder in the blowing away a Devil's Tit Town or what? There I was a feeling proud a myself and being all pumped up, and then Ole Horse blowed at me and said that I should ought to a kilt them three, and that likely I'd be sorry that I didn't sooner or later.

"Oh, shut up, Ole Horse," I said. "I ain't worried about them three a damn bit. I done forgot all about ole Doc back there when we blowed that town away. I meant to get her outa there. We got to go back, Ole Horse. We got to find her if she's even still alive."

He nickered back at me as if to say, "Well, let's get going then," and so I turned his head and we lit out along our own back trail. It come to me then that I had sure as hell been doing a lot a that lately—back trailing. I was a-getting sick of it. We moved along as fast as ever Ole Horse could stand it, and we never stopped for food nor water nor nothing. Now and then we had to really slow it down and walk to keep from killing ourself, but soon as we was rested enough, we moved on out again. We went like that all day. Both our bellies was a-grumbling, but we neither one of us never complained, not once. We just kept on a-going.

Come dark, we never stopped to camp neither. We moved a lot slower, though, on accounta I sure didn't want Ole Horse a-stumbling over nothing and breaking a leg or something. We went along real keerful. That was sure one long night, I can tell you. I got to where I was thinking that it wouldn't never end, and I wouldn't never see no sun again nor any kinda daylight.

"Ole Horse," I said, "this here is the longest night I have ever saw in my whole entire life."

Ole Horse blowed at me, and I swear to God, I heared him clear, and what he said was, "You're just a snot-nosed kid is all."

"Damn it," I said, "you been around ole Zeb way too much."

But we kept on a-going, and it did final come daylight. In just a little ways then, we come across that little crick what I had got to know way too good that one time, and I rid Ole Horse over to it so he could get him a little drink a water. I never bothered, though, for my own self. Ole Horse noticed that, and he cut his own drinking short, and we went on our way. At long last, we come to the Devil town. We stopped at that same little camping spot on the side a the hill, and I looked down over what was left a that place.

There was one building a-standing. It was scorched some on one side, but it was still all there. I didn't see no horses nor dogs nor human beings. I did see some bodies a-laying

around, and it come to me that it would sure be unpleasant
down there with them bodies just a-laying around like that.
It looked for all hell to me like there hadn't been no one
come nowhere near that there one-time town since we had
blowed it all away. They was all kinds a trash and burnt
lumber and furniture and piles a ashes. I wondered what
someone would think who might come along and see the
sight and not know what had happened there. Just what
would they think?

Maybe they'd think that a war had tuck place and they
hadn't never heared about it. It was sure enough a hell of a
mess. Well, a-looking down on all that and not seeing no
sign a life, I got to thinking the worst, and I asked myself
just how the hell could I a rid outa there and not even remembered poor ole Doc, and the onliest thing that I could
possible come up with was that there had been so much
a-going on, and I had to fight alongside them three
a-worrying all the time was they a-going to shoot me in the
back. I had them and the money and—

But then I thunk, if I was to try to explain it all to ole
Doc, what would she think a them kinda excuses? I sure did
feel mean and bad and ashamed and ever' other kinda bad
feeling a man can have.

"Ole Horse," I said, "we got to go down there."

Ole Horse snorted.

"It ain't a-going to be pleasant," I said, "but we ain't got
no choice."

"Well, let's go, then," Ole Horse said, but a course, he
said it by just a-blowing, but I understood him all right. We
moved slow down the hill, and then we rid across that short
open area till we come to what had once been the edge a the
town. It come back into my mind how it had been before
a-riding into town in just this same direction, how loud and
lively it had been. Now it was dead ashes. The wind was
a-blowing just enough to stir them ash piles as we rid betwixt

them. The odor in the air assaulted my poor nostrils, and I'm sure that it did Ole Horse's too on accounta the way he snorted and blowed. I made myself look at each body I seed as we rid along. Then we come up to the one building what was left, and we stopped.

Chapter 18

That there building had been a butcher's shop, and it had been a-standing at the far end a the town whenever they was a town there. I reckon that's the only way what it didn't get burnt down or blowed up, 'cause it set off a little ways all by its lonesome. Anyhow, it surely did look lonesome with the rest a the town a few heaps a ashes and it just a-setting there. Riding through the mess, I had made myself look at all the bodies, and a course, they was some that was in the ruins a the buildings what I couldn't see hardly atall, so I couldn't know ever'thing, but I didn't see none that looked like they coulda been the doc once upon a time. I couldn't see how she coulda survived though, not and still be in that town.

I was a-hoping that she had run off somewheres whenever all the shooting and the blowing up had got started, and I was a-asking myself if she had did that how in the hell was I ever a-going to find her. 'Course, they was that there butcher's shop a-standing, and if she had run off to safety till the war was over, and if she had any good sense about her, maybe she had come back to the shelter a that building. There had oughta be some food in there, too, you know, slabs a meat and such. I set my hopes on that notion, and I tied Ole Horse to the rail in front and went up to the front door. It was a-standing wide open. I didn't take that as no good sign on accounta if she was in there, I figgered, she'd be a-shutting the door behind her to keep the critters and such out. But then, whenever I went to step inside, I seed that the door was just a hanging on one hinge. My hopes went on back up at that.

I stepped inside and went to looking around. I didn't see nothing out a the ordinary. It looked like a butcher shop was all, 'cept only it looked like as if someone had been a-rummaging through it some. I tuck that as a good sign on accounta it didn't make no sense that the shop woulda been rummaged before the war, and that meant someone had survived the war to go rummaging in it. 'Course it coulda been anyone, but I was sure hoping that it was ole Doc. I stepped on in a little further and looked around some more, but I didn't see no clues.

"Hello," I said, kindly tentative. "Hello. Is anyone alive here?"

I heared a noise like someone knocking against something, and I turned around real quick, and a damned ole cat meowed and run acrost the floor.

"Doc?" I called out. "Are you in here? Anyone?"

On the back wall a the room what I was in they was a door what looked to open into a back room, so I walked over there and put my hand on the door handle. I hesitated a couple a seconds, then shoved it open. Nothing happened. I stepped through into the back room kindly cautious-like, and then I heared a inhuman kinda roar, and of a sudden, and I don't know where he come from, they was a monster of a man right in front a me. Why he looked to be as big as a grizzler bear and even more hairy, and his mouth was wide open and dripping slobbers, and his eyeballs was red and ferocious. He was wearing dirty furry clothes, and I figgered him to be some kinda mountain man or buffler hunter or some such damn thing, but mostly I figgered him to be crazy dangerous.

You see, besides he had roared at me like a wild animal, his both arms was up way over his shaggy head, and his both big, dirty hands was a clutching the handle of a wood chopping ax what he was a-fixing to swing right at the top a my head. I yelped like a skeered rabbit and flung myself backwards onto the floor in the front room, and that there ax come down hard and fast and stuck itself in the floor right betwixt my legs. I scooted backwards like a crawdad, a-jerking out my shooter at the same time. He was a-wrenching that ax loose from the floor. I shot him right in the chest, and he stopped a-wrenching for a second or two to look down at the hole in his chest what was a-running red blood, but on him it looked like a little tiny hole, and all it done was it just only made him mad.

He roared out even louder than before and jerked that there ax aloose. I was up on my feet by then, and I had runned back into a corner a the room. He turned and looked at me. I leveled my Colt at him and cocked it.

"Drop that ax," I said, "or I'll kill you."

"I seen her first," he said. "She's mine."

I thunk about giving him another warning, but then I realized that I had done shot one hole in his chest, and that hadn't made no impression on him. I figgered warnings would have about as much effect on him as they would on some wild animal. Then I wondered just how many bullets would it take to slow this big, ugly son of a bitch down some. I shot him again, jut a couple a inches from where I had shot him before. He stopped and looked down at it again, and then he roared again, and he come at me. I run to the next corner a the room, and I decided that weren't doing no good a-shooting him in the chest. I decided to shoot his head, but just as I had made that decision, he flung that damn ax like as if it were a little ole throwing ax, and when I seed that thing a-coming at me, I had to duck, and that throwed off my shot. I hit him low betwixt the legs. Oh lordy, but he did howl.

The ax stuck in the wall just above my head. The monster was a-bent over a-holding his balls or whatever was left of them with both his hands, and blood was a-running all through his fingers. He was a-looking up at me with a real astonished kinda look on his face. Well, there weren't nothing else for it. I couldn't leave a man in that kinda shape. It woulda been too cruel, so I shot him once more, this time right betwixt the eyes, and this time he dropped over dead on his face.

I tell you what, though. I didn't know whether to believe it or not, him being dead. I had just about begun to think that I had final run acrost a man what couldn't be shot dead. I helt my Colt ready, and I walked over to him real slow and easy. I got close enough to reach out and toe him, but I couldn't quite bring myself to do it. I was askeert that he would come alive again and reach out and grab me. He never moved, though, and final I did reach out and toe him. He still didn't move none. I toed him harder. He was dead, all right. I seed enough dead men to know one. Well, I walked over to a chair what was setting against the wall, and I dropped down in it to ketch my breath and to just general try to get over what I had just went through.

After I had tuck me a few deep breaths, it come back to me what I was in there for in the first place, and then I recollected what the monster had said to me when he said that he seed her first. So there must be a woman in there somewhere. I guessed that it coulda been one a the whores from the saloon, but I hoped that it would be Doc, and I hoped even more that he had only just recent saw her and hadn't got a chance to get to her yet before I come up on him like I done. I stood up and headed for that back room again, and even though I knowed the big son of a bitch was dead, I stepped wide around him.

I looked all around in that back room, and I didn't see no sign a life. All it was in there was big slabs a meat a-hanging from the ceiling. I asked myself what could that bastard a meant by what he had said. I holstered my Colt again. I couldn't see no sign a no danger. Then I just stood there a-puzzling over the situation. I decided to check over that whole building real keerful and even turn over ever' desk and table and ever'thing what a human person might could get underneath and hide, and so I walked back into the front and main room and commenced into doing just that. I turned one table over real deliberate onto the body a that human monster in there. I didn't find nothing nor no one.

I went to opening drawers for some reason. I knowed they wouldn't be no one inside a them, but anyhow I did find some money, and I tuck it and stuffed it into my pockets. They was a side room, and I went in there and rummaged all over it, but I still didn't have no luck. Well, that only left that back room with all the meat in it, and a course that had been the room what the monster had been so vicious about defending for hisself. I mighta thunk that he had just been a-trying to hoard all that meat but 'cept for what he had said that he had seed her first. Well, I went back in there, and whenever I stepped through that door, I noticed that my footstep on the floor had a different sound to it from what it had in that front room. I stepped back acrost and stomped on the floor. Then I stepped acrost again and stomped again. It most definite had a different sound to it.

I be damned, I said to my own self, but I think there's a basement underneath this here. I went to walking around the room again a-looking at the floor, and then sure 'nough, back against the back wall, I come onto a trap door. It had a iron ring attached to it for a pull handle, and I tuck holt and pulled, but that there trap was shut tight. I knocked on it. Then I called out, "Is someone down there?" I didn't get no answer. "Hey," I hollered in my louder voice, "this here is

Kid Parmlee. Is they anyone down there alive?" They was a pause, and then I heard, "Kid?" It were a little voice, soft and kindly skeered sounding.

"Yeah," I called out. "It's me. Kid Parmlee. Is that you, Doc?"

"Are you alone?"

"There ain't no one alive up here but me."

Then I heard some scratching and scraping just underneath me, and then that there trap door was raised up just a little like as if someone down there was a-pushing on it. I grabbed onto the iron ring and pulled, and I throwed that door back on the floor, and be damned if Doc didn't poke her pretty head outa that hole.

"Kid," she said. "God, I'm glad to see you."

She reached up at me, and I tuck holt a her and helped her up outa there. Whenever she was out and standing on the floor there in front a me, she throwed her both arms around me and helt me as tight as I've ever been helt. And I seed that she was a-trembling.

"Ever'thing's all right now, Doc," I said.

"I was so frightened," she said. "That man—"

"He's dead. Did he get to you?"

"No. I saw him coming and went down in the basement. There's a bar down there to latch the door from below. He banged at the door and pulled at it. Then he said he was going to chop his way through."

"I reckon that's about when I come up," I said. "He come at me with a ax."

"You came just in time. I don't know what would have happened if—"

"Hey. Don't even think about it. It never happened, and it ain't a-going to. Doc, I feel real bad. I never meant to ride outa here and leave you like I done. I ain't got no excuse neither 'cept only I had me three outlaws along with me, and I had to deal with them. I come back soon as I could."

"You came back in time," she said. "That's all that counts. But—what happened here?"

"Let's get us away from here, and I'll tell you all about it," I said, and I tuck her by the hand and led her on out the building through the front door and outside to where Ole Horse was a-waiting. When he seed me, he give a snort as if to say that it was about time I come out to let him know ever'thing was all right. I started to put Doc up on Ole Horse, but then I had me a thought.

"Say," I said, "I bet you're hungry."

"Yes," she said, "I am."

Well, I had me some trail food, you know, but I thunk about all that meat in that back room, and so I told Doc and Ole Horse to wait just a minute, and I went back inside a there and sliced off a good chunk a beef. I found me something to wrap it up in, and then I went back out. I put Doc in the saddle, and I clumb on behind. Then I rid us out away from that there ugly town what I had give back to the Devil, and I found us a nice camping spot beside a pretty little stream. I built up a little fire and cooked us up a good meal and boiled some coffee, and we et and drunk coffee and just kindly relaxed a bit. I rolled a cigareet, and Doc surprised me and asked for one for her own self. I fixed her one, and the both of us set and smoked. Ole Horse was a doing fine, grazing on nice green grass and drinking outa that clear, running stream.

Well, I final went and told Doc the whole entire story. I admitted to her that I hadn't never been no outlaw, and I told her how me and my temporary pardner ole Cherry had gone into that there Devil Place a-pretending to be outlaws in order to get back that stole Fosterville bank money, but only in order to get it back, we'd had to pretend to rob the stagecoach for ole Wheeler. Then Cherry had gone and turned real outlaw on me. I told her the whole thing, all the details, and wound it all up telling how I had got all the money back. I had done turned the payroll back to the stage line and got them three locked up, and now all I had to do was to just ride all the way back to Fosterville and return the bank money and get my reeward from the bank. That was all.

"And I got me some friends in Fosterville," I said. "The sheriff there, ole Jim Chastain, is a good friend a mine, and the ole banker, he'll like me real good whenever I fetch him back his money. Then there's ole Red, and—well, anyhow, I got me some good friends over there. I reckon we could set you up in doctoring in that town if you'd a mind. They'd go to you if I was to tell them to. What do you say?"

She smiled at me real sweet. "It's worth a try, Kid," she said, "and besides, I don't have anyplace else to go."

Well, it being kindly late in the day by then, we spent the night at that there little cozy camp, and we did have us a good time with her a-showing me just how glad she was to see me and all. And in spite a all a my adventures with wild women, I come to believe that I was just about to fall in love again. I admit to feeling a little bit guilty on accounta ole Red, but I just couldn't help myself. Doc was a fine woman.

The next morning we cleaned up the camp site and headed out towards the west with the both of us a-riding on Ole Horse. I told him I was sorry about that, and I moved us along real slow and easy so as to not wear him out. We stopped to rest now and then, too. It tuck us two days to get back over to the stagecoach road. We camped another night there, and then I turned us south towards the clostest town what was End a the Line. I figgered we could get us a good night's sleep in a real hotel and some real good meals and another horse, and then we could move on towards Fosterville. It was around noon by the time we got to it.

Well, the first thing I done, seeing as how Ole Horse had worked extry hard for me, was to ride right straight to the stable, and I told that stable man to treat Ole Horse the best way he knowed how. Then me and Doc went to walking down the main street a the town. We went into the first eating place we seed, and I bought us both the best steak dinner what they had to offer, and it was good, too. Whenever we had et our fill and drunk all the coffee we wanted, we went back out and found us a hotel. We was lucky to get a room on accounta that little town was a-plenty busy.

But I got us a room all right, and I ordered up a bath for the doc, and whenever she got into it, I couldn't hardly pull myself away from her, but I did. I asked her what size a clothes she wore, and I went out and bought her all kinds a new stuff, pretty dresses and underthings, and even shoes and boots and a new set a riding clothes. I told that feller in the store to wrap them all up and send them over to the hotel. Then I went to the stable and found a fine little filly horse for sale, and I bought it and a saddle for Doc. I left it there in the stable, though, with Ole Horse. Then I bought myself a bottle a whiskey and went back to the hotel room. Doc was still a soaking in the tub. She sure made a pretty picture.

I poured myself a whiskey, and Doc surprised me again by asking for some for herself, and I poured her a glass and give it to her. We was sipping whiskey, and she was a-soaking whenever someone knocked on the door. I went over and opened it just a crack, and it was a kid a-delivering all that stuff for Doc, so I made him hand it through the crack a the door one piece at a time, and I stacked all a them boxes and bundles on the bed. I sent that kid away with a dollar, and I shut the door and latched it again.

"What's all that?" Doc asked.

I went to opening it all up and showing it to her, and it sure did make her happy.

"Kid," she said, "let's go out and walk around the town."

I guess she wanted to show herself off in her new clothes. Women is like that. Well, a part a me didn't want her a-putting on no clothes, but another part a me was real proud

a what I had did for her and wanted to see her all dressed
up and even wanted to parade around with her like that, so
I said, "All right." She come outa that tub and I helped her
to dry off all a her loveliness, and then we picked out some
stuff, and she got all dressed up. She studied herself in the
mirrer some, and she went and told me what a fine job I had
did in buying tasteful ladies' clothes for her, and she did
look fine, I can tell you. 'Course, the man in the store had
helped me to pick out all the right stuff.

Anyhow, we went on out, and we was a-strolling up and
down the main street a-showing her off to ever'one, and I
got to feeling like as if I might oughta have tuck me a bath
and put on some new clothes too, but then, the way I was
a-looking, all it done was it just made her look all that much
better. I figgered that folks was a-looking at us and saying
things like how in the hell did that scruffy little shit get
hisself that there fine-looking woman on his arm? So I was
kindly puffed up my own self. Yes sir.

I noticed the jailhouse while we was a-walking along, and
it come to me that ole Dick Cherry and them two dumb
Duttons was likely in there a-hating my guts. I figgered that
it was still too soon for them to have been give a trial. I
wondered how many years in prison they would get for robbing that payroll and if I would ever run into any of them
again anywhere along the road in this here life. Hell, I hoped
the law would lock them up and then just forget about them
and let them rot away in some dungeon somewheres in the
damn desert.

Anyhow, we strolled on past the jailhouse, and Doc, she
musta been thinking the same thing what I had been
a-thinking just a bit before about my own clothes, on accounta she said, "Look, Kid, there's a store with men's
clothes. Let's go inside and find you a new suit."

I puffed myself up some and said, "Okay."

The store was acrost the street from where we was at, and we stepped down off a the board sidewalk to go over there, and then I seed someone acrost the street point right at me, and he yelled, "There he is right there."

About six men gethered around him then, and they all come at me. I kindly shoved ole Doc away from me, and I braced myself for a fight. I didn't have no idee what it was all about neither.

"Kid, what—"

"Just stay outa the way, sweetness," I said. "I don't want you a-getting hurt."

Chapter 19

The only thing I could think of was how one a them Duttons had tried to tell that there stage driver that I had helped them rob that payroll, which a course was true enough, but only I had meant all along to give it back, what I had did all right, and they hadn't believed him none, but only now with them six men a-coming at me, I thunk, maybe them three had gone to telling that again and someone had decided to believe them after all.

But a course, I didn't have much time for thinking just then. I seed that none a them fellers had their guns pulled out, but then they had me way outnumbered, so I was a-thinking maybe I had ought to pull my shooter to defend myself, but then they was all around me all of a sudden, more than just them six. Some others had come up beside a me and some behind me even, and they was a-slapping me on the back and ever'one was a-talking so I couldn't tell what no one was a-saying, but they was all a-smiling, too. I was sorta astonished, you might say, but then I kindly relaxed whenever I seed that they never meant me no harm.

Well, it come clear final that I was some kinda hero in that there End a the Line, and things kindly calmed down a bit slowly, and the crowd come to be about four main guys what said they wanted to buy me a drink at the saloon, but I told them that I was in the company of a fine lady, and so they said we could go to a fancy resteerant instead.

"We've done et," I told them.

"We can get drinks there," one a the men said. He was a middle-aged feller with a fancy suit on. Well, I asked Doc, and she said okay. I think she was kindly curious about me getting all a that attention from them big-shot-looking fellers. Well, we walked to the fancy place they was a-talking about, and it really was, too. I hadn't never seed a place so fancy just for eating and drinking in, and all that in that little ole End a the Line place.

We got in there and all set down at a round table, and that one feller ordered up a bottle a champagnee, but he seed right quick that I didn't take to it, so he ordered me a whiskey. Doc tuck to that bubbly stuff, though, so I was glad that he had ordered it.

"What's this all about?" I said.

"Well, Mr. Parmlee—"

"Don't call me that," I said. "Just call me Kid. Ever'one does."

"All right, Kid. My name is Stratton. These men are my colleagues. Mr. Long, Mr. Bowman and Mr. Polk. We work for the railroad. That payroll you saved is ours, and you got it back to us in the nick of time. Our workers were just about to walk out on us. If that had happened, we'd be in big trouble. We owe you a lot, and we intend to pay. In fact, if you'll hang around here for a few minutes with us, Mr. Polk here will run over to the bank and draw out the money for your reward."

"Well, I reckon we can afford to set here a spell," I said. I give Doc a look. "What do you say to that, darlin'?"

Doc smiled real sweet. "I think we have the time," she said.

That there Polk stood up then. "I'll be right back," he said, and he hustled his fancy ass outa that place. I noticed that Doc was a-giving me a real kindly curious look. I couldn't quite figger out how to describe it. She was a-smiling real sweet, and she looked like as if she was a-feeling proud a me somehow, but it was more than that, too. I think maybe for the first time she really believed me that I never was no outlaw.

"Kid," that Stratton feller said, "could I interest you in a job with the railroad?"

"Aw, I don't know nothing about railroading," I said.

"That doesn't matter. The job I have in mind is what you might call a troubleshooting job. Kind of like what you've already done for us. You might call it a railroad detective job. We'd pay you real well."

"Well now, I thank you kindly for the offer, Mr. Stratton," I said, "but I got me a job right now what I have to finish up."

"Will it take long?"

"Prob'ly not too long," I said. "I got to ride over to Fosterville is about all. Then I'll be all did."

"Keep us in mind. I'll hold that job open for you."

"I 'preciate that," I told him. I picked up my glass and sipped me some whiskey. "Say, what's happened to them three what stoled that payroll in the first place?"

"Oh, they're sitting over in the jail," Stratton said. "We won't have a judge in town for another week."

"We decided that we'd let them have a trial before we hang them," Mr. Long said, and then they all laughed.

"You fixing to hang them just for a robbing?" I said. "No one got kilt on that job, did they?"

"He's just jawing," Stratton said. "We have no way of knowing what the judge will say. But it was a serious robbery. It brought this community to a standstill for a while. It had a lot of men and their families broke and stopped the progress of the railroad. People around here take that pretty seriously."

"They'll hang," Bowman said.

I give a shrug and tuck me another sip a whiskey, and just then that Polk come back in. He had a bundle a bills in his hand, and he laid them on the table in front a Stratton. Stratton picked them up, counted through them real quick-like and laid them down right under my nose.

"The railroad appreciates you, Kid," he said. "Remember what I said about that job."

Well, them railroad fellers excused theirselfs right after that and left me and Doc setting alone in that fancy eating place. I poured Doc another glass a that bubbling stuff and me another whiskey, and I leaned back looking as pompous as I could look, being as scrawny as I was. Doc looked at me real proud-like.

"You're a hero in this town," she said.

"I reckon so," I said, "but whenever them folks out in the street first come a-running at me, I thunk I was in for a fight."

She laughed at that, and we finished up our drinks. Doc reminded me that we was on our way to buy me a suit a clothes whenever we was interrupted, so we decided to go on ahead and do that. We got up to leave and whenever I went to pay our bill, the man there said that it had done been tuck keer of. We puffed up some more and went on over to that store. Doc made me try on two or three suits a clothes before she made up my mind, and whenever we left there, I was a-sporting a new pair a shiny black boots, a three-piece black suit, a white shirt and string tie, a black hat with a fancy band, cuff links, and a stick pin.

We went back to our hotel room then and ordered up another bath. Whenever it was all ready, we locked our door and got us both nekkid, and we soaked and played and had us a fine time. We fooled around like that till supper time when we was a-getting hungry again, and then we dressed ourselfs up real fancy and headed our ass on back for that fancy eating place. Well, they already knowed us in there on accounta our earlier visit, you know, and they treated us like we was someone real special. We et and drank real good. Why, we couldn't empty a glass but what someone was right there a-filling it up again. I tell you, I never seed nothing like it in all a my whole entire young life.

And whenever folks would come in or go out and they would walk past our table there, they all smiled and nodded and said howdy to us real friendly-like, like as if we was well knowed and prominent citizens a their town. It come to me that I could get to liking that kind a life with all a that respect and attention and such. It sure as hell beat getting throwed out a hotel winder stark nekkid, I can tell you that. The other thing was, it got me to thinking kindly hard about ole Stratton's offer of a job with the railroad. It come to me that if I was to take that there job a his, why, I would move on down there to End a the Line, and I'd get paid good, and all a these folks would treat me like that all a the time. It sure was a tempting me.

"Doc," I said, keeping my voice kindly low, "what do you think about that there job that feller offered to me?"

"It could be dangerous," she said.

"My whole life has been dangerous," I said. "The only difference, it seems to me, would be that I'd be a getting paid for it. Well, I been paid for it before, like with this here reeward, a course, but Stratton's way, it'd be regular, you know. Steady like. I reckon I'd always have money in my pockets."

"With a steady job, Kid, you could have money in the bank. You could buy a home. You could become a real success."

That there word she said then just went straight into the middle a my brain and set there like a lump. Success. I'd thunk about a lot a things, being a outlaw, finding a gold bonanza, bounty hunting, but I hadn't never actual thunk a being what folks would call a success. And in that there town a End a the Line, I was already being treated like a success, and I was being offered a chance a being one for real and for permanent. What did ole Stratton call it? A troubleshooter, or a railroad detective. Why, it started in to sounding better and better.

Then another thought come to me. I had been bragging to ole Doc about all the friends what I had me in Fosterville, and I did have some, that's true enough, but I didn't have nothing in Fosterville to compare to what I had right in that there town where I had never before set foot till that day. Why, hell, I thunk, I could have it all right there. I decided to put it to the real test. Whenever we finished up in there, I paid up, and I asked that feller in the red vest what had been making over us so much, "Say, where would I find that there Mr. Stratton?"

"He has his railroad office right across the street," the feller said, "but he's not likely there this late in the day. If he's not there, you might try the hotel. He stays there. Or the saloon."

"Thanks, pard," I said, and I give my arm to Doc, and she tuck it, and we walked outa there.

"Are you going to talk some more about that job?" Doc asked me.

"Not just yet," I said, "but I got me something else to talk to him about. If it works out, I'll let it be a surprise for you."

I walked her back to the hotel, and then I went a-hunting Stratton. I found him in the saloon. He smiled real big whenever he seed me a-coming at him. He had them same other fellers with him, and he invited me to set with them, and he poured me a drink a real good whiskey.

"Have you reconsidered my offer?" he asked me.

"I been thinking on it," I said. "That's for sure. I still got to finish that there other job what I told you about, but I'm a-thinking real hard about coming back here once I've did it."

"Good."

"But that ain't how come I come here a-looking for you."

"Oh?"

"I got me something else to ask you about."

"Ask away. I'll help if I can."

"Mr. Stratton, you know that there lady what is with me?"

"Yes."

"I call her Doc, you know. It's a kind of a nickname I give her, but I give it to her for a real good reason. You see, she really is a honest-to-God doc. She's went to school for it and ever'thing. Only problem is that folks out here don't want to give a chance to a woman doc. If she opens her up a office, they won't come to see her. I'm a trying to help her find a place where she can settle in and do her doctoring business, and—"

"I suspect that if your lady friend gets an office here, and if she gets patients coming to her, that will be the more reason for you to come back. Am I right?"

"Well, yes sir, you got that right."

"Kid, say no more. I can have her set up in practice to-morrow."

"It might could take longer than that," I said. "The last place she was at kindly got burned up, and she lost all a her doctoring tools. Likely she'll have to send off for more."

"We can help with that, too. Bring her over to my office first thing in the morning, and we'll talk business."

I stood up a-grinning wide, and I reached out to shake ole Stratton's hand, and whenever I got aholt of it, I pumped it up and down real good.

"Thank you, Mr. Stratton," I said. "I sure am obliged to you for that. We'll be over and see you first thing. The two of us. And, Mr. Stratton, I'll take that job. Soon as I get this other tuck keer of, I'll be right on back here, and I'll take that job."

Well, I had went and did it almost without thinking. Now there weren't no backing out. I had to keep my word. I couldn't change my mind whenever I got back to Fosterville and Chastain and ole Red and ever'one. Ole Zeb, he was likely off somewheres in the mountains looking for his mother lode, but them others would be there, and they'd likely be a wanting me to stick around, but I wouldn't be able to. No, sir. I had blurted me out a promise, and so I had to keep to it.

But that was all right, on accounta I had fixed things up for ole Doc. I had been secretly a-worrying some on how things was going to work out in Fosterville with me a getting Doc set up there in the same town with ole Red. So this here was a relief to me in a couple a ways. I knowed, too, that ole Stratton and them would have a whole hell of a lot more influence on what doc the folks in their town would go to than Jim Chastain and ole Red would have there in Foster-ville. Things was a-working out real well, and I hustled my ass back over to the hotel to tell Doc about it.

She weren't asleep, neither. She was a-waiting for me. Whenever I give her the news, she sure was happy. It was just what she had been a-wanting, and I was sure happy that it was me what had been able to get it did for her. She was so excited about it all that she hugged me and kissed on me till I thunk that I might pass out from it. Final, she broke away loose from me a bit.

"So I'll stay here now," she said, kindly asking, but not quite, "while you go on."

"Well, yeah," I said, "like I told that Stratton, I got me a job I got to finish. It's what I come out this way for in the first place, you know. I come out a-chasing bank robbers and meaning to return that stoled bank money. Well, I kilt the robbers, and I got the money. All I got to do now is to just take it back to the bank, but just as soon as I get that did, I'll turn right around and come back here, Doc. I promise you that. Why, hell, I done tole ole Stratton that I would for sure take that job."

"You did?"

"Right after he promised to do what he's a-fixing to do for you, I tole him, I'll be a-coming back. I'll take that job."

"Oh, Kid," she said, and she throwed her arms around me so hard and fast I fell over backwards on the bed. Well, she didn't need no more hint than that, and I ain't a-going to tell you no more.

The next morning, me and Doc strolled over to Stratton's railroad office, and we found him there all right. He stood up and shuck our hands when we come in.

"Good morning," he said. "Have you two had your breakfast?"

"No," I said, "we come straight over here like I said we would."

"Good. I haven't either. Let's go over to the restaurant. We can talk over breakfast and coffee."

Well, we done that, and what we found out was that Stratton had done picked out a office in town for Doc, and he had done fixed it for her to be the official doc for the railroad crew. He asked her where to send off to for the tools and stuff she needed, and he tuck notes whenever she told him, and he said that he would order all a that stuff. Doc, she told Stratton where to write to in order to get what she called her creedentials so he would know for sure that she was for real, and he said that he didn't need to do that, but she insisted on it, so he final agreed to it, and he tuck down all a that there information, too.

Well, betwixt the two of them, they had my head a-spinning, but I sure did like the way things was a-going, and I never did see me a woman so happy and so excited and so all fired businesslike all once and at the same time. Doc was really something. Then just as I thunk that they had everything figgered out and tuck keer of, Stratton come up with something else.

"Staying in a hotel can be expensive," he said, "and less than private. I know of a little house at the edge of town you could get for a good price, and I'm sure the bank will cooperate—if you're interested."

"I'd love to look at it," Doc said.

So whenever we finished our breakfasts, what ole Stratton paid for all of them, we walked out, and we went and tuck a look at the office what Stratton had in mind, and Doc said she sure did like it, and he said it was settled then, and then we walked on to the edge a town and seed the house. It was a nice little house, and Doc was real happy for that, too. From there we went on over to the bank where ole Stratton got his way again. The banker feller come up with the money for the house right away. And I was glad to notice over at that there little house, that they was a nice little stall for a horse out back and a bit of a fenced-in place for a horse to run around some in.

Once ever'thing was settled, me and Doc walked down to the stable where I paid up and saddled up Ole Horse and that little filly what I had bought for her. Then we mounted up and rid on back to her house, just the two of us this time, and she had the key.

"It's really mine," she said.

"It sure is."

"Let's go in."

I couldn't turn down that offer, so I tuck the two horses out back and put them inside the fence, and me and Doc went into her house. I had just stepped inside the door, and I run smack into her a-waiting for me with her arms opened out wide. She hugged me tight and kissed my mouth.

"Just one thing, Kid," she said.

"What's that?"

"We called this my house."

"Well, it is, ain't it? I mean, you got to pay that banker feller back the money, but whenever you get your business a-going, you won't have no trouble doing that. And I can help you whenever—"

"That's not what I meant," she said.

"What then?"

"It's your house, too. It's ours."

Chapter 20

Well, I seed to it that ole Doc, she got settled in, all right. She had her a nice little house with furniture and all, and ole Stratton give her the key to the office he had picked out for her, and he set a sign painter to work a-fixing up a sign for her to hang out front. He ordered up all the things she would need in order to outfit her office all proper, and I moved her little horse to the stall out back a her house. I couldn't think a anything else there was to be did, so I told her, "Darlin', I hate to leave you, but the sooner I get going, the sooner I'll get back here to you."

She didn't argue with me none, and she give me a real swell good-bye smooch, and I clumb up on the back of Ole Horse and we headed north on that stagecoach road. I rid through the day, and I had to make me a camp for the night, and the next morning I got started early again. Around noon, I didn't know it was a-going to do it, but that road swung northeast. Now, I had to go west to get back to Fosterville, but I sure did prefer a real road to just riding across wild country. For one thing, you know that a road is a going someplace, and it's possible for a feller to get hisself all turned around slaunchways just out in the open like that. So I figgered a stopover in a town wouldn't hurt me none, and I had to come to some place or other where a east–west road would join up with that there stagecoach road. I stayed on it, even though it were taking me some outa my way.

In another hour or so, I come on a little town. A sign beside the road called it Etter, and I come well into Etter before I realized that I had been there before. It was the same damn little one-horse town where I had met up with ole Dick Cherry the first time, and where we had tuck that outlaw Girt and formed up our ill-fated pardnership. Well, that was all right with me. I knowed that I could take the west-going road outa that place and get my ass on back to Fosterville all right. I brung back to mind the little boarding house in Etter where I had stayed before, and I rid over there and got me a room for the night. Then I tuck Ole Horse over to the stable, and when I went to leave him there, he snorted a good night to me. I found the eating place there without no trouble, and I had me a bowl a beef stew what was pretty good. Had some corn bread with it. I drunk a few cups a coffee to finish it all off.

When I got up to leave, I paid the man, and then headed for the door, but before I had reached it, it come open and I reckernized the big ugly bastard a-coming in. He reckernized me too, and he give me a hell of a look. It was that there Moose Marlowe what I had humiliated the last time I was in that town. I recalled that whenever I had not bothered to kill ole Moose, Dick Cherry had told me that I was too soft. I reckoned he was right about that, too. Most likely, I shoulda kilt Moose that time, and I had oughta have kilt ole Cherry, too, at least one of two different times.

I stopped and touched the brim a my hat in a greeting and smiled, and I said, "Howdy, Moose." He kindly grunted at me. "Don't you recall my name?"

"Howdy, uh, Kid," he said.

"Say," I said, "when you finish up your eating here, come on over to the saloon, and I'll buy you a drink."

I didn't make him answer me that time. I just walked on past him and out the door. I figgered right then that I would have to watch my back the whole time I was in Etter. Ole

Moose, he wouldn't face me, but he would dearly love to back-shoot me. I knowed that. I walked on over to the saloon and got me a bottle and two glasses. Then I found me a table where I could set down with my back to the wall. I poured me a little drink a whiskey and set it down on the table. I weren't in no hurry to drink it.

I tuck the makings outa my pocket and rolled me a cigareet and lit it, and then I just set there a smoking and looking over all a the faces in the saloon. I kindly reckernized some of them from the last time I come through. The sheriff what didn't have no use for bounty hunters come in and looked around, and he spotted me right off and give me a straight hard stare. I smiled and touched my hat brim to him. He turned around and left the place. Final, I tuck me a sip a whiskey.

Then a little gal come a walking toward me a-smiling real wide, and I reckernized her as the one what had made up to ole Dick Cherry before and had went upstairs with him. She come on over to the table and set her ass down right beside me, a-leaning over toward me real suggestive-like.

"Is that glass waiting for me?" she said.

"It's a waiting for a friend a mine," I said, "but if you wanta fetch yourself another one, I'll be tickled to buy you a drink."

She set back a little like as if I'd insulted her, but then she recovered from it right quick and smiled again. "All right," she said, and she got up and headed for the bar. She come back fast with a glass and put it on the table. I poured her a drink. "So," she said, "you're waiting for someone."

"That's right," I said.

"I know you from some place."

"From right here. I was in here a while back with ole Dick Cherry. You oughta remember ole Dick. You tuck him upstairs with you."

She wrinkled up her nose like as if she was a-thinking real hard. "I don't recall the name," she said. "I take a lot of men upstairs."

"I bet you do," I said. "Well, ole Dick, he was a wearing all black, and sporting two six-guns. He was doing all he could to look like as if he was a bad gunfighting man."

"Oh, yeah. I remember now. Yeah, you were sitting right here with him. Now I recall it, it turned out that you were the real gunfighter of the two. They called you—Kid. Kid something."

"Kid'll do," I said.

"Well, Kid, I think maybe I went upstairs with the wrong man last time. You want to go upstairs with me now?"

"I told you I'm waiting on a friend."

"Not Dick Cherry?"

"No. He's in jail waiting to be tried for robbing a stage-coach of a fat payroll."

"Did he do it?"

"He sure did."

"What'll they do to him?"

"Prob'ly stick him in a prison cell for about a hunnerd years is all."

"Oh, that's too bad."

"Say," I said, "if you wanta hang around here and drink my whiskey with me, we can go upstairs after a while whenever my friend shows up and I buy him a drink is all."

"Okay," she said. She had done finished her first one, and I poured her another. I was still a-sipping at my first one. I didn't have no intention a getting my ass drunk, leastways not yet that early in the evening.

"What do they call you?" I asked that gal.

"Lulu."

"I ain't been in a saloon yet anywhere in this big country what didn't have a Lulu a-working in it," I said.

"You never found one as good as me," she said.

Now, you might be taking me for a pretty terrible bad feller seeing as how I had just a couple a days before said that I thunk that I was a-falling in love with a real fine and respectable lady, and I had went and got her settled in a house and a office and ever'thing, and had even gone so far as to say that I would take me a job and get my ass back to her just as soon as ever I could, and here I was already a-fooling around with another whore. All I can say about all that is that I did say I was a-falling real hard for ole Doc, and I really was, too, but I was a long ways from dead, if you get my meaning.

Just about then, ole Moose Marlowe come a-walking into the saloon, and he stopped just inside the door and commenced to looking around. He seed me final, and he stood there like as if he weren't sure what to do. I lifted up my bottle towards him, and he come a-walking over. When he come close, I said, "Have a seat, Moose," and I poured him that extry glass full and shoved it over to him. He set, and he picked up that glass and tuck him a drink.

"That's good whiskey," he said.

"I only buy the bestest," I said.

"Thanks, Kid," he said, and he tuck another drink. "That's real big of you."

I give a shrug. "What're friends for?" I said. You see, I was a-trying to see what ole Moose would do, and how he would react to the way in which I was a-treating him. Like I said before, I knowed that he wouldn't try to fight me face to face when I had my gun on me, but I did figger that he would try something sooner or later if ever he could slip up behind me. I didn't mean to give him that chance, but I was a-thinking that maybe I could make him think that he had that chance but only I'd really be ready for him to try something. Anyhow, he finished off that drink, and I poured him another.

"Say, Moose," I said, "I'd kindly like to go upstairs with

ole Lulu here for a little while, you know, but I really hate
to lose this here table and 'special my chair here. If I was to
go on upstairs, and if I was to leave you this bottle a good
stuff, would you set here and drink my whiskey and save
my table and chair for me?"

"Yeah," he said. "You can count on me."

"Thanks, ole pard," I said, and I stood up taking Lulu by
the arm, and she stood with me. "Come on, sweetness. Let's
go on up there."

"All right," she said, a-smiling wide and a-hugging my
arm. "Let's go."

We started in a-walking toward the stairs, and I heared
someone back behind me say, trying to keep his voice low,
but I still heared it, "Hey, Moose, who the hell is that?"

"That's my good friend, Kid Parmlee," Moose said. "And
if you know what's good for you, you won't rile him. They
say he's a regular Billy the Kid, but I'm here to tell you,
he's more than that. Way more."

I reckon ole Lulu heared it too, 'cause she squeezed my
arm real close then and kindly laid her head over against me.
We clumb on up them stairs, and she led me down the hall
to her own room. We went in, and she closed the door. I
watched to make sure she set the latch from inside. Well,
she stripped off right quick, and she sure was a pretty little
thing all nekkid like that, and her hair was all blond, and I
mean, all of it. Well, we was at it for might near a hour, and
she give me the best time what she knowed how to give.

I felt a mite guilty though on accounta my Doc, you know,
and I went and give that little Lulu twice as much money as
what she asked for. I tell you what, I sure enough made her
happy when I done that. She washed us up some, and we
got dressed back up. I strapped on my Colt and set the hat
on my head, and we went back downstairs. I seed right off
that ole Moose was still a-setting at my table, and he hadn't

let no one else set there, neither. He smiled whenever he seed us a-coming.

"You got to go circulate now or what?" I asked Lulu.

She give a pretty little shrug. "I don't have to," she said.

"Well, come on back and set with me a spell if you've a mind."

"Be glad to."

We made our way back to my table and set back down.

"Thanks, Moose," I said. "Say, you do know ole Lulu here, don't you?"

"Yeah," he said. "I know Lulu. Hi, Lulu."

"Hi, Moose."

"A feller I know come over here and wanted to sit down and drink some of your whiskey," Moose said, "but I told him no and made him go away."

"Good for you," I said. I looked at the bottle. "Hell, Moose, you didn't drink much of it your own self."

"I didn't want to drink too much."

His glass was damn near empty, so I picked up the bottle and poured it full. I looked at Lulu and she nodded, so I poured her another one. Final I poured my own glass full. I started to just only take me a sip on accounta not wanting to get my ass drunk, you know, but then I got me this real kindly strange feeling about ole Moose, and I went and tuck a good gulp. I leaned over close to Lulu and whispered in her ear.

"Say, did you ever take ole Moose upstairs?"

"No," she said. "He spends all his money on whiskey."

"Would you take him up?"

She give one her cute little shrugs. "If he had the money."

I tuck some outa my pocket and give it to her, and her eyes popped way wide open.

"Go on," I said. "Ask him."

"Oh, Moose," she said, and she smiled wide and batted her eyes at him.

"What?"

"You want to go upstairs with me?"

"Oh, I ain't got that kind of money."

"Come on, Moose," she said. "It's all taken care of."

"What do you mean?"

I give him a nudge with a elbow. "Go on," I said. "Go with her. It's all right."

Ole Moose, he turned damn near purple in his face, but he got up, and then Lulu got up and walked over to him and tuck him by the arm and led him acrost the floor and up the stairs. I felt good about that, and I went on ahead and drunk my whiskey like I didn't have no worries in the whole world. I knowed I would have some time to pass before them two come back, and so I rolled me a cigareet and lit it and set there a-smoking and a-drinking whiskey.

I seed that damn sheriff come back in, and this time he come right on over to me where I was a-setting. He never waited to be invited. He just pulled out a chair and set down a-giving me a long hard look.

"Set down, Sheriff," I said. He ignored me.

"Where's your partner?" he said.

"In jail."

"That's a good place for him. As far as I'm concerned, it's where you belong, too."

"You got a right to your opinion, Sheriff," I said, "but if you was to ask them down at End a the Trail, they'd tell a sure enough different tale on me."

"Oh yeah?"

"That's right. Why don't you ask them sometime? By the way, it was me what put ole Dick Cherry in jail. Figger that one out if you can."

"I don't have time for games," he said. "How long are you planning to be in town?"

"I'll make you real happy and ride outa here at first day-light," I said.

He shoved back his chair and stood up. "See that you do," he said, and he turned around and walked away.

"Hey, Sheriff," I called out, and he spinned around fast a-drawing out his shooter, but I was just a-setting there with my both hands up and empty. He looked a little embarrassed, and he put away his gun. Then he tuck a couple a steps back towards me a-looking real mad.

"What?" he said.

"What the hell's your name anyway?"

"Go to hell," he said, and he stormed on outa the place. A few folks laughed or sniggered at him as he left. I tuck me another drink a-draining my glass, and so I poured it full again. I had finished my smoke so I went and rolled another one. I fooled around like that till I final seed ole Moose and Lulu a-coming back down the stairs. Ole Moose sure had him a big grin on his face, and Lulu was a-looking up at him like as if he was something real special. I wondered when I seed that if it was a for real look or if she laid that on all a her customers after they was all did. I tried to recall did she look thataway at me, and I sure couldn't call it up. Anyhow, I had drunk me enough, that I was sure glad they was a-coming back to save me my table again, on accounta I needed real bad to get up and go out back. I reckon you know how come. When they set down, I told them. I got up and started in toward the back door when I heared the familiar sound of a revolver a-being thumbed back ready to shoot. It flashed through my head that ole Moose was a whole lot smarter than what I had give him credit for being, a-waiting for just that time to draw down on me. As I was a-reaching for my Colt and spinning, I heared a voice call out.

"Kid Parmlee, you son of a bitch."

I whirled ready to shoot, but I never had time. You see, it weren't ole Moose atall what had drawed down on me. It was a total stranger what I had never before saw in my whole entire life that I could recall, and he was sure as hell ready to blow a great big hole in my bony back. He mighta too, 'cept that ole Moose, he acted real quick. He seed what that bastard was a-fixing to do, and he was up on his feet with a chair in his hands and over his head in a flash, and he brung that chair down hard on that would-be shooter's head. God, but it made a sickening sound, and I guess it crushed that ole boy's skull. He dropped like a sack a shit.

Well, ever'one in the place commenced to talking all at once, and someone run out the door, I guessed to fetch the sheriff. Lulu, she went and hugged onto Moose. I was about to piss my pants, so I said, "I'll be right back," and I went on and done what I had set out to do in the first place. When I come back in, the sheriff was there, all right.

"I knew there'd be trouble when I saw you here," he said to me.

"I didn't do a damn thing," I said.

"He never either," said Moose. "I hit that man. He was fixing to back-shoot the kid."

"I can back Moose up there," I said. "I heared the click a the hammer and turned around in time to see the shooter aimed at me, but ole Moose here got him before I could draw and fire. He saved my life."

"Well, he won't get a medal for that," the sheriff said. "Who else saw it?"

Several folks spoke up, and all a them backed up Moose, and so the sheriff cussed some more and got a couple a boys to haul out the carcass. Then he give me another one a them looks.

"First thing in the morning," he said.

I set down and picked up my drink as the damned sheriff was a-walking off.

"Who was that man, Kid?" Lulu asked me.

"I never seed him before in my life," I said. "Likely his name was Pigg or Hooks, though. There don't seem to be no end to them two families."

"You really leaving in the morning?" Moose asked me.

"I got to," I said. "I got me a chore to finish up in Fosterville."

"Can me and Lulu ride along with you?"

"What? What for?"

"Me and Lulu, we want to get hitched up." He looked down at Lulu, and she looked up at him and smiled. "Ain't that right, Lulu?"

"It sure is, Moose."

"Well, I be damned," I said. "Who'd a thunk it? Well, yeah, that's fine, but how come you don't just get hitched up right here?"

"Lulu's gonna quit this kind a work," Moose said, "and I just thought it would be easier for her if we got out of here, you know."

"I reckon you're right about that," I said.

"And I need to go find me a job."

"Yeah. That makes sense, too."

"There's one other thing."

"What's that, Moose?"

"Someone has got to watch your back for you."

Chapter 21

Ole Moose got a couple a horses and saddles for him and Lulu to ride on, and we waited till the next morning after we had us a big breakfast, and then we lit out west a-headed for Fosterville. Now in case you're a-thinking that I'm some kinda blockhead, I ain't. I told them two that I weren't about to settle on down in Fosterville on accounta I had me a good job lined up over in End a the Line. I never told them about ole Doc though. Anyhow, I did tell them that we'd be a-making a long trip and then just turning around and re-tracing a bunch a steps to get back out to End a the Line, but ole Moose, he said that didn't make no difference with him. He was a-trailing along with me to watch my back, and Lulu was a-trailing with him, and that was that. So I never argued with him none about it. Actual I was kindly glad for the company. A long trail can get right lonesome.

And it was sure enough interesting about ole Moose anyhow. I mean, for someone what wanted to kill me so bad to a done a total and complete turnaround the way he done and become a good friend and a perteckter like that was unusual to say the leastest and just about downright amazing to contemplate on. He sure was a-looking after me. Whenever we stopped to make a little camp and fix us up some vittles, why, he even pulled the saddle offa Ole Horse on accounta he said I was too little for heavy work like that, and then whenever we got ourselfs ready to move on, he'd saddle Ole Horse back up for me. It was kindly nice in a way, but in another way it was embarrassing as all getout. Hell, I can saddle a horse all right. I reckon you know that well enough about me by now.

We had made us a camp for the night the first night out, and the next morning we was a-fixing us up some food and coffee. Now in case you was to get some other idee about it, I want to tell you that Moose and Lulu was just as nice and polite as they could be during the night. They made theirselfs separate bedrolls and each one slept the night in his and her own bed. They wasn't about to do nothing else, if you get my meaning, with me alone there in the same camp with them. I thunk that was real admire-able of the two of them.

Anyhow, the next morning, like I said, we was whomping us up some breakfast, and I was a thinking back on ole Zeb's biscuit and wishing that we could a had some, and ole Moose, he kindly stiffened up and stared off at our back trail.

"Two riders coming," he said.

I turned around to look, and he was right all right. They was two riders a-coming straight at us. They was yet a ways off, and they was moving along real casual. I figgered it was going to take them a little while yet to get on up to us. The coffee had boiled long enough, and I poured me a cup. Moose, he wouldn't have none. All a his attention was on them two riders. He just stood there a-staring at them and a-waiting for them to come on up close. I seed him kindly check the slide a his shooter in its holster, and I thunk that if it was to come to a shooting, he'd just as well stay out of it. He weren't none too good with a gun.

I stood beside Moose a-sipping my coffee and watching. Lulu poured herself a cup and stood to Moose's other side. "Who are they?" she asked.

"Could be anyone," I said. "This here is a fairly good-traveled road."

"You reckon it's someone on your trail?" Moose asked me.

"Might could be," I said. "There's a-plenty of them out there."

"If they come after you," he said, "they'll have me to deal with, too."

"I appreciate that, Moose," I said, "but if it should come to a shooting, you just get Lulu and get off over there to one side outa the way. I don't want neither one a you getting hurt in a fight a mine. I ain't seed no two gunhands that I couldn't take at the same time, nohow."

Them two riders come in close enough then to reckernize, but I didn't know them none, only I heared Lulu give a kinda gasp and outa the corner a my eyeball I seed her grab tight onto ole Moose.

"Moose," she said, "I know them. They work for Harvey."

"It ain't your fight, Kid," Moose said. "It's mine."

"How come?" I said. "Who the hell's Harvey?"

"Harvey owns the place where Lulu worked. He thinks he owns Lulu too, and all the girls that work there. I reckon he sent them two to bring her back."

Well, I started in to tell Moose again to move off to one side, but then it come to me that he wouldn't do it, him a-thinking that this coming up was his fight and not mine, so 'stead a saying anything more, I kindly started in to sidling my own self away from ole Moose. He was a-standing to my right side, and I went to sidling off to my left, and I got myself several feet off to the side. Them two rid on up and stopped their horses. For a minute they just set there a-staring.

"Lulu," one of them final said, "you're coming back with us."

Moose, he shoved Lulu back behind hisself, and he puffed up his chest real big, and he said, "She's with me. She ain't going back."

"Now, Moose," the feller said, "we got no quarrel with you. Harvey sent us to fetch Lulu back. That's all. You just step aside and stay out of this."

"No, sir," said Moose. "I ain't going to."

"Moose," the second feller said, "don't be a damn fool. We ain't getting off these horses to do no fistfighting or wrassling with you, and you can't beat either one of us, much less both, with a hand gun."

"I can take the both of you before either one gets a shooter out," I said.

Both a their heads turned and looked at me.

"You got no call to interfere in this," said the one guy. "Lulu belongs to Harvey."

"Well," I said, "I don't know no Harvey, but I do know that no one belongs to no one else in this here free country. Lulu don't want to go back, so you two just wasted a trip out here. Turn around and go back and won't no one get hurt."

"We can't do that."

"I ain't had my breakfast yet," I said, "and I don't really want to kill no one. Do you two fellers know who it is you're a-messing with?"

"Some punk kid."

"You got the 'Kid' right. I'm knowed as Kid Parmlee."

I seed them two exchange quick looks, and it sure looked to me like as if I seed a little fear and doubt in them looks, but then they both looked back at me with hard and mean stares. Then they swung their ass down outa the saddle right together, and they stepped out in front a their horses and then moved off to one side like as if they wanted to get them horses outa the line a fire. Whenever they done that, they moved over in my own direction away from Moose and Lulu, and I was glad a that.

I stood there as calm as you please, and I seed them two a-flexing the fingers a their gun hands. Then they stepped away from each other in order to split my targets apart. I knowed what they was a-doing all right. I couldn't keep my eyeballs on the both a them at once. That didn't bother me none, though. I had faced men like that before. I was ready. I tell you what. I ain't necessary proud a the fact, but I had come to be real casual when it come to a killing. I mean, if it was a man what was a-looking for it. Anyhow them two spread out real good so as to kindly split up my concentrating, you know.

"Well," I said, "is either one a you two shitty-ass fuck-faces going to do something, or do you think you can just stare me into the ground?"

Well, a good cussing almost always causes fast action, and both a them rannies went for their shooters. My trusty Colt was out in a split-up second, and I drilled the first one right through the middle a his chest. My second shot went right into the nose a the other'n, and he hadn't even cleared leather yet. I don't mean to brag, but I was sure enough fast when it come to using my Colt. They was both a-laying there dead.

"I ain't never seen nothing like that before," said ole Moose.

"It weren't much," I said. "They weren't no shucks."

"Kid, thank you," said Lulu. "I wasn't going back with them no matter what. They'd've had to've killed me first."

"Ain't nobody going to go killing my friends if I'm around to do something about it. But what I want to know is, do you reckon that there Harvey is a-fixing to let it go now?"

Lulu kindly shuck her head. "I don't know, Kid," she said. "He's not one to let go real easy."

"That's all right," I said. "Don't let it worry you none. We'll just have to keep our eyes peeled for him or anyone what goes around licking his boots. That's all."

Now, we had done started our breakfast whenever ole Moose had spotted them two a-riding towards us, and distasteful as it were, we went on ahead and finished it up even with them two a-laying dead not far from where we set down and et. When we finished our coffee and cleaned up our camp, I started in to getting us ready to move on out.

"What about them?" Lulu said.

"What about them?" I said back to her.

"Shouldn't we—do something?"

I looked over at them two bodies, and then I looked at their two horses. "You're right," I said. "There is something we'd oughta do." I walked over to the horses and pulled the saddles off and the bridles and slapped them on their ass. Then I walked on over to Ole Horse and clumb up on his back. "Y'all ready to ride?" I asked.

The rest a the ride over to Fosterville was mostly just boring. We seed a few travelers and talked a little bit with them, but mostly we just rid along talking to each other now and then. One time whenever we stopped to let Lulu run off into the bushes for some privacy, me and ole Moose was a-setting there a-waiting. There had been something on my mind for a while, and I decided that was as good a time as any to get it said out loud.

"Moose," I said, "if I'd had me any idee how things was a going to turn out betwixt you and Lulu, I wouldn't never a tuck her upstairs that one night. I feel awful bad about that, and I—"

"Don't feel bad," he said, interrupting me. "She was doing what she was doing. She ain't doing it no more, thanks to you. Besides, I'm just as glad that the last one in her old life was you. You're my friend. I wouldn't a wanted it to be no one else."

After three days a riding, we come onto Fosterville, and I tuck us to the stable first to get our horses fed and rubbed and put to bed for the night. Then I led the way over to the saloon, and soon as we walked in there I seed ole Chastain a-setting at a table with ole Red. Well, my anxious riz up seeing Red there like that, but I done my best to control myself. I tuck Moose and Lulu over to the table and inter-duced them all around. I told them how Moose had saved me that time from a back-shooting son of a bitch by cracking his skull bone, and I told them as how Moose and Lulu was fixing to get theirselfs hitched. Jim and ole Red congratulated them two real hearty. Then I throwed my saddlebags down on the table right under ole Jim's nose. He looked up at me real curious.

"That there's what I went after," I said. "Them that had it is dead."

I tell you what, that was a great relief offa my mind and like a big weight tuck offa my shoulders all at the same time. I had did the job I set out to do, and all the stole money was now back where it belonged. The outlaws what stoled it was either dead or in jail waiting to get hanged up by their necks. I set down, and ole Jim grabbed up them saddlebags and opened up their flaps. He kindly shuffled through all that money in there, and then he smiled and looked up at me. He stuck a hand acrost the table for me to shake. I tuck it and shuck it.

"Thanks, Kid," he said. "You did a real fine job."

"All I done was just only what I said I would do," I told him.

Jim waved his hand and called for three more glasses, and the barkeep brung them over. Jim poured them each full a whiskey and shoved one at me, one at Moose, and one at

Lulu. We all tuck them up real grateful and begun to slurp at that fine brown liquid. Then ole Jim looked around, and he spotted a feller a setting a couple a tables over from us. He motioned to the feller to come on over, and then he said, "Do you know where to find Mr. Throne?"

"Sure," the feller said. "I think so."

"If you'll fetch him over here to me," said ole Jim, "I'll buy the next round for your table."

"You got a deal, Sheriff," the feller said, and he went a-hustling off outa there. I heared what Jim said, and I figgered he just only wanted to show off to ole Throne what I had did, and that was just fine with me. Mostly though I was happy for the time being a-setting back and sipping that good whiskey. Well, I'd had me two drinks by the time that feller come back with Throne, and that ole banker set down and Jim showed him the money, and ole Throne's eyeballs like to a popped plumb out the front a his face. He counted that money, and then he tuck a little notebook outa his pocket and done some fast ciphering. Then he counted out my percentage right outa that there money on the table and give it to me. He writ out a paper and had me sign it that I had tuck that money. My deal was all did, and I was free to head on out to End a the Line and my new job. But I was sure a-ogling ole Red. Only thing was, I was a getting real hungry, and I was sure enough tired a all a that damned ole trail food.

"Say," I said, "how about we all go over to the eating house and have us some good steaks?"

Well, ever'one agreed, even Jim and Red, and we adjourned our ass from the saloon and walked over to the eating place. We had us a fine steak dinner what I paid for all around, and now with my belly full a good food, I was a thinking more on ole Red, but another thought come into my head.

"Jim," I said, "can we scare us up a preacher at this time a night?"

"I think so," he said, and sure enough he done it, and we had us a wedding for Moose and Lulu. Then I give Moose some money for a wedding present and told him where to go to rent a nice room for the night. I told him to have a bath drawed for them and to take along some good whiskey and some good champagnee for them. Well, he blushed red, but he tuck the money and said that he would take all my suggestions for sure. Then them two went off to do their honeymooning.

That there was my chance, I figgered. I was a fixing to make a move on ole Red. Me and her hadn't never worried about no wedding bells nor nothing like that before, so I figgered I wouldn't have no trouble a-getting together with her in a upstairs room at the saloon. I hadn't never had no trouble along them lines before, but then just as I was a-fixing to come out with my most eloquentest words, ole Jim, he stood up and he tuck holt a Red's arm. She looked up at him in that there special kinda way a woman can look and she stood up alongside of him, and then he said, "Well, Kid, I think me and Red are going to call it a night, too."

I think my face like to a fell down on the floor, but if Jim and Red noticed it, they never let on.

"I'm glad you're back, Kid," Jim went on. "Thank you for what you done. By the way, there's rewards for each of those Dawson brothers. Come by the office in the morning, and we'll fill out some papers and see what we can do about it."

"Yeah. Sure," I said. I just set there kindly dumbfloundered while ole Jim Chastain and my own sweet little ole Red walked outa there together like that without no word a explanation nor nothing. Like as if there weren't nothing to it and it had been thataway all along, and I shouldn't be surprised about it none. When they was gone out the door, and I was just a-standing there with my mouth a-hanging open, I said out loud but just only to my own self, "Well, I be God-diddly-damned right down to the bottomest floor a hell."

I walked on back over to the saloon with my head a-hanging down like a kicked dog, and I went inside and got me another bottle and a glass and went and set at a far back table with my back to the wall. I poured me a drink. I was a-thinking, there is other gals in this place, and I thunk about getting me one for the night, but I didn't really feel like it no more. Not after ole Red a-walking off from me on the arm a ole Chastain the way she done and not saying nothing to me about it.

'Course, my plan, such as it were, had been to take her upstairs for a long night a fun, and then to just ride off from her the next morning and get my ass on back over to End a the Line and to my newest sweetie, ole Doc. I guess, thinking back on it, I was a-fixing to do her more dirtier than what she had did me, but just then I weren't really a-thinking along them lines. I was a-feeling like as if I had been did dirty, and whatever it was that I had in my own mind to do weren't really all that bad. You know, us human beans is like that.

Anyhow, I was a-setting there a-feeling thataway and fixing to get good and sloppy drunk, when of a sudden in come a-walking ole Zeb Pike hisself. And he come in a roaring, too.

"I hit it," he hollered. "I hit the big bonanzy, by God. I done it. I hunted it all these years long, and be dagnabbed and befuzzled if I didn't final at last sniff her out. Barkeep, buy ever'one in the place a drink on ole Zeb Pike."

Well, he went and slapped some money on the bar, and the whole place went up in a roar, and I couldn't a got his attention in a million years just then. So I just set there a-feeling good for him. He had done did what he wanted to do most in his entire life. He had found his mother lode. That is, if he were a-telling the truth. You know, a course, the first thing he ever told me was a damn big lie whenever he said that he was ole Zeb Pike and had a mountain named after him. But I was a-hoping that he weren't a-lying about his bonanzy. I waited till ever'one kindly settled down again with their fresh drinks what Zeb had just paid for, and then I stood up a-grinning. It tuck a little while, but he final looked in the right direction and seed me.

"Kid," he roared, and he come a-running for me. When he come to me, he throwed his arms around me, and I throwed mine around him, and when we final come apart and stepped back to get a look at each other, he said, "Kid, you little shit, you shoulda gone with me like I wanted you to do in the first place. I found her. I actual found her. The mother lode. The bonanzy of all bonanzies. I'm a rich son of a bitch."

Then he went to hopping and spinning around in circles and singing. "A rich son of a bitch. A rich son of a bitch."

Final he cut out the hopping and singing, and he set down a-panting for breath. I poured us each a drink.

"I'm glad you found her, Zeb," I said. "Who's watching the place for you? Who's working it?"

"I don't know and I don't keer," he said. "I found it and that's all I give a damn about. Hell, Kid, I sold the claim."

He reached in his pocket and pulled out wads a money, and it looked almost like that bank money or that payroll. Other than them two bunches a money, I never seed as much as what ole Zeb had on him.

"Put that away, you silly old son of a bitch," I said. "You want someone a-knocking you in the head?"

"Oh, hell," he said, "who'd dare to bother ole Zeb now with his pard Kid Parmlee back in town?"

"Well, I don't know," I said, "but don't go showing it off like that. I might not be a-sticking around for too much longer, nohow."

"Oh, I reckon you'll stick all right," he said.

"What makes you say that?"

"I reckon when you find out who's over yonder in the jail, you'll be a-wanting to do something about it."

"Who?" I said. "What the hell're you a-talking about?"

"Come back from Texas," he said, kindly singing it. "Come back from Texas. Your ole paw, that's who, come all the way back from Texas."

Chapter 22

"You floor-flushing ole fart," I said. "You're a-trying to bluff my ass."

"I swear I ain't," Zeb said. "He come back from Texas, or else he never went back there in the first place. He's over there, all right. Right now. Go look and see if you don't believe your ole pard."

"Damn it," I said. There weren't a damn thing a-going the right way for me of a sudden. "How come him to be in the jail house? What the hell'd he do?"

"Ah, not much. He got drunked up and he got mouthy with ole Chastain. Chastain throwed him in the jug for a few days since he didn't have no money to pay his fine."

"You coulda paid it," I said.

"He ain't my ole paw."

"Shit."

"You going to get him outa there?"

"I oughtn't to," I said. "But I guess I will. Then I'm getting outa this damn town for good."

"You air? How come? Why, hell, I figgered this here was kindly like your home."

"Well, it ain't no more."

Then I went and told ole Zeb how Red had went off away from me a-hanging onto ole Jim's arm the way she done and never saying nary a word about it, and then ole Zeb, he said that while I was gone Jim and Red had married up.

"What?"

"That's right."

"Well, how come they never told me?"

"Maybe they just hadn't figgered out the right words to use in the telling," he said. "Or maybe they was afraid that you'd go to shooting or something. How the hell would I know?"

"Well shit. Well anyhow, that's all the more reason for me to get outa this here town. Besides, I got me a job. And another woman."

"What kinda job?"

I told ole Zeb then about how that there Stratton had made me that offer of a job for the railroad being a troubleshooter on accounta I had brung him back his stoled payroll money and all, and then he asked me about the woman, and I told him all about how I come acrost ole Doc.

"A real doctor?" he said. "A female doctor for real?"

"That's right," I said, "and I got her a job too a-being the official doc for the railroad crew there in End a the Line."

Then I went and told him about ole Moose and Lulu and how they was a-planning to string along with me on down to End a the Line.

"I figger I can get ole Stratton to put Moose on," I said. "Moose is a strapping big son of a bitch."

Ole Zeb went to wrinkling and scratching at his face. I knowed he was a-thinking some deep thought.

"I reckon I'd best string along, too, then," he said final. "You getting yourself surrounded by all a them strangers, someone had best come along with you to watch over you."

"Aw, hell, Zeb," I said, "you don't need to—"

"You trying to get rid a me? You think you got yourself a new pardner and don't need ole Zeb no more? Ole Zeb a-getting too old for you? Is that it?"

"No, Zeb, hell no," I said. "I was just only a-thinking that now you're rich and all, you might just want to set back and take it easy for a spell, but come to think on it, you had better come along with me before you go to blabbing too much and someone busts your old stupid skull bone in and steals all a your money."

"I can damn well take keer a myself," he said. "And I can take keer a you, too. When are we a leaving?"

"Sometime in the morning," I said. "I got to go see ole Chastain and collect my reeward money for them Dawsons, and I reckon I'll see about ole Paw while I'm at it. I don't want to bother them two what's honeymooning, neither, so I'll kindly wait around till they show theirselfs. But right after that for sure. I don't want to hang around here no longer than I have to. What about you?"

"Hell, I could ride out right now. Ain't nothing a-holding me back."

"Zeb," I said, "let's you and me get drunk as hell. What do you say?"

"I say bring on the whiskey, ole pard," he said, and then he let out the damnedest whoop I had heared in a hell of a long time. Well, we commenced in to do just exact what I had suggested, and I got to say that I lasted damn near as long as ole Zeb did that night. I figgered that I must a been a-getting a little better at it, and I had got me in some practice. I don't really recollect how nor when it happened, but I got me into a room and a bed sometime, or someone done it for me, 'cause whenever I waked up the next morning that's where I was at.

I got my ass up kindly slow, and I splashed some water in my face from the bowl what was a-setting on a table in the room. I hadn't never really undressed the night before. All I had to do was just strap on my Colt and pull on my boots and set the hat on top a my head. There weren't no one else in the room with me, so I just went on out and down and made my way over to the eating place. I found ole Zeb in there and I set with him.

"I was a-wondering if you was still alive," he said.

"I'm alive, and I'm hungry."

We et, and then we headed down for the stable to get our critters ready to go. Ole Zeb, he got out his Bernice Burro and I saddled up Ole Horse and them other two horses, and I paid the man for the lot of them. We commenced to walking on over towards ole Chastain's office a-leading all a them critters, and along the way I seed Moose and Lulu a-walking out on the street. I told them where to go get some breakfast and went to give them some money, but Moose said they had a-plenty left from what I had done give them. I told them where we was a-going and said for them to take their time a-feeding their face. Over at the sheriff's office, we tied all a them animals to the rail and went on inside. My ole paw seed me come in right off, and he went to caterwauling from inside that cell.

"Goddamn," he said, "it's about time you come to get your own old man outa this damned ole jail cell. Where the hell you been, Kid? Tell that fucking sheriff to let me outa here."

"Shut up, Paw," I said, "or else I'll just leave you in there to die and rot."

Chastain looked up from behind his cluttered ole desk and grinned. " 'Morning, Kid," he said. "You come about the paperwork for those Dawson brothers or about your ole paw?"

"Let's take keer a that there paperwork first," I said. I never said nothing about him and Red, and he never, neither. I figgered it was best left thataway. Well, he filled out some papers and had me to sign them, and I got me a reeward for them guys all right. Then I looked over towards ole Paw a-scowling from the cell.

"His fine's fifty dollars," Jim said.

"I oughtn't to do this," I said, but I went and hauled out the fifty and tossed it on the desk in front a Jim. He stood up and went for the cell keys and then walked over and opened up the door.

"You're free to go," he said.

"It's about Goddamned time," Paw said.

I said, "Shut up, Paw. From what I heared you got your ass throwed in there in the first place for a-cussing the sheriff. If you do it again, I ain't paying no fine. You got a horse?"

"I had me one," Paw said, "but I don't have no idee what become of it whenever this—sheriff—throwed me in here."

"Down at the stable," ole Jim said. "There'll be a charge to get it out."

I give ole Paw some money. "Go get it and saddle up and get your ass back down here," I said. "We're a-riding out."

Paw tuck off.

"Likely he'll go straight to the saloon," Zeb said.

"If he does," I said, "we'll just leave his ass here."

"You leaving town already, Kid?" Chastain asked me. I told him about my job with the railroad in End a the Line.

"There's some places on this here earth where I get respect," I said. "I'll be seeing you—maybe."

Well, I tell you, we was quite a crew a-riding outa Fosterville that day with me a-riding in the lead and ole Zeb alongside a me on his Bernice, and then my nasty ole paw and Moose and Lulu. Zeb had been right about one thing. Paw had not just only got his horse bailed outa the stable, he had also managed to get hisself a bottle a rotgut whiskey, and he was a-sucking on it as we rid along. Zeb was a-grumbling at the size a what he called our contingent. I didn't have no idee what that meant, but I reckoned it meant something like a gang.

I was real glad for it whenever we stopped to eat around noon on accounta ole Zeb done all a the cooking, and right then it come to me just how much I had missed his cooking whenever I was out like that on the trail and away from civilization. He was sure the bestest damn camp cook I ever knowed.

"Where the hell're we a-going anyhow?" ole Paw said.

"Didn't you hear me telling ole Chastain about I got me a job?" I said.

"Hell no," he said.

"Well I did. I got me a job with the railroad. Trouble-shooter, they call it, or else railroad detective. It's a damn good job, too. We're a headed to where my job is at. Place called End a the Line. I guess if I can't trust you to go on back home to Maw, then you'll just have to come on along with me."

"I go where the hell I want to go," he said. "Who the hell's the paw here anyhow, and who's the kid?"

"All right," I said. "Climb up on your horse then and get the hell outa here."

"You're free to go," Zeb said.

"Aw, hell," Paw said, "I reckon I'll tag along for a spell."

"When's the last time you seed Maw?" I asked him. "Did you even go back to Texas after I told you to? Did you go back or not?"

"Well, I—"

"Tell me the truth now, you old bastard. Did you go home and see Maw?"

"Naw, I— Well, hell, something come up."

"You ever send her any money?"

"Well, no."

He was a-muttering, and he was a-pissing me off something terrible. I was so mad at him I coulda kilt him 'cept that he was my ole paw, and I damn sure was a-wishing that he weren't.

"What the hell's she living on?" I said. "Weeds and bugs?"

"Oh, it ain't all that bad."

"How would you know if you ain't been back? Now listen here, old man. Whenever we gets to End a the Line, I'm a going to find you a house to live in, and then I want you to go and fetch Maw up to the house. I'll give you some money now and then, and you're a-going to use it to take keer a Maw. You understand me what I'm a saying?"

"That sounds real good, Kid," he said.

Now, least you get the wrong impression a me and think that I were a real good kid what loved his ole maw, let me remind you that the last impression and memory I had a that old woman was whenever she slapped me real hard acrost the face right before I lit out from home at the age a thirteen with only ten dollars and a sway-backed horse. There weren't hardly no love lost betwixt me and Maw, no more than what there was betwixt me and Paw, but the hell of it was that she was my maw, and there weren't nothing I could do about that. That's how come me to be a-hounding ole Paw about her the way I done.

I actual had more genu-wine feelings for my friends than what I had for my own paw and maw, but ain't that just the way things is? I mean, you picks your friends out, but you ain't got no say in who's a-going to be your maw and paw. But I didn't mean to go getting philosophical-like on you there. I just can't help myself from a-getting into them deep kinda thoughts ever' now and then.

Anyhow, I tried to shove my troubling thoughts, what was mostly about Maw and Paw, outa my head and dwell more onto thoughts about my coming-up new situation down in End a the Line what with old Doc in that there nice new little house and my new job with a good boss what had real respect for me and what I could do for him and a big outfit like the railroad a-backing me and likely alla the money I could ever spend in my whole entire life. I tried to think a my own self as a big-shot railroad detective. The sound a them words was pleasuring to my ears and thoughts. I couldn't quite imagine it for real though.

Well, we rid for the rest a that day and camped for the night without much to tell about, just only some bickering from Paw and Zeb, and we headed out early the next morning. I noticed that ole Paw's bottle was a-getting low, so I figgered we'd be a-hearing him cry around pretty damn soon. Sure enough, the old son of a bitch emptied the bottle and throwed it away. It weren't five minutes later, I swear, till he said, "Say, anyone in this here outfit got a drink?"

No one answered him, and he kept quiet for a few more miles. Then he blurted out, "How damn soon are we a-going to get to some town? Huh? I need to get me another bottle. Well? How fur's the next goddamn town?"

"We won't come to no town till sometime tomorrer, Paw," I said. "So just shut your yap about it."

"Anyone bring along a bottle?"

No one said nothing.

"What kind a chickenshit outfit is this anyway?"

I stopped Ole Horse and turned right quick on ole Paw, and I jerked out my shooter and shot the hat right offa his head. His eyeballs popped wide and his jaw dropped.

"That could just as easy a been your good ear," I said. "Now I want you to cut out your Goddamn grousing or else ride off from here on your own. I don't even give a damn no more if you ride towards Texas or China. I just don't want you a-spoiling the peacefulness a this here traveling group no more. You got that? Next time you feel like squawking, either bite your damn tongue or ride away. One or t'other. I mean it."

Now, I admit that I embarrassed myself some by that what I done and what I said to my own paw, and I was so damn mad at him that I just didn't want to hang around no more for a spell. I shoved my Colt back down in the holster and turned Ole Horse around again. I rid up beside ole Zeb, and

I said, "I'm riding ahead a ways. I'll let y'all ketch up to me in a while." Ole Zeb, he unnerstood, I guess, on accounta he never argued none, and I spurred Ole Horse ahead. We moved along right fast for a ways. Then I slowed him down again. He blowed a chastisement at me.

"Damn it, Ole Horse, I know I made a kinda fool outa myself back yonder, but ole Paw makes me so damn mad sometimes that if he was anyone 'cept my own ole paw, I'd kill him. I swear it."

Then he nickered, but only he weren't answering me back. It was something else. Some kinda warning. He stopped right there in the middle a the road. I looked up ahead, and I be damned if we weren't a-fixing to ride right up to that there spot where me and them others had robbed the stage a that there payroll. Well, I figgered if there was any danger up ahead it would be hid in them self-same rocks where I was hid that other time. I squinnied my eyes at them rocks real hard, and damned if I didn't see a little motion up there, just a little and like a shadder, but it were enough.

"Ole Horse," I said real low, "I think you're right. I think there's someone a-laying in them rocks up there. Let's you and me move real slow till we get down yonder where them clumps a brush is on the other side a the road. Then I'll jump off and take cover. You run way back outa rifle range."

He blowed a unnerstanding response at me, and we moved on ahead. I kept on a-eyeballing them high rocks to my right, and I seed a glint a sunlight off a rifle barrel. If they was someone up there after me, I was gonna have to be real keerful. They'd have the advantage on me with rifles and me with just only my Colt sidearm. We come close to them clumps on my left, and Ole Horse, he just turned sudden and run right smack into the middle of them, and I jumped off, and he kept on a-running.

When I hit the ground, I rolled, a-hoping that no one would be able to tell just where I was at when I quit rolling.

I come up behind a thick clump a sagebrush with my Colt in my hand, and I squinnied up at them rocks. Just then about five rifle shots sounded, and bullets kicked up dust all around me. They couldn't see me, whoever they was, but they sure enough had the range, and they might could get lucky just a-sprinkling the brush like that. Me, on the other hand, I couldn't a hit no one up there at that range even if I was a looking at him. And I couldn't see no one.

"Hey," I hollered, "who the hell's up there, and who do you think you're a-shooting at?"

I heared a weird laugh then.

"Hey, Kid," come a answer. "It's Dick Cherry, your old pard. Me and the Dutton boys. We want that payroll."

"Well, that's tough shit," I called out, "on accounta I ain't got it. It's back where it belongs. I turned it in."

"Now that's too bad, Kid," Cherry hollered. "I might be able to let it go by because of the past, but the Dutton boys here feel differently about it. If they can't have that payroll, they want your hide. And there's someone else. We picked us up a new partner, name of Harvey. He says you got something of his, and he wants it back."

"Is he talking about Lulu?" I yelled. "Is it that Harvey?"

"That's me, Kid," come a new voice.

"You can't own a person," I said.

"We'll see about that."

"Well, I'm down here all by my lonesome. Why don't you chickenshits come down and face me?"

"We ain't stupid, Kid," Cherry yelled. "It's easier like this."

Well by God, it come a-raining rifle bullets, and they was a-kicking up dust all around me. I figgered it was only a matter a time before one of them got lucky and hit me. I figgered my number had done come up, and that just when my future was a-looking so bright, and all accounta I let myself get so pissed off at my ole man. Then I heared a shot what for sure weren't no rifle shot, but it come from up there where them bastards was at. It sounded for all hell like a shotgun to me. Then I heared someone up there call out, "Hold it right there."

"Don't shoot," come a answer.

I raised up to get me a look, and that just in time to see ole Moose stand up tall right on top, and he had that Harvey by the shirt collar in one hand and by the seat a his britches in the other, and he just tossed him out over the edge. That there Harvey screamed something terrible as he went a-flying, and whenever he landed, he was all smashed up. I heared a little more commotion from up there and then another couple a shots. Then I heared ole Dick Cherry's voice real clear.

"Don't shoot. I quit."

I stood up, and Ole Horse come a-running. I mounted up, and we rid on over to the road, and by then here come my ole paw, Zeb, and Moose all from around the bend. They had to a gone down the backside a that there hill and walked around the far end to get on the road. Walking in front of them was ole Dick with his hands held high. He stopped and looked at me and grinned. I looked at Zeb.

"The rest is all dead," he said.

I looked back at Cherry.

"Howdy, Kid," he said.

"Who's got his guns?" I asked.

"I got them," said Paw.

"Give them back to him."

Paw didn't hesitate. He done what I said.

"What is this, Kid?" said Cherry.

"I reckon you know, all right," I said. "Say, how come you three to get outa jail?"

He shrugged. "Lack of evidence," he said. "You sure you want to do this?"

"You know I am," I said. "It's your move."

By God, he didn't wait none atall after I said that. He whipped out his shooter, and he were fast. Just as I snapped off my shot, I heared his whizz right close by my left ear. Mine smashed his chest bones though, and he dropped. I walked over to him where he was a-laying. He looked up, still a-grinning.

"Kid," he said, "I never really knew till just now which one of us—"

He croaked then without getting to finish what it was he was a-trying to say, but I reckon I knowed, all right. I looked around at all my pardners. I was sure proud of them, all of them.

"Say," I said, "where's Lulu?"

"I left her back out of the way of danger," Moose said. "I'll go get her right now."

He tuck off a-running, and I stood there a-thinking that now there didn't seem to be nothing nor no one a-standing in the way a the new life what was a-waiting for me and the rest a my bunch a pards on down at the end a the trail.